SHADOWS OF THE MIND

BOOK 6 IN THE JOSEPH STONE OXFORD CRIME THRILLER SERIES

J R SINCLAIR

Copyright 2025 © J R Sinclair

All rights reserved. This book or any portion thereof may not be reproduced or used in any manner whatsoever without the express written permission of the publisher except for the use of brief quotations in a book review.

This is a work of fiction. Any names or characters are fictitious. Any resemblance to actual persons, living or dead, or actual events, or organisations, is purely coincidental.

Responsible person: Nicholas Patrick Cook.

Address: 2 Bailey Hill, Castle Cary, England, BA7 7AD

Email: contactme@jrsinclair.net

Published worldwide by Voice from the Clouds Ltd.

www.voicefromtheclouds.com

In memory of Mike Chalwin, the man who was instrumental in igniting my passion for books, and everything that has led to it, including my love of writing.

CHAPTER ONE

DCI SIMON HART got out of his unmarked BMW police car, mentally bracing himself for what lay ahead of him. Based on what his superintendent had briefed him about, it sounded as though this crime scene was as bad as they came.

Banbury's morning rush-hour traffic crawled past, the drivers slowing to gawp at the cordoned-off area. The DCI noticed a school minibus was among them, children's faces pressed against its glass as they took in all the excitement in what was meant to be a relatively quiet Oxfordshire town.

Until last night.

In the spring sunshine, the Major Crime Unit (MCU) van was parked up in the street, surveillance cameras and antennas visible on its roof. Its presence was also testimony to just how serious this incident had been.

Half a dozen police had been joined by ambulances. It would be down to their crews waiting in silence to be permitted to enter. Permission for that would be down to the chief SOCO, Amy Fischer, who was already on site with her colleagues. Once her forensic team's painstaking work to unpick what had happened was done, the ambulance crews would be allowed to start the grim task of retrieving the bodies.

Within the police cordon was the focus of all the attention, a well-kept, unremarkable, three-bedroom terrace house. It was almost identical to every other home along this main road in Banbury. That had probably been the point of the gang who had chosen it. Its ordinariness was its camouflage, helping it fly under everyone's radar—especially the police's.

The stove-in front door, for once not the work of the tactical team attempting to gain entry, was the only clue to the massacre that had happened within its walls during the small hours.

God, I need a cigarette, Simon thought. His mouth tingled with the phantom taste of tobacco, an echo of a habit he'd managed to leave behind over a year ago. But the DCI had a strong hunch this particular murder scene would be enough to make his resolve falter. Today, of all days, Simon could forgive himself for breaking his promise to his wife, Julia, to quit.

A few commuters had stopped, phones out, taking photos of what would probably be the highlight of their day. With one notable exception. A woman with dark hair, who didn't give the house, or the gathered police vehicles, a second look as she headed along the pavement towards the DCI.

Simon didn't think anything of it until she was alongside him. 'Metamorphous,' she said without stopping.

'Sorry?' Simon asked.

But the woman didn't pause and was already heading away.

Then he smiled to himself as he realised the woman had probably been in a conversation on her phone via her earphones. People talking to themselves didn't raise anyone's eyebrows these days.

A throbbing headache started pounding behind the DCI's eyes. He grimaced as he pinched his nose.

'Boss, are you okay?' called out DI Alex Roberts, his close

friend. His colleague was wearing white protective coveralls as he emerged from the broken front door.

'I've got a bloody splitting headache, out of nowhere. I don't suppose you have any paracetamol on you?'

'No, but I'm sure one of the paramedics can sort you out.' The DI gestured with his chin towards one of the waiting ambulance crews.

'Maybe later. First, I need to see the crime scene. So how's it looking in there?'

'Like the bloody gunfight at the OK Corral,' his friend replied. 'There are bullet holes everywhere, not to mention all the bodies.'

The stabbing sensation intensified behind the DCI's eyes. 'No survivors then?' he asked, trying to ignore the grinding pain in his head.

Roberts's expression darkened as he shook his head. 'This one's as bad as it gets.'

The DCI's gaze was drawn to a pop of light in the landing window. That was probably one of Amy's team at work with a camera, gathering evidence.

'Okay, I suppose I better get suited and booted,' Simon said.

'I'll see you in there,' Alex said, turning and heading back inside.

The DCI breathed deeply, gritting his teeth as the headache notched up another level and he moved to one of the storage crates beside the SOCO van. He pulled on the forensic suit, before ducking under the cordon tape with a nod to the PC on guard.

Even with a mask on, the smell hit him immediately as he entered the house—a sickly mix of cordite and the unmistakable iron scent that struck the back of his throat. He didn't have to look far for the source.

Just inside the doorway, a body lay sprawled against a chest of drawers, a dark pool of blood seeping from beneath him. The young man couldn't have been more than nineteen, skin marred by fresh acne, eyes wide and frozen. His right hand still clutched a zombie knife, useless against the weapon that had ended his life.

As they say, never bring a knife to a gunfight, Simon thought as Alex approached from the back of the house.

'What a bloody waste,' Alex muttered under his breath, shaking his head at the lad's body.

'Tell me about it. So where are the rest of the victims?'

The DI gestured up the stairs. 'One up there on the landing and three more in the weed factory in the attic.'

Simon nodded, but regretted it immediately as his brain pounded against the inside of his skull. 'And the neighbours had no idea of what the gang were up to in here?'

'Absolutely none. They only had a few complaints about loud music in the middle of the night.'

'So much for the local bloody Neighbourhood Watch then,' the DCI replied, having spotted at least two of the stickers on nearby windows.

A faint smile cracked his colleague's face as he began to lead the way. 'Yep, vigilant as always, and the immediate neighbours didn't hear a thing last night.'

'That suggests whoever attacked this drug gang probably used muzzle suppressors, which suggests a professional hit.'

Alex nodded as they reached the landing.

Simon took in the next dead body, this time a young woman. Her thin arms were wrapped around her middle as if she'd tried to shield herself from the bullets that riddled her body. The DCI's professional mode kicked in, partly as a way to cope, as he took in the other details of the woman barely older than a girl—the cracked lips, hollow eyes, and gaunt face. It all hinted at a life ravaged by addiction. Scattered around lay her personal items—lipstick, an old mobile, and several disposable syringes that had all fallen from her open bag.

This whole awful mess was being photographed by a female SOCO, her blonde hair tied back with a scrunchie. The forensic officer was pure focus, capturing every detail of this poor woman's murder with her camera.

'Okay, I better see the other bodies,' Simon finally said to Alex, as the pain behind his eyes ratcheted up another level to the point of making him feel nauseous.

The DI nodded and led the way up a ladder leading up into the attic, where bright blue light was spilling out of the open hatch.

The scene waiting for Simon up there was almost surreal.

Rows of towering cannabis plants filled the attic space beneath a gantry of lights intended to stimulate their growth, casting everything with an eerie hue. There was an earthy, almost pungent scent clinging to the air. Bullet holes were everywhere in the ceiling, each one letting in a fine pencil beam of light to crisscross the confined space.

Three more SOCOs, looking for all the world like astronauts exploring a tropical alien world in their white suits, were examining several bodies. Their blood was splattered over the leaves of the plants that had once been their livelihood.

Simon had seen enough death over the years not to be squeamish, but even so, the scale of this slaughter made the air catch in his throat.

'They killed everyone... and left the product untouched?' the DCI asked, gesturing towards the marijuana plants.

'That's certainly what it looks like,' Alex replied.

The DCI sighed. 'Then we know what that means.'

Alex gave him a sombre nod. 'A turf war between rival drug gangs.'

'And that's increased tenfold across the country in recent

months. Based on the number of bullet holes up here, it suggests the use of submachine guns. Whoever it was, certainly wasn't messing around.'

Even as Alex nodded, Simon's gaze shifted to one of the SOCOs, who, even with her mask on, he recognised as Amy Fischer. The woman was carefully lifting what looked like a Beretta from next to one of the victims. As Amy moved the pistol to deposit it in the evidence bag, something deep inside the DCI's mind shifted. It was like a switch had been thrown. His surroundings blurred and his headache suddenly thundered inside his skull.

Somewhere in the distance, Alex's voice drifted through the haze descending over the DCI's senses. 'Are you okay, Simon? You look really pale all of a sudden,' his friend asked with obvious concern.

The DCI tried to answer, but his mouth seemed glued shut. Then his body began to move on its own, like he'd become a puppet with someone else pulling the strings. Unable to stop himself, he seized the Beretta from Amy's hand. Her mouth opened and closed, but whatever she was saying, Simon couldn't hear the words.

Trapped inside his own brain, the DCI found himself watching the events unfold, the cold metal of the Beretta's grip pressed against his palm.

What the hell am I doing? he thought.

He tried to stop himself, to seize control of his hijacked body, but it was like he was watching events unfold on a TV screen, unable to intervene. This other version of himself raised the weapon and turned it towards the DI, aiming it straight at his friend's chest.

Alex's eyes widened. The DCI might not have been able to hear any words in this silent movie, but he could still lip-read the single word that formed on the DI's lips,

'Don't,' Alex said, as he raised his palms.

But there was a cold fury building up inside Simon, a feeling he knew didn't belong there. This alien thought was shouting at him that the man standing before him was responsible for everything that had ever gone wrong in Simon's life.

What the hell? the rational part of the DCI's mind asked, confused about where all this madness was coming from.

But events were unfolding in awful slow motion. Simon could feel the weight of the trigger beneath his finger and the slight give as he pulled it. Then the blood, so much blood, spraying from his friend's chest. Alex's hands clutched at his wound as he stumbled backwards, eyes horrified.

Around him, the SOC team scattered. Two backed away, staring at the madman who'd just shot his best friend. Only Amy advanced towards him, her hand outstretched for the weapon, saying soundless words to him as she closed.

Simon watched, his mind screaming at himself, as the puppet-controlled version of himself whipped the Beretta around and gave Amy a sharp blow to the side of her head. The SOCO's eyes fluttered as she slumped to the floor and didn't move.

Then the DCI found himself aiming the pistol once again, this time at his best friend's head as he lay helpless on the ground. In that moment, Alex's eyes met Simon's, widening in that split second before his friend pulled the trigger and a bullet hole appeared in the DI's forehead.

What the fuck is happening? Simon's mind screamed at himself as Alex slumped to the floor.

But this hijacked version of himself wasn't done yet. This other Simon was now turning the pistol around and pointing it under his own chin.

The man trapped in the prison of his mind, winced when his finger pulled the trigger. Nothing happened. The other

Simon tried again, and got the same result. The Beretta was out of bullets. But any relief for the DCI was short-lived because the other Simon's legs were moving again, propelling him towards the ladder. Sound started to return then, and he was able to hear the dull thud of his boots on the metal rungs against the background of muffled shouts.

As he reached the landing, a uniformed officer lunged for him, reaching out to wrestle the Beretta from his grip. The other Simon's arm swung the butt of the pistol down again with the force of a hammer. He heard the sickening crack as the weapon struck the officer's skull and the man crumpled to the ground.

The landing seemed to stretch endlessly before the DCI, a place of blurred lights and disembodied voices. His vision swam, morphing and shifting until the world around him became a dizzying, half-formed kaleidoscope. He barely registered the moment he found himself passing under the cordon tape, ignoring the PC who gave him a shocked look as the officer registered the pistol in this other Simon's hand.

The DCI fought with every ounce of will he could summon, thrashing against whatever invisible force still held him. His vision blurred as tears welled up, but his body still refused to obey.

Simon felt the smooth tarmac of the road beneath his feet as he stepped off the pavement. He could feel the faint vibration from nearby traffic, but in this out-of-body experience, none of it felt real.

An engine grew louder, breaking through his mental haze. The DCI turned around to see the delivery van barrelling straight towards him. For a heartbeat, he glimpsed the driver's face, eyes wide, knuckles white as he gripped the steering wheel.

Time seemed to fracture in those final seconds and stretch into an eternity as the vehicle's tyres screeched. But rather than tense, the DCI felt his muscles relax, his mind almost welcoming its release from this nightmare. A brief surge of heat and pain erupted through his body as the van slammed into him. Then darkness, thick, absolute, swallowed the DCI and carried the consciousness that had been Simon Hart away into an endless void.

CHAPTER TWO

Joseph stood back to properly take in the gleaming beauty of the silver Aston Martin DB5 sitting in DCI Chris Faulkner's garage. His inner wannabe James Bond definitely appreciated the stunning vehicle they'd just finished restoring.

'So, are you ready for the big moment for me to fire her up?' Chris asked, taking the keys off a hook in his garage.

'Yes, although I'm still going to be keeping everything crossed that her engine doesn't explode in a cloud of black smoke.'

'I have every faith in our combined mechanical skills, especially yours. It seems I have a lot to thank your dad for.'

'He certainly taught me a thing or three about engines back in the day,' Joseph replied.

'For which I'll be ever grateful,' Chris said, heading past his Triumph TR4, another restoration project of theirs, towards the Aston Martin.

'She certainly looks the part,' Joseph replied, admiring the car's swooping lines. And the DB5 really did. Months of work had finally come together, and the engine they'd put so many hours into was hopefully ready to roar back into life.

It had been a labour of love, restoring this classic vehicle from the wreck they'd first started with. Joseph had also been by Chris's side nearly every step of the way, helping to ensure everything had been done to the best possible standard. But now came the big test as his friend inserted the key into the ignition.

'Okay, keep everything crossed,' the DCI said through the open window of the DB5.

Joseph nodded. 'I don't know if I can take it if she doesn't start after all this effort.'

'Think positively,' Chris replied.

Even so, Joseph grimaced as the DCI turned the key.

The starter spun—a second, then two.

Joseph frowned.

But Chris shook his head. 'Just give her a moment for the fuel to prime her system.'

The words had barely left his mouth when, with a slight cough, the engine burbled into life with a glorious growl.

Joseph couldn't tell whose grin was wider, his or his boss's. He stuck a hand through the open door of the Aston and shook Chris's hand. 'Grand job.'

'Steady there, or we'll be hugging next.'

Joseph snorted. 'God forbid.'

The DCI revved the engine, his grin reaching his ears. Joseph more than understood because the sound of the engine was a low, throaty rumble demanding she be driven.

'So are you really going to take her out on the racetrack like your Triumph TR4?' Joseph asked. 'Personally, I don't think I'd take the risk.'

'As I've told you many times over, it would be a crime not to,' Chris replied. 'Yes, the DB5 might be worth a small fortune now she's been fully restored, but the engineers built this car to be driven, and that's exactly what I intend to do. Okay, maybe not as my daily ride, but otherwise, hell yes.'

Joseph couldn't help giving the DCI a look at the mention of money. 'Talking of small fortunes, you know, for a while I was convinced the only way you could afford a car like this was because of some backhander from the Night Watchmen.'

Chris frowned. 'Yes, I realise how that must have looked.'

Joseph gave the DCI a hard look, as the man seemed to be skirting the underlying question and looking a tad embarrassed.

'So how did you afford it? A secret lottery win? Or is this all part of your NCA cover for your investigation into the Night Watchmen, and they're footing the bill?'

'If only. But if you really want to know, it was an inheritance I received from my dad. He died just before I moved to Oxford.'

Joseph felt slightly taken aback at that because it sounded like a very impulsive use of money. 'I suppose that's one way to spend the family silver.'

His boss held up his hands. 'Don't be too quick to judge. My dad dreamed of owning a DB5 his entire life, but never felt he could justify it, especially to my mum. Even when she died, he still couldn't bring himself to do it. But he did spend plenty of time tinkering with old bangers and taking me out with him on track days. That's where my love of restoring and racing cars comes from. Hopefully, Dad would approve of this purchase because I bought her partly as a way of honouring his memory.' Chris patted the steering wheel.

Joseph nodded. 'Hearing that, something tells me he absolutely would. Just do your best not to dent her, for both our sakes.'

The DCI snorted as he turned the ignition off and the engine burbled into silence. 'Anyway, talking of the Night Watchmen, something happened I need to bring you up to speed about. I'm afraid there was another rival gang hit last night, this time over in Banbury. And once again, it has the sticky fingerprints of the Night Watchmen's handiwork all over it.'

'Jesus H. Christ, not another fecking one. That's the fifth attack since they took down the Shotgun Raiders before Christmas.'

'Don't I know it. Thanks to that, my bosses at the NCA are talking about wrapping up our investigation, even though we don't have enough evidence yet to guarantee bringing the whole gang down.'

Joseph sighed. 'In other words, stuck between a rock and a hard place. But the problem, as I see it, is if they move too soon without sufficient evidence, there's a real danger that some of these arsewipes will walk free.'

'Tell me about it,' Chris said as he got out of the DB5. 'And right at the top of that list is Chief Superintendent Amanda Kennan. The sooner we get rid of her and her lackeys embedded in the Thames Valley Police Force, the better for everyone. But the good news is, slowly but surely, we're getting closer to having a watertight case.'

'So what's the plan, assuming there is one?' Joseph asked.

'The NCA obviously has lots of surveillance operations going on, including wiretaps. You and I need to keep our ears to the ground to see if anything useful turns up. Maybe one of these gangland hits, including this latest one, will lead to a breakthrough. But then, of course, there's Amy and her part in all of this, perverting the course of duty by altering evidence at the crime scenes, and guess what?'

'She was at this latest Night Watchmen hit?'

'In one. Who knows what she's managed to hide that might have confirmed a direct link to the crime syndicate?'

Joseph sucked the air between his teeth. 'For feck's sake. I'm certainly not going to shed any tears when that woman goes down.'

Chris nodded. 'I know, although, with my NCA agent hat on, I just wish you could have kept up with the pretence of dating her.'

'Sorry, but that was just too big an ask, especially after I discovered Amy was using me. Besides...'

A knowing smile filled his friend's face. 'With Kate back on the scene, I doubt there was little chance of you staying with Amy for much longer, was there?'

'Aye, I can't deny it. Besides, it's hard enough for me to be around her now, even as a colleague, knowing how she played me.'

'I can certainly understand that. At least Amy seems none the wiser that we're onto her. Anyway, the needs of the investigation aside, I'm just really happy for you and Kate. So, any plans for you two to move in together?'

'No, we're taking it slowly, not rushing anything and rediscovering who we are after all these years.'

'That's good to hear, although I'm surprised there's been no blowback from Derrick about any of this, especially as technically he's still married to her.'

Joseph pulled a face.

Chris stared at him. 'You're not going to tell me he's still in the dark about you two being an item again?'

The DI shrugged. 'Kate's insisting on holding off on having that tricky conversation until she feels the time is right to break it to him.'

The DCI blew his cheeks out. 'Bloody hell, that could blow up in your face.'

'That's what I keep telling her, but Kate insists she needs to do it her way. The problem is, I'm not particularly comfortable with this strategy, because, despite all the odds, there's been a considerable thawing behind the scenes between Derrick and me.'

'You'd never know that at work. He's still trying to break your balls at every opportunity.'

'Yes, but that's mainly for show these days, so there's no way the Night Watchmen are tipped off that we're working against them. Talking of which, I'm not entirely comfortable that we haven't made Derrick aware of the NCA investigation and your involvement in it.'

'I'm sorry, Joseph, but that's just the way it has to be. My bosses have insisted on it. It's just safer all round if Derrick's not brought into our confidence until we're ready to start prosecuting people.'

'You do realise you can trust him?'

'I do, but my superiors still think otherwise.'

'And I get a pass, even though I was the one who handed over the Shotgun Raider files to the Night Watchmen?'

'Yes, but only because I covered for you. But the truth is, as we both well know, that was only a test by the Night Watchmen of your loyalty as they already had access to that information via Kennan.'

'Well, I certainly owe you one for not dropping me in the shite over it.'

'No, you don't, because you're a good copper through and through. You certainly didn't deserve to be dragged down by something you were basically set up for. I'm afraid Derrick was just too far down that path for me to be able to help him in the same way. But with a plea bargain, I'm sure we can make things easier on the DSU when this all eventually comes to light.'

'Just do whatever you can for the man.'

'I promise I will. Anyway, what do you say to a celebratory stout after firing up the DB5 for the first time? I've got a fresh brew ready to go.'

'As long as it's only half a pint,' Joseph said. 'Your homebrew's grand and all that, but fecking hell, it packs a punch.'

Chris grinned. 'Just as it should.'

Joseph and Chris sat in his conservatory, sipping their stouts, and looking out across Cumnor Valley and over Farmoor Reservoir towards Wytham Woods.

The DI pulled an appreciative face after his third sip of the stout. 'This is one of your best batches yet. With these kind of skills, you should think about opening a microbrewery.'

Chris smiled at him. 'I could think of worse ideas for a retirement plan. Fancy going in with me on that particular endeavour?'

'Now there's an idea.' Joseph raised his glass and clinked it against the DCI's.

They sipped in companionable silence for a while, taking in the view, before Chris turned to Joseph. 'Look, I don't know quite how to ask you this, but I could use your advice about something.'

The DI glanced over his shoulder and then pointed at his own chest. 'Who, me? Nobody ever wants my advice about anything. But I'm happy to listen if you need to bend someone's ear. Is this work-related?'

'Not quite, although it does have everything to do with Megan.'

'I see,' Joseph said, realising where this conversation was headed. It had been clear to him for some time that the DCI held something of a candle for his colleague. He settled back in his seat. 'Go on then, fire away.'

Chris was now pointedly looking anywhere but at the DI. 'I was just wondering if Megan was seeing anyone right now?'

'Not that I'm aware of. But what about the TVP's police

code of conduct about dating someone on the same team? Doesn't that rather throw a spanner in the works here?'

'For now, it does, at least whilst I'm undercover. But at some point, the NPC's investigation into Night Watchmen will end, and so will my undercover role right along with it. So I was thinking when it does, I would ask Megan out.'

Joseph felt mixed emotions at hearing this, not least because he hadn't considered the fact the man would end up leaving St Aldates one day. He would certainly miss his steadying force in the department, not to mention his friendship. But as far as Megan went, he could see the two officers hitting it off together.

He met the DCI's expectant gaze. 'When circumstances allow, I say go for it, although there is someone else you should know about who is rather keen on her.'

Chris frowned. 'Don't tell me, our very own pathologist, Doctor Rob Jacobs?'

'How did you guess?'

'Probably the same way you did. He's not exactly subtle.'

Joseph nodded, keeping quiet about the time Rob had asked him the very same question about Megan.

He met his colleague's expectant gaze. 'For what it's worth, I know Megan has Rob very much in the'—he scratched air quotes—'friend zone.'

Chris visibly brightened at hearing that. 'Has she now?' Then he frowned. 'I don't suppose you know if that also applies to me?'

'God knows, but I'm sure you've big enough nads on you to find that out for yourself. If you want my advice, I'd say go for it. Nothing ventured, nothing gained and all that.'

'Wise words—'

The DCI was cut off by Joseph's phone ringing. When the DI saw Derrick's name on the screen, he took the call straight away.

'I'm afraid I have bad news, Joseph,' Derrick said the moment he picked up.

'Shite, what is it?' Joseph asked, bracing himself because a direct phone call from the big man was very much not business as usual.

'There's been another gangland hit over in Banbury and it bears all the hallmarks of another Night Watchmen hit.'

Joseph held his tongue because he obviously already knew about it from Chris, but flicked his phone to speakerphone so the DCI could listen in.

'How can you be sure, Derrick?' he asked, playing along.

'It has their MO all over it, including the use of MP5 submachine guns based on the recovered bullet casings. But that's not actually why I'm ringing. Two officers who were attending the forensic investigation led by Amy were killed this morning.'

Joseph's blood iced. Even though he had every reason to loathe the SOC officer as she'd played him for a fool, it didn't mean he'd completely stopped caring about her.

'Shite—you're not saying Amy was one of the people killed?' he asked.

Chris's eyes widened at hearing that.

'No, Amy's fine, although she was attacked. However, a firearm recovered from the crime scene was discharged and killed one of the detectives. Needless to say, Amy's very shaken up by what she's witnessed.'

'I'm not surprised.' The cogs in Joseph's brain were well and truly spinning, although what he was about to ask didn't make much sense. 'So you're saying the Night Watchmen tried to take the investigation team out as well?'

'That would be easier for me to get my head round. That's why I'm ringing you.' The DSU took a deep breath. 'I'm sure you remember Simon Hart and Alex Roberts from back in the day.'

'It would be hard not to when we were all freshly minted PCs working the Oxford beat together. Those two were always something of a double act...' Joseph's brain caught up with where this conversation was headed. 'You're about to tell me one of them was the officer killed, aren't you?'

'Yes, I'm afraid I am.'

'But who, for feck's sake, shot him, or was the weapon discharged by accident because some arse wipe didn't realise it was still loaded?'

'I just wish that was the case. But the truth is, Simon seems to have suffered some kind of mental breakdown. He grabbed the firearm from Amy, who was about to bag it, and shot Alex twice with it.'

Joseph traded a shocked look with Chris. One shot could be explained away as an awful accident, but not two.

'Why the hell would Simon do something like that?' Joseph asked.

'If only he could tell us. I'm afraid it gets even worse, Joseph. After turning the pistol on himself, only to discover it was out of bullets, Simon walked straight out of the house and into the path of a van. He was killed instantly.'

Joseph's mind whirled even faster as he tried to process what he was being told. 'But that doesn't make any fecking sense. Apart from anything else, those two were always the best of mates.'

'None of this makes sense to me, either. That's why I want you to be my eyes and ears on the ground over in Banbury. An Independent Office for Police Conduct investigation is already underway, led by Geoff Flynn. I was thinking because of your connection to both men, you may be able to turn up something they might otherwise miss. That's why I want you to be my liaison officer during their investigation. However it's done, we need to get to the bottom of why a serving officer, someone who was awarded the King's Police Medal for distinguished service no less, could end up killing himself and his best friend. The only thing I know for certain is none of this sounds like the actions of the man we both knew.'

'No, it doesn't in any way, shape, or form,' Joseph replied. 'I'll head over there right now and start digging.'

'Good. Just do whatever you have to do to get to the truth of what was going on between those two, not least for the sake of both men's widows. But I also know this is a lot to ask of you; you'll be heading into a world of grief and pain. So if you want to decline, I'll more than understand.'

'No. Now I've heard about it, there's no way I can sit this one out. I owe it to both men's memories.'

'I'd hoped you'd say that,' Derrick replied. 'So best get yourself over to Banbury as quickly as possible, and take Megan with you. Two sets of eyes and all that.'

'Will do.'

'Thank you for this, Joseph. I really appreciate it.' The line clicked off.

Chris raised his eyebrows at Joseph. 'Sounds like bad business.'

Joseph sucked the air through his teeth as he nodded. 'Aye. I better get going. I'll need to go to St Aldates first to pick up a vehicle.'

Chris gave him an unreadable look before sticking his hand into his pocket and then tossing him a set of keys. 'You best take these now then.'

Joseph gawped first at his boss and then at the Aston Martin. 'You're going to let me loose in her?'

Chris rolled his eyes. 'God no. Those are the keys to my TR4. It struck me that now you're a driving man again, you really could do with your own set of wheels. I've been thinking about this for a while, about letting you borrow the TR4 on a permanent basis, especially since I will be racing the DB5 from now on.'

'But you use that car to commute.'

'Not anymore, as I've finally cracked and bought myself an Audi S4 with working air conditioning, ABS, and all the toys. It's being delivered tomorrow. Anyway, I don't want the TR4 languishing in my garage. She deserves more than that. That's why I want you to drive her from now on, Joseph. See it as a thank you for all your help restoring both vehicles.'

'Even though I was the one who totalled the TR4 during that racing accident, you'd seriously still trust me with her for day-to-day use?'

'I do, but dent one panel, and you'll pay for it.' A grin cracked Chris's face.

Joseph raked his hand through his hair. 'Then I don't know what to say.'

'Maybe a good bottle of Irish single malt would suffice.'

'Done. And thank you for this, Chris, seriously. Although, I'm not giving up my mountain bike anytime soon.'

'I realise that, but for moments like now, pedal power isn't always the best option, certainly not for getting all the way over to Banbury.'

A smile curled the corner of Joseph's mouth. 'You're not wrong there.'

He set down the rest of the lethal homebrew and, with a nod to the DCI, headed toward the TR4 parked in the garage. He couldn't help running his fingers over the red bonnet, just wishing this first solo drive in her was under much happier circumstances.

CHAPTER THREE

THE WIND WHIPPED through Joseph's hair, leaching the body heat from his head. The DI was seriously starting to wish he'd brought a hat with him. Despite the decidedly nippy three-degree Celsius spring evening, he hadn't been able to resist lowering the soft top.

'Are you sure the heater in this thing doesn't go any higher than flipping lukewarm?' Megan asked, zipping her wool jacket right up to just beneath her chin.

'I don't think the heater is the TR4's strongest aspect, at least with her roof down,' Joseph replied. 'But having said that, you've got to agree this car was designed to be driven like this.'

Megan gave him a sceptical look. 'Maybe in the height of summer, but now?' She gestured to the night-time frost still lingering on the shadow-covered side of the hedgerow next to the road that the sun hadn't been able to reach. 'Look, don't get me wrong. You know how big a petrolhead I am, but there's a time and a place for going topless.'

Joseph chuckled. 'I know, but just indulge me on this, her maiden work-related road trip.'

Megan let out a mock sigh. 'Fine, but you so owe me dinner

for putting up with this ordeal. Or better still, let me take the wheel.'

'Only if Chris agrees to it, as don't forget this is a loan vehicle,' the DI replied as they passed the sign for Banbury and began heading through the outskirts of town.

'Oh, I'm sure I can butter him up.' The DC cast him a sideways look. 'I have to ask, why did Chris lend you his precious set of wheels for your very own runaround, anyway?'

'I certainly didn't see it coming, but who am I to look a gift horse in the mouth?'

'Lucky you. But I suppose if Morse had his jags, Stone can have his Triumph. It's only a matter of time before you treat yourself to some leather string-backed driving gloves to complete your new look.'

Joseph snorted as he glanced at the satnav on his phone clamped to the dashboard.

'Not far to go.'

Megan's expression grew serious. 'I did a quick search online of DCI Hart as I was waiting for you to pick me up. There's nothing there but praise for him.'

Joseph let out a long breath and nodded. 'He was certainly one of the good guys. That's why none of this makes any sense, Megan. I spoke to the lead IOPC investigator who's been assigned to this case, Geoff Flynn. His initial assessment is that there's no obvious motive. Everyone at the Banbury station said Simon seemed as upbeat as usual. But then again, Simon wouldn't be the first person to hide problems he might have been having, even from those closest to him.'

'Okay, I can understand that with a bit of depression. Most people don't want to share that sort of stuff. But based on what you've already told me about Simon, for him to kill DI Roberts, somebody who was meant to be his best mate, surely that doesn't make any sense?'

'I know, I know. How dark a place must he have been in? That's why I'm hoping Simon's wife, Julia, may open up to us in a way she hasn't already to the IOPC investigators, to help shed some light on what happened.'

'Talking of the IOPC, what exactly is our role here, Joseph? Aren't we in danger of stepping on their toes?'

'Basically, Derrick has sent us over as an extra set of eyes, which can't hurt. He's also hoping because of my connection to both men, I might turn something up, especially as I also knew both their widows as well.'

Megan shot the DI a grim look. 'That's going to be a very difficult conversation, especially so soon after their husbands' death. But if anyone can, it will be you, Joseph.'

The DI blew out his cheeks. 'Thanks for the vote of confidence, but we'll see. I'm not sure even the softest words can ease heartbreak at a time like this.'

The satnav chimed and said, 'Turn left onto Meadowfield Close. Then your destination is a hundred yards on the left.'

'Ready for this?' Joseph asked.

'No, but I'll do it anyway,' the DC replied.

A few moments later, they pulled up in front of a brick, three-bedroom house with an extension built over the garage.

The first thing Joseph noticed as they got out of the car was that all the curtains were closed despite it still being a sunny spring evening outside. A small pile of Amazon parcels also sat outside the front door.

'Are you sure anyone's home?' Megan asked as her gaze swept over the closed curtains as well.

'I spoke to Julia earlier, and she's expecting us,' Joseph replied. 'She's probably just trying to keep a low profile.'

'Understandable in the circumstances.'

'Aye. At least the press hasn't tracked her down yet, although that's only a matter of time.'

Joseph took a deep breath as they headed up the drive. He couldn't help but notice there wasn't a weed in the flower beds or any moss between the immaculate paving stones. The windows looked as though they'd recently had a fresh lick of paint as well. Simon had always been one of those officers who kept every aspect of his work life meticulously organised to the point the others had teased him that he was in danger of being OCD. Certainly, judging by the well-tended appearance of the DCI's home, that ordered approach had also extended to his personal life.

Joseph pressed the doorbell and he mentally braced himself as they heard a chime somewhere within the house. A moment later, a shape moved beyond the frosted glass. The door opened, and a young woman with red hair, wearing a jumper and jeans, looked out at them.

'DI Stone and DC Anderson?' the woman asked.

'Yes, and you are?' Joseph asked.

'PC Sarah Collins. I'm the liaison officer assigned to Julia to look after her.'

Joseph was relieved to hear the Banbury team hadn't abandoned one of their own. Julia would certainly need all the support she could get right now.

'Good to hear. So how's she doing?'

'As badly as you might expect and still very much in a state of shock. Her GP has already given her a course of sedatives, but she's refusing to take any.'

Sarah looked past them, her eyes narrowing as a vehicle approached with a tabloid logo on its side.

'Great, here come the vultures. I better go and deal with them. If you'd like to see yourselves in, Julia is in the living room.'

'Good luck with those feckers,' Joseph said, casting a scowl towards the vehicle as it pulled up behind the TR4.

The PC nodded and she scooped up the parcels, placing them in the porch, before heading down the driveway to confront the journalist and photographer getting out of their car.

The two detectives headed through the hallway and into a darkened lounge. Julia Hart, a dark-haired woman in her forties with a drawn expression and red-rimmed eyes, looked up at them from the armchair she was sitting in. The moment she saw Joseph, she let out a half-sob before standing, closing the distance, and throwing her arms around him.

'Oh, Joseph...'

The DI felt her whole frame shaking in his arms as he wrapped them around her. 'I am so sorry, Julia. I just don't have the words.'

'No one has. And I still can't believe Simon's gone—and Alex, too,' she said, her breath catching in her throat.

Megan watched, her expression full of compassion. The two of them stood like that for several moments before Julia finally pulled away, wiping her tears away with her hand.

'I'm so sorry about that, but the grief keeps coming up from nowhere,' she said.

'Nothing to be sorry for,' Joseph said with a gentle voice, rubbing her arms.

Megan looked between them. 'If there was ever a time for a strong cup of tea, this is it.'

'Oh, of course. Where are my manners?' Julia started to head for the door.

Megan shook her head. 'Please let me make it.'

Julia gave her a lost look and then nodded. 'That would be wonderful. And you are...?'

'Sorry, I'm DC Megan Anderson, a colleague of Joseph's, and I like to think his friend,' she said, reaching out her hand.

Julia shook it. 'Then I'm very pleased to meet you, Megan.

Any friend of Joseph's is always welcome here. I just wish it wasn't like this.'

Megan nodded, squeezing the woman's hand with both of hers, before heading off to the kitchen.

Julia's grief hung heavily in the living room as she cradled a large mug of tea to her chest. The two detectives sat opposite on the sofa. Sarah had joined them, having read the tabloid journalists the riot act, sitting on a stool to one side.

To Joseph, it seemed like pain exuded from every pore of Julia's being. She was every bit the victim that Alex, not to mention his widow, Carol, was. The only blessing was that neither family had children to mourn the loss of their fathers as well.

'Julia,' Joseph began gently as Megan opened her notebook, 'are you all right to answer a few questions?'

The woman let out a long, low sigh. 'I've already done plenty of that with the IOPC investigator, Geoff Flynn. He was a lovely man and very sympathetic. But he did a very thorough job of questioning me about why Simon did any of this. I'm not sure what else there is to say.'

Joseph nodded. That's exactly what Geoff had told him on the way over. The investigator had brought the DI up to speed with the state of play so far, including the fact that Julia had been able to provide Simon's password, making it a fairly quick task to unlock his laptop. The forensic technical team had already pored over it, but so far, nothing had emerged from the secrets buried in its drive to suggest a motive for DCI Simon Hart's actions.

Joseph looked at the woman he'd last seen at Simon and

Alex's going-away bash at the Scholar's Retreat twenty years ago, before they'd transferred to the Banbury station.

'I'm sorry to have to go over this again, but I'm just hoping we can turn up something that Geoff might have missed. To start with, I thought Simon and Alex were the best of friends, so was there some falling out between them?'

'As I told Geoff, not that I know of,' Julia replied. 'They were in the five-a-side football match together on Thursday evening, something they did every week, the night before all this happened, and there was certainly no trouble then. As you know, Joseph, our families were as closely knit as it's possible to be. We even went on holidays together.' She looked down at the cup of tea she clutched like a lifeline. 'I've tried to reach out to Carol this morning, but she doesn't want anything to do with me.' She looked up to search the DI's face. 'I suppose you'll be talking to her as well?'

'Yes, although once again, according to Geoff, she didn't know anything either.'

'In that case, when you do talk to her, please pass on my condolences and tell her just how heartbroken I am for her.'

Joseph couldn't help but be moved by this act of compassion from a woman who had also just lost her own husband. 'Of course I will.'

Megan leaned forward a fraction in her seat. 'Can you tell us whether there was any sign your husband was under any strain when he left for work this morning?'

'Not that I noticed. We'd even been talking that morning over breakfast about him taking early retirement so we could open the B&B we'd always dreamed of running by the seaside in Cromer.' She clutched her hands tighter around her mug. 'We really had everything to look forward to, Joseph, which is why I just don't understand any of this...' She looked at the detectives, eyes blinking rapidly. 'I just need to know why? I keep asking myself if there was something I could have done, said, that would have stopped him.'

'Just so you know, everyone at the station feels the same way,' Sarah said. 'The problem was, your husband seemed fine right up until what happened this morning.'

Julia nodded, the lines deepening around her eyes. 'The only thing I can think of is Simon was suffering from some sort of mental health problem he somehow hid from me.'

Joseph kept his expression neutral because he'd heard exactly that same theory suggested by Geoff during their phone call.

'Is there anything you can think of, however trivial, that might have suggested he was having that sort of problem?' Megan asked.

'Absolutely nothing at all,' Julia replied. 'All I can tell you is that the man who shot Alex and then stepped in front of that van, isn't the same man I married. And you know Simon, Joseph. He was as grounded as they came. Alex, too, for that matter. I certainly can't think of anything he might have done to make my husband want to murder him.'

'In that case, is there anything in his personal possessions that might give us a clue as to his state of mind?' the DI asked.

'Geoff and his team have already taken anything of interest, including Simon's laptop and notebooks from his study. But feel free to look through it again in case they missed anything.'

'Thank you, we'll do that,' Megan replied.

'Then if you wouldn't mind, I'd rather stay here. It's too painful for me to go into his study. I can't bear seeing the sight of his empty desk in what Simon jokingly used to call his man cave.'

'I can show you where it is,' Sarah added.

'Thank you, then we'll take a look at it now,' Joseph replied.

A few moments later, as they climbed the stairs following

Sarah, Joseph noticed a framed photograph on the landing. It was a picture of a smiling Simon and Julia with a tropical beach in the background. Happier times in a different lifetime.

'Just through here,' Sarah said, gesturing to a door to the left of the landing.

Joseph and Megan entered a small room to find a desk facing the window. For such a small space, it was stuffed full of things, from golf clubs to fishing rods. There was also a small collection of rather good single malts and a cut crystal tumbler next to them. Next to that was a bookshelf overflowing with books and photos, mostly of family, but some work-related ones too. It was among these that Joseph recognised a much more youthful version of himself, along with Derrick, Simon, and Alex in the Scholar's Retreat. It had been taken back in the day when they were still serving as PCs. They each held a pint in their hands as they gurned at the camera—a tight-knit group back then with plenty of banter and laughter.

It struck Joseph that this photo was evidence of just how easy it was to let friendships drift apart if you didn't put the legwork into maintaining them. That was certainly something he'd been guilty of after Simon and Alex had moved to Banbury station to become the Starsky and Hutch team of the Cotswolds, as they'd called themselves. How times had changed.

A chime came from the doorbell, and Sarah crossed to the window to look down at the driveway. 'Wonderful, yet more journalists. I better deal with this.'

Joseph nodded and as the PC departed, he and Megan set to work searching the study. Not surprisingly, after the IOPC's visit, the room had been picked clean of anything of real interest, so there wasn't exactly a lot left to examine. The desk itself was almost empty apart from a few pen pots and the faded outline around a dark rectangle, presumably where Simon's laptop had sat until that morning.

'Anything useful yet?' Joseph asked after a few minutes as he opened a filing cabinet that turned out to be empty.

'The only thing I can tell you so far is that Simon loved his golf and fishing based on the number of books he has about them. Oh, and there's this.' The DC held up a self-hypnosis book. 'It's for quitting smoking by that famous mentalist, Damien Storme.'

Joseph nodded. 'When I knew Simon, he was a twenty-a-day man, and tried kicking the habit several times. I can imagine he tried absolutely everything to try and help him stop.'

'Well, maybe this was what did the trick. I wonder if this guy does one for sleep because I often have trouble nodding off. Of course, I blame the job.'

'Aye, you wouldn't be the first officer that suffers like that, present company included. Anyway, as far as I can see, there's nothing obvious in here. We should head over to see Alex's wife.'

'Shouldn't we check in with Geoff Flynn at the Banbury station?' Megan said.

'That will be the next thing on our list. Come on, we better say our goodbyes and get going.'

As they headed downstairs, Sarah was standing at the front door, berating the fresh crop of journalists. She raised her eyebrows at the two detectives as they passed her.

The detectives walked back into the living room to find Julia staring into space, her cup of cold, untouched tea clasped in her hands.

'Julia?' Joseph said gently.

She blinked as if surfacing from a dark place in her mind. 'Did you find anything at all useful?'

He shook his head. 'No, nothing, I'm afraid.'

'I see,' she murmured. 'But you will be attending Simon's funeral, won't you?'

'You can count on it,' Joseph replied. 'Anyway, we better head off as we have other people to see. But if there is anything, anything at all you need, you call me day or night.' He handed her his card.

The broken woman gave him a small nod. 'Thank you. Just please do your best to clear Simon's name. I realise how this must all look, that my husband suffered some sort of mental breakdown, but as I keep telling everyone, none of this equals the man I know—I mean, knew—and loved.'

Joseph held her gaze, feeling her desperation as he would if he'd been in her situation. 'We'll do our best, Julia. You have my word.'

A few minutes later, the two detectives were back in the TR4, heading towards Carol Roberts's house just a few streets over, but this time with the soft roof firmly up and the cabin actually verging on cosy.

Megan glanced at her notebook and shook her head. 'Why would a good man throw everything away without a reason?'

'Fingers crossed the IOPC team has turned up something by now,' Joseph replied as he turned the car onto another residential road, getting ready to have another difficult conversation with another grieving widow.

CHAPTER FOUR

AFTER A TREMENDOUSLY DIFFICULT, but largely fruitless, visit with Alex's wife, Carol, Joseph and Megan sat across from the IOPC investigator, Geoff Flynn. He was a grey-haired man with a well-lined brow, square-framed glasses, and a jaw to match. The detectives were sitting with the man and the rest of his investigation team in the temporary incident room allocated to them at the Banbury Police Station.

The DI had already made a point of sticking his head around the door of another room in the station where a parallel investigation was being held into the cannabis farm hit, to share his condolences with Simon and Alex's colleagues. To a person, the detectives' faces had all looked drawn. To lose one officer always hits everyone hard, let alone two. And to lose them under such awful circumstances... It would take everyone a long time to mentally and emotionally process that. But Joseph had been impressed that the team had knuckled down with their own investigation. There was still a job to do, and that's exactly what Simon and Alex's colleagues were doing. It spoke volumes about their professionalism and the calibre of the officers involved.

Joseph focused his attention on the IOPC incident board.

From what he could see, it was filled with lots of speculation about why DCI Simon Hart would have been at the epicentre of this earthquake that had ripped through the Banbury station.

'Looks like you are just as in the dark about all of this as we are,' the DI finally said.

Geoff Flynn looked over the top of his glasses at the board and nodded. 'We've found nothing so far in the way of a possible motive for any of this. Certainly, based on the testimony of both men's widows, Simon and Alex really were the best of friends outside work.'

'And what about at work?' Megan asked.

'Everyone here says exactly the same thing. Apparently, only yesterday, the two men were talking about both their families getting tickets for the Reading Music Festival later this year.'

'That doesn't sound like the actions of two mates who had fallen out,' Joseph said.

'Precisely, and that's backed up by the picture we've been able to build about the two men by trawling through their laptops, phones, and work computers. There's absolutely nothing there to suggest there was any issue between the two men either. If there was a grievance, it was certainly a well-hidden one.'

Joseph noticed Megan chewing her lip. He immediately recognised the tell-tale sign she had something she wanted to say. 'What are you thinking there?'

'I hate to suggest this, but I don't suppose there's a possibility that Alex might have been having an affair with Simon's wife, is there?'

The DI stared at her, but then his expression softened. 'I suppose we do need to consider absolutely every angle, however unlikely. But for what it's worth, back in the day, I know how devoted Simon was to his wife, and her to him. Based on that, at least, I find the idea of any sort of affair unlikely.'

Geoff was already nodding. 'It's something we've already considered. But once again, there's nothing to hint at anything like that going on based on what we've been able to find out so far. I can tell you, that was a very sensitive conversation to have with two grieving widows.'

Joseph sucked air between his teeth. 'I can imagine, although knowing them both well, I suspect they understood why you needed to ask them about that.'

'They did, and talking of which, in light of your personal connection to both families, did either woman say anything to you that they might have held back from us?'

'Which is the real reason we're here. But I'm afraid they really are as much in the dark as the rest of us.'

'Yes, that's exactly the impression that I was left with.' Geoff's gaze flicked again to the incident board and the list of possible motives, all with question marks after them. 'I'm afraid that leaves us with one of three conclusions.'

'The first being DCI Hart suffered some sort of mental break?' Megan asked.

The lead investigator nodded. 'That's what I would lean towards, apart from the fact there's no prior evidence to suggest Simon was struggling with mental health issues. He even attended one of those optional police wellbeing courses recently. There was nothing reported there to suggest any sort of psychological issues.'

'When I knew Simon, he was as grounded as they came,' Joseph added.

'So if you're leaning towards ruling that out, what's the other possibilities?' Megan asked.

'Perhaps he had some sort of drug problem that no one knew about.'

'I suppose that's something we can't ignore,' Joseph said. 'So what about the third possibility?'

'That Simon could have had some sort of medical issue like an undiagnosed brain tumour that made him act so out of character. Doctor Jacobs is specifically going to be looking for any evidence of that during the autopsy.'

At hearing that, Joseph felt something relax a fraction inside him. Somehow a medical issue was easier for the DI to get his head around than any of the previous suggestions.

'Hopefully, that will deliver results and means we're on the verge of getting to the bottom of this catastrophe,' Joseph said. 'In the meantime, I don't think there's a lot more we can do to assist you, at least for the time being. Obviously, on a personal level, I intend to support both families as best I can.'

'I think they both need all the help they can get right now,' Geoff replied. ' I think you'll be happy to hear you won't be alone in that effort, especially with Julia. There's already a groundswell of support for her from the Banbury team here. Officers who knew both families intend to help both widows in any way they can.'

'That's good to hear,' Megan said.

Joseph nodded. 'Then we best be away and back to St Aldates to report in. Please keep us posted about how you're getting on, and if you think we can be of any more assistance, just let us know.'

'I will,' Geoff replied, reaching out and first shaking Joseph's hand, then Megan's.

As the two detectives headed out of the door, they almost ran straight into Amy, emerging from an interview room opposite.

In a glance, the DI took in the ashen face of the SOCO. 'Are you okay?' he asked.

'Not really. It's been a bit of a morning...'

'That sounds like the understatement of the century, but at least you and your colleagues are okay,' Megan said.

Amy drew in a shaky breath and nodded.

It was the first time Joseph had ever seen Amy so badly shaken. Angry on occasion, but never like this.

'It must have been shocking to witness,' he said.

'With a weapon Simon seized from me, Joseph,' Amy added, ashen-faced. 'I keep rerunning things in my head about how I should've tried to snatch it back, tried to stop him.'

'Tricky to do, when, from what I hear, he knocked you out first,' Megan said.

'I know, but if I'd moved faster, been better——' A choked-off sob cut off the rest of her words.

Despite all the reasons Joseph had to loathe the woman standing before them, just like that, his emotional armour was pierced and he found himself reaching out to squeeze her shoulder.

Amy responded at once, burying her head into his shoulder. As she shook in his arms, Joseph glanced at Megan.

She gave him an understanding look. 'I'll see you back in the car, Joseph,' she said. Then she gently rubbed the SOCO's back. 'Just try not to second guess yourself, Amy. You did all you could.' Then she grimaced at Joseph before heading away along the corridor.

Amy finally pulled away from the DI. 'Sorry...'

'Don't be. I more than understand. But apart from being knocked out and badly shaken, you're okay otherwise, aren't you?'

'I'll probably suffer from some nightmares after this.'

Joseph gazed into her eyes. 'I think most people would.'

'Apart from you, maybe. You seem to have nerves of steel when it comes to this sort of thing.' She gave him a small smile.

'I'm not so sure about that. I'm actually finding this all hard to process, as I knew both men. I just can't get my head around him doing anything like this.'

'Then, for what it's worth, Simon didn't seem like himself when he seized the gun from me.'

Joseph gave her a questioning look. 'What do you mean exactly?'

Amy dipped her chin towards the room she'd just emerged from. 'As I just told the IOPC investigator, it was like he was zoned out and, I realise this is going to sound strange, but almost like he was sleepwalking.'

'First thing in the morning, I don't think so... Unless...'

Amy peered at him. 'What is it?'

'The IOPC team are already considering the idea that Simon was suffering from some sort of medical issue like a brain tumour.'

'Now, there's something I hadn't considered,' Amy replied. 'It would certainly fit in with the zoned-out state I saw him in.'

'Well, hopefully we'll know for sure one way or another when Rob does the autopsy later today. Meanwhile, you should get yourself home and get some rest.'

The SOCO shook her head. 'No, the best thing I can do is push through this by getting back to work. Besides, I need to help the others analyse the forensic material we recovered from the house and the assassination of the crime gang.'

Just like a switch had been thrown inside him, Joseph felt a pulse of anger at hearing that. No wonder she was so keen to get back to work. If the Night Watchmen had been involved in the hit, Amy had a job to do. Based on previous experience with the SOCO and her actions at the Shotgun Raiders crime scene, no doubt she'd go out of her way to make sure that any critical evidence linking this latest hit to the crime syndicate would never come to light.

The DI kept his expression as neutral as possible in an attempt to not give away his internal thought process. 'Okay, but just try not to push yourself too hard.'

She gave him a small shrug. 'You know me.' Then she leaned in and kissed him on the cheek before heading away.

Joseph watched her go with conflicting emotions. Part of him felt genuinely sorry for the ordeal Amy had gone through. But the bigger part was extremely wary. After all, this was the same woman who had so expertly manipulated him into doing the bidding of the Night Watchmen.

As God was his witness, when the time came, Joseph would do whatever it took to help Chris and the NCA investigation to bring Amy and the other corrupt officers, along with the Night Watchmen, all tumbling down.

'This is a bad business,' Derrick said to Joseph in his office back in St Aldates.

'It is,' the DI replied. 'I keep looking for an explanation, and I have to say I'm putting my hope in Rob discovering some sort of previously undiagnosed brain condition.'

'In other words, to suggest he didn't really know what he was doing?' the DSU asked.

'That would at least fit with the behaviour Amy observed. She said it was almost like he was sleepwalking. If it was a brain tumour, it could explain an awful lot.'

Derrick nodded, but Joseph couldn't help noticing the troubled look on the man's face.

'What is it?' he asked.

'I was looking through Simon's record to see if there might be any explanation for what he did. There was nothing there, but there was something that triggered a memory about a case I hadn't thought about in over twenty years. That commendation that Simon got for finding that crucial piece of evidence in the Samuel Dawson case we all worked on together. He was that very successful psychologist who murdered his wife by slitting her throat. Do you remember?'

'Of course I do. It was the first murder scene we ever attended together.' Joseph decided to keep quiet about Derrick throwing his guts up. 'If I remember correctly, there'd been heated arguments overheard by neighbours, including one where Samuel actually threatened to kill her in their garden. But that was all circumstantial evidence until we were tasked with a sweep across the area, and Simon found that box cutter with Eleanor's blood and Samuel's prints on it.'

It had been thrown over a hedge a couple hundred metres away from the house. After that, all the pieces slotted together, and it was an easy prosecution for the CPS.

'Despite all of that, there was one dissenting voice—yours,' Derrick replied.

'Aye, there was just something about the way Samuel kept protesting his innocence. Then he took his life a year later in prison, leaving that letter saying he'd been framed.'

'Yes, but do you also remember what the forensic psychologist said at the time?'

'That Dawson had mentally blocked out what he'd done as a coping mechanism.'

'And he certainly wasn't the first, nor will he be the last. After all, if you listen to half the cons in prison, they're all bloody innocent.'

Joseph smiled. 'Aye, you're not wrong there.'

Derrick nodded as he turned and took a bottle of whiskey out of his desk. 'Fancy one to toast Simon and Alex's memories?'

'No, I'm grand. Thanks all the same.'

The DSU poured himself what Joseph looked like a triple before turning back towards his screen and gesturing toward it. 'So I was looking through the notes on Samuel's case when I came across something rather surprising in the Holmes 2 database. That's actually why I bought up Dawson. Do you remember the senior crown prosecutor who worked on it?'

'Laura Whitcombe, if I remember correctly?' Joseph said.

'That's the one.'

'I'm not going to forget her in a hurry. She was a regular wolf in court and really went for Dawson's throat.'

'Well, you're not going to believe this, but she died a month ago.'

Joseph shot the big man a surprised look. 'I take it, by you mentioning it at all, we're not talking about natural causes here?'

'Not if you take into account that Laura fell headfirst off the top of a multi-storey car park.'

'Feck, not a great way to shuffle off this mortal coil. Any evidence of foul play?'

'Not according to a CCTV camera that caught her final moments. She walked up to the top level of the car park and, as casually as you like, climbed onto the wall, and leapt off. The thing is, and the reason I bring it up now, is that just like Simon, no one could find any obvious reason for Laura to take her life.'

'Okay, that really is one hell of a coincidence.'

'Which is probably all it is. But I just thought I should mention it. Anyway, this latest tragedy aside, do the cannabis farm murders look similar to the other Night Watchmen hits?'

'I'm afraid so. From what I've been able to gather, the MP5 submachine gun bullet casings are identical to their other shooting sprees.'

'Bloody hell, when is all this bloodshed going to stop? The sooner we bring them down, the better. Talking of which, you're still a hundred percent sure Chris isn't in the Night Watchmen's pocket?'

Joseph didn't hesitate. 'Completely certain.'

'And I don't suppose you're going to tell me how you know that, exactly?'

'It's better you don't know. Just take it from me, Chris is one of the good guys.' He had to bite his tongue about Amy, not to mention DCI Charlton from the Cowley station, also being in the Night Watchmen's pay. Chris had explicitly told Joseph he needed to keep any information regarding the investigation to himself. Apart from that, the DI couldn't help but feel like the less that Derrick knew, the safer it would be for him.

'Okay, I'm going to have to trust you on this,' Derrick said. 'But it doesn't make me any happier about sitting on my hands, especially when we have every reason to believe all these ongoing gangland massacres are connected to the Night Watchmen. Just knowing Kennan is involved makes me sick to my stomach.'

If only you knew who else, Joseph thought to himself. Out loud he said, 'Look, the moment we have concrete evidence, the sooner we'll be able to bring her and the others in, but we're still not there yet.'

'I know, but I'm not comfortable with this wait-and-watch approach. I bet Kate isn't either.'

'Oh, I can assure you, she isn't.'

'So you've seen her then?' Derrick sat up straighter.

'Just on and off,' Joseph replied with a deliberate effort to avoid telling him the truth about the fact that the two of them were an item again. He'd also sworn Chris and Megan, the only people at work who knew about him getting back together with his ex-wife, to secrecy for the time being.

'And how's she doing?' Derrick asked.

'Working too hard at the newspaper as usual, but otherwise, she seems fine.'

'That's good to hear,' Derrick replied, taking a long sip of his whisky.

Joseph nodded, trying to avoid the searchlight gaze of the

DSU. 'If you don't need me for anything else, I need my bed. This has been a long day of it.'

'No, that's all. Another date night with Amy, is it?'

'Something like that,' Joseph replied, completely and deliberately ducking the question.

Just like the situation with Kate, this was another one he was playing close to his chest. For now, he and Amy had kept very quiet about their breakup to try to avoid the inevitable office gossip. But he knew it was just a matter of time before everything regarding his personal life came to light. Probably when someone saw him and Kate together.

Yes, the sooner she came clean with Derrick, the better, as far as he was concerned. He was certainly going to bring it up again with Kate when he saw her on Tús Nua for their date-night dinner. To say he felt duplicitous lying to Derrick's face, would be the understatement of the year.

'Then have a good time,' Derrick said. With that, he returned his attention to his screen and his whisky.

Taking that as his cue to make a swift exit, Joseph headed for the door before he could tangle himself up in any more half-truths. He'd had quite enough of those for one conversation.

CHAPTER FIVE

Joseph's narrowboat neighbour, the one and only Professor Dylan Shaw, cast a beady eye over the DI's culinary efforts in his galley kitchen on board Tús Nua.

'Are you sure you didn't rush the roux, and you remembered to stir it for a good twenty minutes until it was the colour of peanut butter?' his friend asked as he peered into the slow cooker pot.

'You can relax; I did. I also made sure I properly browned the chicken and fresh chorizo sausages first thing this morning. Then I caramelised what you called the holy trinity of onions, peppers, and celery, before adding them in. In other words, I followed your very precise recipe to the letter.'

A relieved smile filled the professor's face as though Joseph had been attempting brain surgery rather than just preparing a meal.

'Good, good. Then everything should be on track for an exceptional culinary experience. But the real test is in the tasting. Do you mind?' The professor gestured with a spoon towards the pot.

'Knock yourself out,' Joseph said as he prepared the side dish of okra.

The DI couldn't help but keep a sideways look on his friend as he scooped up a portion with the wooden spoon and raised it to his mouth. As Joseph waited for his reaction, he tensed a little. Dylan set a very high bar indeed when it came to cooking. Thankfully, a smile filled the professor's face.

'That, my dear man, is exceptional. I certainly couldn't have done better myself. I would pay good money for that in any New Orleans restaurant.'

'That's a relief and high praise indeed when coming from you. But do you think Kate's going to enjoy it?'

'Without a doubt. If food could sweep someone off their feet, this dish would manage it. I'm certain that your wooing efforts with this gumbo will be highly appreciated.'

'Wooing now, is it? You're so firmly minted in the last century.' Joseph smiled as he took the cornbread he had baked to accompany the meal, also at his friend's suggestion, out of the oven.

Dylan chuckled, as he leant in to examine the freshly baked bread. 'That looks perfect, but I have to warn you, cornbread is addictive stuff. You'll find yourself using any excuse to make it after this.'

'I don't think there's much danger of that,' Joseph replied. 'The gumbo alone has been stressful enough. For any future dates, I'll be taking Kate out to restaurants.'

Dylan pulled a face. 'If you want to win her heart, a home-cooked meal will beat a restaurant every time.'

'Will you stop with all this wooing advice already?'

The professor chuckled as Joseph's phone rang.

When he saw Geoff Flynn's name on the display, he immediately took the call.

'Joseph, I thought you would want to hear the results of

DCI Hart's post-mortem,' the IOPC investigator said. 'It's just come through from Doctor Jacobs.'

'Then don't keep me in suspense.'

'Despite the massive trauma from the impact of the van that hit the DCI, it turns out Simon's brain hadn't been damaged. But I'm afraid Doctor Jacobs found absolutely no sign of any brain tumour. He also said the lab report showed there weren't any traces of any drugs in his bloodstream, either. You do realise what that means?'

Joseph sighed. 'That Simon really did suffer some sort of mental break.'

'Exactly. I realise that's not the answer you probably wanted to hear.'

'Aye, you're not wrong. But thanks for letting me know anyway.'

'No problem. I'll let you get on with the rest of your evening. Goodnight.' Geoff ended the call.

Dylan was looking at the DI. 'I caught most of that. I hope you don't mind me asking, but this sounds like a new case?'

'Yes, but it's actually an investigation into one of our own that Derrick asked me to liaise with the IOPC about. It involves the death of an old friend, DCI Simon Hart. He committed suicide after shooting his colleague, DI Alex Roberts, another old mate of ours.'

'Good grief, Joseph, I'm so sorry. Do you know what his motive was yet?'

'That's the thing, Dylan, no one can find one—at least so far. It's certainly not often that I find myself wishing that someone had a brain tumour like I was hoping to hear from Rob's autopsy findings. The thing is, I'd find that easier to deal with rather than the alternative.'

'Some sort of mental breakdown, based on what I just overheard?'

Joseph nodded. 'That's the only plausible explanation we're left with, unless there was some feud between the two men that nobody's been able to discover so far. But there is one rather strange coincidence. Back in the day, both men worked alongside Derrick and me as young PCs. There was this investigation we were all assisting on, where a psychologist called Samuel Dawson was accused of murdering his wife. Derrick and I were actually the first on the scene after her screams were heard by their neighbours. The thing was, I was never happy that Samuel was our man.'

'And you were eventually proved right?' Dylan asked.

Joseph shook his head. 'If only. You see, Samuel Dawson took his own life in prison. The psychiatric report at the time was very black and white about him not being able to live with the guilt, even though he continued to protest his innocence in a suicide note.'

'But you still think he was innocent?'

'I'm a lone voice when it comes to that, and it's only based on instinct.'

'An instinct that has proven to be very insightful, time and time again.'

'Maybe, but there was no evidence to support it this time round.' Joseph looked out through the cabin window at the towpath, where his cat, Tux, was sitting in a puddle of spring sunlight. 'Anyway, about that strange coincidence, I mentioned. It turns out that Simon and Alex aren't the first people who were involved in that investigation to have died. A T-Rex of a crown prosecutor, Laura Whitcombe, someone who was instrumental in getting Samuel convicted, died a month ago when she leapt from the top of a car park.'

'So we're talking another case of suicide, then?' Dylan asked, giving his friend a thoughtful look.

'That's apparently what the CCTV footage from the car

park showed. But, just like with Simon's death, there seems to have been no motive for her taking her own life.'

'Alright, that really is quite a coincidence. But then again, I suppose statistically this is just one of those strange things that life occasionally throws up. After all, there are a lot of people out there who are maybe more troubled than they let on, even to those closest to them.'

'You're not wrong there,' Joseph replied, thinking about his own struggles after the death of his baby son, Eoin, which he'd kept very much to himself for years.

Dylan gave him a look that suggested he knew exactly what Joseph was thinking, before he glanced at the clock. 'I better leave you to it. Kate will be here any moment.'

'Thank you again for all your help. Before you go, there's been one thing I've been meaning to ask. How are you and Iris getting on? Have you got around to any wooing of your own and arranging that first date yet?'

The professor scowled at him. 'As I keep telling you, it's purely a platonic friendship, Joseph.'

The DI made a scoffing sound. 'So says you. I've seen the way you are around each other. Ask her out already, or I'll do it for you.'

Dylan stared at him. 'You wouldn't dare.'

'Wouldn't I?' Joseph crossed his arms. 'Unless you want to test me, I suggest you get on and get cracking before I'm forced to do some sort of intervention on your behalf. Maybe I'll enlist Kate and Ellie's help as well, just like you've done with me over loosening up about my daughter dating a police officer.'

'Well, you needed a nudge when it came to John. Tell me it wasn't right for us to give you a nudge to make him feel welcome?'

'Aye, he's as good a man as I could hope for my daughter to

date. So like then, when you weren't wrong to intervene, the same applies to me now, regarding you and Iris.'

Dylan pulled a face at him. 'And I thought you were my friend.'

'I am indeed, and that's why I'm going to give you a kick up the arse to encourage you to get your act together.'

The professor held up his hands. 'Alright, alright, message received and understood.'

'You promise you're going to actually do something about it? After all, a crossword is all well and good, but it doesn't exactly keep you warm in your bed at night.'

The professor arched his eyebrows at his friend. 'It seems I'm going to have to arrange a date with her, if only for a quiet life from you. Anyway, I'm not so sure I should give you your gift now.'

'A gift, is it? Oh, go on, you know you want to.'

A small smile curled the corners of Dylan's mouth. 'Well, it would be a waste of a lot of research on your behalf.' He dug into the canvas bag and withdrew a bottle of gin. 'A present for your and Kate's enjoyment—a bottle of Opihr Oriental Spiced Gin to go with your meal tonight.'

'Sorry, you're seriously suggesting there's a gin to go with gumbo?' Joseph said, examining the bottle with a sceptical look.

'I'm not saying it didn't present a greater challenge than usual, but I got there in the end. You see, Ophir is infused with cardamom, coriander, and black pepper. Thanks to that, it will perfectly mirror the gumbo's warm spices.'

Joseph gave his friend an impressed look. 'I doff my imaginary hat to you yet again for your knowledge of gin and food pairings. Thank you for this, and I'm sure Kate's going to appreciate it as well.'

'Just try to maybe keep a glass or three back for me, so I can try it. And maybe a portion of that rather excellent gumbo as well to go with it.'

'Consider it done, my friend.'

'Then I really better get going. I hope your dinner date with Kate is everything you hope it to be.'

'I have a feeling it will be, and in no small part due to your help,' Joseph replied. 'Maybe I can reciprocate by choosing some Irish poetry for you to read to Iris on your own date.'

Dylan's lips thinned. 'I'm not about to start spouting Yeats to her anytime soon.'

'Actually, I was thinking more of Bono from U2. A contemporary poet to rival the old greats. I tell you, play her, All I Want Is You, and she'll be putty in your hands. Works every time with Kate.'

Dylan eye-rolled him. 'Thank you for that suggestion.'

Joseph grinned. 'Anytime, my friend.'

Shaking his head, the professor grabbed his bag and opened the door to find Kate standing there, her hand raised to knock on the door, and Tux winding himself around her legs.

Kate lowered her hand. 'I'm not too early, am I?'

'No, very much fashionably on time,' Dylan replied. 'Anyway, I must love and leave you both to enjoy each other's company. Have fun.'

He winked at Joseph before squeezing Kate's hand and heading out through the door. As he closed it behind him, the professor started whistling a tune Joseph was absolutely certain was All I Want Is You. The DI couldn't suppress a smile as he turned to Kate, and offered to take her coat.

'Something smells delicious in here,' Kate said, sniffing the air as she shrugged the coat off to reveal she was wearing a black dress.

Joseph tried not to stare too hard as he took in the dress's perfect fit that showed off Kate's lovely figure. 'Wow, don't you look something?'

'What, this little old thing?' Kate said, doing a little twirl and grinning at him.

'Well, it's actually what's inside it I'm particularly admiring. Obviously, I'm talking about your soul.' He grinned at her.

Kate laughed and pulled him into her arms for a very passionate, fill-your-boots kiss. When she finally pulled away, without so much as a pause, she took him by the hand and led him towards the bedroom.

Joseph cast an anxious look towards the slow cooker. 'But the food is ready to serve.'

'And it smells absolutely delicious, but I'm sure that it will keep. Let's start with dessert.'

Joseph raised an eyebrow at her. 'Are you trying to seduce me?'

'God, yes, so get a move on.' She pulled more impatiently on Joseph's hand. Smiling, he allowed himself to be towed towards his bed, his heart fuller than it had been for years.

CHAPTER SIX

Tux's paddy-pawing dance on his chest woke Joseph from a very deep sleep the following morning. Despite his cat's best efforts to rouse his member of staff into feeding him, the DI resisted. That had everything to do with the wonderful blonde woman curled up next to him, her right leg hooked over his.

A deep sense of peace pervaded Joseph to the depth of his bones, along with a sense of coming home. He took in the ray of gold sunlight sneaking through the gap in the curtain. It seemed even the weather was in a good mood. He certainly didn't want this magical moment to end. His cat, unfortunately, had other ideas.

Tux walked right up to his face and let out an indignant meow.

Next to Joseph, Kate stirred, cracking an eyelid open and peering up at the cat through a muddle of hair. 'Who needs an alarm clock when we've got you around, hey, buddy?'

'Aye, isn't that the truth,' Joseph said. 'But I suppose, like they say, there's no rest for the wicked.'

'Wicked you say?' A mischievous smile filled Kate's face as she began to walk her fingers down his chest beneath the duvet.

If they had been alone, there would have been an inevitability to where this was all headed. However, Tux was having none of it. He pounced on Kate's hidden hand, driving just enough claw through the duvet to make her snatch it back with a scowl. Then the cat meowed at Joseph again, this time at a far louder volume, as if to say, you're not getting any as long as I haven't been fed.

'Okay, okay, I get the message,' Joseph replied, reluctantly sliding out of the bed.

Kate laughed. 'I can see who's captain of this boat.'

'You better believe it. Anyway, once I've fed the beastie, I'll return with coffee.'

'Now that sounds like a plan, although don't be too long,' Kate said. Even though she didn't quite lick her lips, there was enough encouragement for Joseph to feed the cat, get the coffee made, and get back to her in double-quick time.

A little while later, after they'd made up for being so rudely interrupted, Kate sat crossed-legged on the bed as she drank her coffee, giving Joseph a thoughtful glance.

'I don't know about you, but I'm starting to think we can really make it work this time,' she said.

'I believe that with every fibre of my being,' Joseph replied, leaning over and kissing the side of her head.

She leaned into his shoulder. 'In that case, I was wondering if we should move in together.'

Kate said it in such a matter-of-fact way that it took a moment for Joseph to process not only what she was saying but also the magnitude of it.

'You think we've reached that point? Aren't we in danger of rushing things? I thought we'd agreed to take things slowly to check if this is really what we both want.'

'Well, I'm already there, but if you're saying you've got reservations...?'

Joseph quickly shook his head. 'You know I haven't, although some might say you're coming over as a bit needy.' He grinned at her.

Kate mock-punched him in the arm.

'But seriously, the sooner the better, as far as I'm concerned,' Joseph said. 'But you understand I'm not comfortable with the idea of moving into the house you and Derrick lived in together?'

Kate frowned. 'I can understand why you would feel like that, and I have to admit I wouldn't mind moving out, either. To be honest, a huge part of me feels very guilty for driving him out of his home. The more time I've had to think about it, I think it's only fair that I should be the one to move out so he can live there if he still wants to.'

Joseph immediately picked up on the finality of her tone. 'So you're saying that's it, then? There really is no trying again with Derrick?'

'I did just say I wanted to move in with you, didn't I? That should have been a pretty big clue.'

Joseph raised his shoulders. 'I just wanted to make sure this is what you really want.'

She looked into his eyes. 'You know I do.'

He smiled at her. 'Then that makes two of us. But it's hard not to feel sorry for Derrick. I know we're going to agree to differ on this, but in many ways, I feel it was the Night Watchmen that actually broke you two up.'

Kate immediately shook her head. 'No, that was still down to some very bad decisions by Derrick. If he'd chosen to be honest with me at the time about how they were blackmailing him, things might have turned out differently. But unfortunately, Derrick didn't, and instead ended up lying to my face. I can't forgive him for that.' She gave a small head shake as though trying to get free of a cobweb of a thought. 'But that's all in the past now.'

'Nearly all in the past. There's still the massive elephant in the room about not telling him we're dating again. My guilt has been made even worse by the fact he's been halfway decent towards me recently. I'm certainly feeling very two-faced with Derrick right now. You do realise it's only a matter of time before he hears I've split up with Amy and puts it all together. We really do need to tell him.'

'I know, but I'm still just trying to find the right moment, Joseph.'

'Then please do, and sooner rather than later, if only for the sake of my conscience.'

'And mine.' Kate took another sip of her coffee. 'Anyway, where are we going to live when we do move in together? Maybe a rental place whilst we're looking. Obviously, it doesn't need to be too palatial as it's only the two of us.'

Joseph frowned. There was another implication he wasn't at all keen about.

Kate caught his expression. 'What is it, or are you about to tell me you're not ready to commit after all?'

He quickly shook his head. 'No, it's nothing like that. It's just that I've built a real life for myself here in the community on the canal. I've got Dylan next door, Tux loves it here, and I adore the lifestyle. This feels like home, Kate.'

She gave him a straight look. 'Chemical toilets and all?'

He smiled. 'Okay, maybe not so much that aspect, but it's amazing what you end up not batting an eyelid at when you've been dealing with it for a while.'

Her gaze took in the small bedroom they were in. 'I know I said it didn't have to be palatial, but if you're suggesting I move in here with you, isn't it going to be a bit cramped?'

Joseph was starting to feel really uncomfortable about where this conversation was heading.

'What, you're saying you don't think it's an option?'

'I'm just saying I've got reservations, that's all. Look, let's park this conversation there for now. We each need to have a good think about this and work out a plan that works for both of us.'

'Okay...' Joseph replied, realising that leaving Tús Nua and everything it represented would be a bitter pill for him to swallow.

Kate's phone buzzed on the shelf next to the bed. She reached across and took hold of it. As she scanned the text that had landed, her expression became troubled.

'Okay, now it's my turn to ask; what's wrong?' Joseph said.

Kate's forehead ridged as she looked at him. 'A colleague just told me the story she has been working on is going to be on the front page of today's Oxford Gazette.'

'Which is?'

'I didn't want to raise this last night so as not to upset you, but have you heard about our old friends from your work, Simon and Alex, who died yesterday? That's what our front page leader is all about.'

'Yes, unfortunately, I know about it all too well. Derrick assigned me as the liaison officer with the IOPC team who is looking into it. So I take it you already know all the grim details?'

'The ones the police are admitting to publicly, at least, that both officers were killed whilst attending a crime scene, which sounds like another of the Night Watchmen's gangland hits. That aside, our journalist has already spoken to eyewitnesses who saw Simon walk out in front of a delivery van. Even though they haven't officially come out and said it, the speculation at the newspaper is that Simon murdered Alex before taking his own life. Of course, we'll wait for the official version rather than print idle speculation, unlike some of our tabloid brethren. But strictly off the record, care to give me a heads up?'

'I believe the IOPC team is going to make an official statement later today about their initial findings, so you'll have your answer soon. But since I know I can trust you not to print anything ahead of that, there's no harm in telling you in the meantime. Simon did indeed shoot Alex before committing suicide.'

Lines spidered out from the corners of Kate's eyes. 'Oh my God, but that's awful. But what possible reason could he have had for doing anything so terrible?'

'That's a very good question. So far, as I was telling Dylan last night, we've found absolutely no motive whatsoever. The only thing that seems to fit is that he suffered from some sort of mental breakdown. But if you want to hear something really strange, the same thing happened to Barrister Whitcombe. She took her life a month ago by jumping from a car park rooftop when she had everything to live for.'

'Hang on, I remember that name,' Kate said. 'Wasn't she a prosecutor on the Samuel Dawson case all those years ago...' Her face paled. 'Oh my God.'

'What is it?' Joseph asked.

'Do you remember a tabloid journalist called Jackie Cross?'

'That tabloid journalist who could give Ricky Holt a run for his money?'

'That's her. She was the one who wrote a hatchet piece about Samuel Dawson.'

Joseph had a growing sense of unease about what Kate was about to say. 'Okay, what about her?'

'This is starting to sound like more than coincidence. Jackie slit her wrists and was found dead by her girlfriend in their bath.'

'Jesus, when did that happen?'

'This is where it gets very strange; it only happened two weeks ago. And here's the really odd thing. It sounds like it was a very similar situation to Simon and Laura. By all accounts, Jackie apparently had absolutely no reason to take her own life. In fact, she and her partner had been given permission to adopt a child literally the day before. Until that moment, everyone was under the impression she had everything to live for.'

The significance had already slammed into Joseph's brain. 'Fecking hell, this can't be a coincidence then. Two suicides I could swallow as a statistical anomaly, but not three, and if you include Alex in that headcount, it makes it four people who were all involved in that Dawson case, who are all now dead.'

Kate peered at him. 'Hang on, you're not suggesting Simon believed there'd been some sort of miscarriage of justice in the Samuel Dawson case, and was behind all of these deaths?'

'That might make sense, apart from the fact I was the only one who thought Dawson might have been framed. Simon, like everyone else on the case at the time, thought he was guilty. Also, and here's the clincher, Laura Whitcombe clearly took her own life based on the CCTV footage. Apparently, there was no one else anywhere near her when she jumped from the top of the car park.'

'Then I don't know what to think, other than this is all obviously very suspicious. What if someone else was blackmailing all of them, including Simon?'

'No evidence has come to light of that so far. But just because it hasn't, doesn't mean that's not the case. But one thing's for certain, I'm going to need to take this to Derrick. This is starting to have the hallmarks of being a much bigger case than any of us realised at first.'

Kate chewed her lip and nodded, but remained mute. Joseph could clearly tell she wanted to say something else.

'Okay, tell me what you're thinking?' he asked.

'If this has something to do with the old Dawson case, and this is some sort of vendetta based on his wrongful conviction and suicide, you and Derrick are going to have to watch your backs as well.'

Joseph shook his head. 'Good luck to anyone trying to blackmail me into taking my own life.'

Kate's frown deepened. 'With all due respect, you can't afford to think like that. Just think of what the Night Watchmen were able to persuade you to do when they hung Ellie's and my lives over your head. If this is blackmail, who knows what the person or people behind this threatened Simon and the others with.'

'Okay, there you make a very good point. We're certainly going to need to dust down the Samuel Dawson case in a hurry and do some serious digging about anyone who might be holding a grudge against everyone involved in that case. The sooner we dig up a name, the better.'

Kate reached over and took Joseph's hands in hers. 'Please do, because I'm not about to lose you after we've just found each other again.'

'Don't worry, I plan to be around long enough to enjoy growing old together,' Joseph replied, pulling the woman who meant everything in the world to him closer and kissing her.

CHAPTER SEVEN

AFTER JOSEPH ARRIVED at St Aldates and told Derrick about the other suicides possibly being linked to the Samuel Dawson case, the wheels quickly spun into action. That was why the DI was now sitting with Megan, Ian, and Sue in an incident room. They'd all been assigned to what now hinted at being a full-blown murder investigation of a potential serial killer.

Derrick was standing with Chris next to the admittedly very sparse evidence board, their heads bent together in conversation.

The DSU finally turned to face the team. 'Okay, let's get this briefing underway.'

Joseph wasn't surprised that the big man wanted to be closely involved. For all they knew, Derrick and Joseph, along with every officer who'd worked that original investigation, could be in the murderer's sights.

Derrick gestured to the four photos on the board listing the names above them of DCI Simon Hart, DI Alex Roberts, Barrister Laura Whitcombe, and journalist Jackie Cross. 'Right now, we can't be sure there is any link between the deaths of all these people, but there is one common denominator between these murders.' He nodded to Chris, who'd already been assigned as SIO to the investigation.

He picked up a marker pen and wrote, The Samuel Dawson Case, at the top of the evidence board. 'All of these people were involved in some capacity in the prosecution of this man.'

Ian piped up at that point. 'So are we talking about someone being convinced Dawson was wrongly accused then?'

Derrick glared at the man. 'Only in their warped brains. The facts still fully supported Dawson's conviction, and to this day no new evidence has emerged to challenge that view.'

'All I can tell you is everyone assigned to that investigation did their best based on the evidence we had at the time,' Joseph added. 'If there is someone who knows better out there, they certainly didn't share that information with us at the time.'

'So what are you thinking, that there could be a revenge motive here from someone who believed Samuel was innocent?' Megan asked.

'That would seem to be the most likely explanation,' Chris said.

'Hang on, if a friend or relative was after vengeance because of a perceived miscarriage of justice, why wait all this time?' Sue asked. 'Didn't this all happen over twenty years ago?'

'Yes, and that's a very good question.' Chris wrote it up on the board. Why the twenty-year gap?

'Well, if we really do have a murderer out there, they're on quite a killing spree,' Megan said. 'For all we know, they may still have some scores to settle.' She shot Joseph and Derrick a concerned look.

The DI raised his hands. 'Okay, we hear you. But what I can tell you is that no one's attempted to contact me regarding the Dawson case, and certainly no one's tried to blackmail me, either.'

Derrick was already nodding. 'And the same goes for me.'

'At least that's something—so what's our next step?' Sue asked.

'As both Simon and Alex's partners have already been interviewed, we should make it a priority to interview those of Laura Whitcombe and Jackie Cross, too,' Chris said. 'Joseph and Megan, I'd like you to talk to Jackie's partner, Molly Parsons. Sue and Ian, you go and talk to Laura's husband, Jason Whitcombe. I want you to find out if there's even the faintest shred of evidence to suggest either Laura or Jackie might have been coerced into taking their own lives.'

'And if we don't find anything?' Sue asked.

Chris shrugged. 'Then maybe this is going to be a very short investigation indeed, if it turns out to be nothing more than an extreme case of a series of unfortunate coincidences.'

Even though Joseph nodded along with the others, a large part of him doubted that was what they were dealing with. To start with, it just seemed so improbable that Simon would want to kill Alex, let alone take his own life. But if there was coercion involved, what on earth could anyone dig up to persuade one person, let alone so many, to take their own lives? Was that why he and Derrick hadn't been targeted, because there wasn't sufficient dirt on them that the murderer knew about? One thing was for sure, the sooner he had the answer to that particular question, the happier he'd feel.

Joseph and Megan sat in the conservatory of a terrace house in Bicester. All the window ledges had been filled with Deepest Sympathy cards, along with several fading bouquets that, based on the look of them, should have been thrown out weeks ago. Not that Joseph gave them much attention as he was focused on the Chihuahua, currently baring its teeth at him from the safety of its dog basket.

'Hey, little fellah, will you take it easy?' Joseph said, with what he hoped was his best dog-calming voice.

That only resulted in the miniature hellhound barking at him with wild-eyed aggression, suggesting it was seriously thinking about ripping the DI's throat out. Thankfully, it was at that moment, the dog's owner, Molly Parsons, appeared with a tray of mugs of tea and a pile of chocolate Hobnob biscuits.

'Alright, Bear, that will do,' Molly said, setting the tray down on the coffee table before the detectives. 'Sorry, you mustn't mind her,' she continued. 'Jackie always said her dog had delusions about being a Rottweiler.' A sad smile filled her face as her gaze flicked to a photo on the bookcase of a red-haired woman on a Ferris wheel at a fair.

Although it had been years since Joseph had last seen the journalist, he recognised the woman at once as Jackie Cross, who was actually smiling in this photo. That was something he hadn't seen her do once in real life. He remembered her as being hard-nosed as they came. But this behind-the-scenes suggested a much softer side to the woman in her private life.

As Molly handed them their teas and proffered the biscuits to which Megan helped herself to three, Joseph was already sitting forward in his chair.

'I just wanted to say how grateful I am that you agreed to see us at such short notice,' he said.

Molly gave him a small smile. 'I'm more than happy to talk to you if it will help get to the bottom of what really happened to Jackie.'

'You're not convinced it was suicide, then?' Megan asked.

'Absolutely bloody not,' Molly said.

As she sat down, Bear ran straight over and leapt up onto

her lap like he was the sweetest dog in the world, and one who certainly didn't have a bloodlust for DIs.

'You sound very certain about it not being a typical case of suicide—why's that?' Joseph asked.

'That's because I am. You see, Jackie was on a real roll recently with her work. She'd just got a scoop about a CEO who'd been embezzling money from a well-known charity. But before you ask, and I know you will, he had an alibi for the time of her death. We were literally about to adopt a beautiful baby girl the month after she died. In fact, we got approved the day before. Jackie adored helping me set up the nursery. I honestly don't think I've ever seen her so excited about anything in her life. If she'd been even vaguely considering throwing her life away, trust me, I would have spotted the signs. Does any of that sound like someone who would want to take their own life?'

'Not at all,' Joseph replied. He took a mental breath because he knew his next question was an incredibly sensitive one, but he still needed to ask it. 'You were the one who found Jackie in the bath that day, weren't you?'

Molly visibly shuddered and wrapped her arms around herself. 'That's a sight that will haunt me to the end of my days. But there's another thing you should know about that. Jackie was one of those people who was furious at those who did that sort of thing. Apart from anything else, she wouldn't have wanted to put me through that sort of anguish. My partner may have been many things, and okay, not universally liked because of the nature of her job, but she certainly wasn't a hypocrite.'

'So what are you suggesting, then?' Joseph asked, trying to make sure that he didn't put words into this woman's mouth.

'That Jackie was murdered, plain and simple. That's the only thing that makes any sense to me.'

Megan checked her notebook again. 'That's what you told the original investigation team, isn't it?'

'Yes, not that they agreed. But to give them credit, the forensic team did a thorough sweep for any evidence, including taking DNA samples, just in case someone had broken in and made Jackie's murder look like suicide.'

'But they only found yours and her DNA, didn't they?' Megan asked, who'd made a point of getting up to speed with the original investigation notes before they headed over.

'That's right. But as I told the original investigation team, I know that with every fibre of my being that Jackie wouldn't have voluntarily taken her own life.'

Joseph couldn't help but be struck by how similar this testimonial was to what Julia had said about her husband. Once again, these suicides didn't make any sense unless someone else had been responsible.

The DI was gazing into the middle distance when he noticed something familiar on the bookshelf. He jumped to his feet and headed straight for it. He pulled the self-hypnosis book from the shelf. Despite it being about managing stress and anxiety, the design of the book was familiar to him. It was in the same series as the one that Simon had for giving up smoking, and by the same author, too, the mentalist, Damien Storme.

Joseph turned to show the book to Megan, whose eyes widened. One book he might overlook, but not two.

He presented it to Molly. 'Did this belong to Jackie, by any chance?'

'Yes, it did. She relied on it a lot over the last year when things at work were getting a bit tough. There's a QR code in the book which links to an online video she used to watch all the time.'

'And where did she get it from exactly?' Megan asked.

'She was actually sent it through the post as a free introduction to a self-hypnosis course,' Molly replied. 'It was strange. It arrived just when Jackie was really struggling with anxiety issues, and this book helped her get on top of it. She used to joke that it was destiny.'

'I see,' Joseph replied, trading a weighted look with Megan. 'Would you mind if we borrowed this?'

'Of course, but why? You don't think it's connected to her death, do you?'

'It's probably nothing, but it might indicate what her state of mind was like when she died.'

Molly's lips pinched together as she nodded. 'Oh, I see.'

Joseph stood. 'Anyway, you've been a great help, but I think we've taken enough of your valuable time.'

Megan quickly downed the last of her tea, before she helped herself to another couple of Hobnobs.

Jackie, who'd visibly paled during their conversation, started to stand.

Joseph shook his head. 'Don't worry, we'll let ourselves out.'

As the detectives left the room, accompanied by the good-riddance barks of Bear, Joseph noticed Molly pick up the framed photo of Jackie and her eyes fill with tears. Yes, there was far too much heartbreak to go around right now.

The moment they were out the front door, Megan turned to Joseph. 'It can't be a coincidence that Jackie read a Damien Storme self-hypnosis book just before she died too.'

'Aye, I know. And there's that word coincidence again. It does seem to love cropping up in this investigation a lot. That's why I want you to ring Ian and ask him to look for any self-hypnosis books at Laura Whitcombe's home when they interview her husband. Meanwhile, I'm going to ring Julia to tell her we're going to need to have Simon's self-hypnosis book as well.'

'You think we're onto something?'

'That's what my instinct is telling me,' Joseph replied as they headed back towards the TR4. 'There's definitely a pattern here. That's why, as a matter of priority, we're going to be looking into those books and specifically the author behind them, Damien Storme.'

CHAPTER EIGHT

MEGAN AND JOSEPH arrived back in the car park at St Aldates almost at the same time Ian and Sue did, parking the Volvo V90.

The triumphant look that Ian was giving them was no doubt due to him being able to grab the vehicle of choice from the carpool. But that expression quickly faded as he spotted the TR4 his colleagues were getting out of.

'How the hell did you persuade the boss to let you drive his car?' Ian asked as Sue joined them.

Joseph didn't miss a beat. 'Blackmail, obviously. I have some serious dirt on our DCI that he doesn't want to be made public, specifically his obsession with pigeons.'

Ian's eyes rounded. 'Really?'

Sue did a mock clip of his head. 'God, you're so gullible sometimes.' She turned to Joseph. 'And the truth is?'

'I've got the TR4 as an extended loan because I helped him restore it and the DB5.'

'Bloody hell, it's alright for some,' Ian muttered.

'Well, you should have seen the wreck they started with,' Megan said. 'Joseph certainly put the hours in, so it's only right he gets to drive it.'

'Well, I'm not at all jealous,' Sue said, holding her finger and thumb a fraction apart as Ian practically glowered at the vehicle.

Joseph chuckled. 'Car envy aside, how did you both get on with Laura's husband, Jason?'

Sue pulled a self-hypnosis book out of her bag. 'Ta-da. The moment we mentioned it to Jason, he fetched this for us from their bedroom. Apparently, Laura swore by it for weight loss.'

'Yes, apparently as a snack it has fewer calories than a box of chocolates,' Ian added.

They all just gave him the look.

Sue ignored her colleague's contribution. 'According to Jason, the hypnosis course was far more effective than anything else Laura tried, and she was full of praise for it. She watched the linked video every week.'

'Did she now?' Joseph replied, sensing that they might really be onto something here. 'Then we better check out these hypnosis videos for ourselves to see what all the fuss is about.'

A short while later, they were in the incident room, shrugging off their coats.

Chris headed over from the evidence board he'd been staring at. 'Any joy?' he asked.

'It looks like we may have struck gold, boss,' Joseph replied.

Chris gave them a surprised look. 'What flavour of gold?'

Megan took out Jackie's Managing Stress and Anxiety book and handed it to Chris. 'This flavour. It turns out that all of the people who took their lives had self-hypnosis books from that famous mentalist called Damien Storme.'

The SIO glanced at the title and frowned, then did the same when Sue presented him with the other book from Laura's home.

'You're seriously suggesting hypnosis is somehow linked to three different people taking their own lives and one killing a friend before walking out in front of a van?'

'Hopefully, we'll find that out when we watch the video courses linked in the back of these books,' Joseph said. He dipped his chin towards Megan. 'You better do the honours, as you're far better with tech than I am.'

'You do realise it's only a case of pointing a camera at a QR code?' she replied.

'Aye, but even so.' He gave her an apologetic shrug.

Megan rolled her eyes at him as she took the book and opened it to the back page. Within moments, and certainly far less time than it would have taken Joseph to get his head around it, she had her phone's display mirrored to the big screen in the incident room.

Joseph felt a sense of anticipation as the DC clicked on the link. But rather than any sort of video appearing, there was only a Can't Find Server message that came up on the screen.

'Well, that's something of a letdown,' Ian replied.

'Hang on, why is this self-hypnosis video suddenly inaccessible? It must have been viewable at some point, if Jackie watched it,' Megan said.

Chris nodded. 'Yes, that's certainly suspicious, although it could just be a technical glitch.'

'Then let's try Laura Whitcombe's book in case that one still works,' Sue suggested, handing it over for Megan to try.

No one in the room looked surprised when that came up with a broken link as well.

Ian frowned. 'Okay, so what do we do now?'

'To start with, I think this confirms that we need to look seriously into this Damien Storme character,' Joseph said.

'Isn't he that guy who had his own hypnosis series on TV at one point?' Ian asked.

'That's him,' Megan said.

'Then we need to start looking into his professional career

and personal life,' Chris said. 'Specifically, whether he has any connection to Samuel Dawson.'

Ian pulled a sceptical face. 'So we're really going down this hypnotism route, then?'

Joseph shrugged. 'As implausible as it sounds, I think we have to consider every angle. But maybe we should also consider consulting a forensic psychologist to get their take on it and whether something like this is even possible using hypnotism.'

'Okay, good thinking. Anyone got any other ideas of angles we should be looking at?' Chris asked.

'If these people all used their computers or phones to access this website, isn't there a chance there might be some files still stored on them?' Megan suggested.

'But surely the digital forensic teams would have turned something up by now?' Sue suggested.

But Joseph was already shaking his head. 'Not necessarily. Remember, if the working assumption was suicide, a lot of time and resources wouldn't necessarily have been spent on looking for alternative explanations. The digital forensic team may have just done a basic sweep of the laptops and phones.'

'Yes, forensic budgets only go so far in cases, as Amy delights in frequently telling me,' Chris said. 'But I'll see if Derrick is agreeable to releasing sufficient funds to do a more thorough analysis this time round.'

'Hang on, I may have an idea here that could save a few pennies and could actually be quicker,' Joseph said. 'Why don't we contact Neil Tanner, that white-hat hacker we used back on the Hidden Hand Club case? He made short work of tracking down those files on the people's phones who were caught up in that case.'

'Then let's do that,' Chris replied. 'I'll also ask the IOPC team to release Simon's laptop to us and get it couriered over. I'll also do the same with the laptops and phones of Laura Whitcombe and Jackie Cross. Joseph, can you arrange a meeting with Neil Tanner, once we have the laptops in our possession?'

'Leave it to me, boss,' the DI replied, taking out his phone to pull up Neil's contact details.

When Neil Tanner opened the door of the Victorian three-storey home in North Oxford, he looked almost identical to the last time the DI had seen him. Certainly, his curly blond hair and neatly trimmed beard were the same. In the case of the latter, Joseph suspected the programmer might own one of those hipster miniature combs for specialist grooming. The only real difference was in his wardrobe choice, specifically the faded T-shirt with the old arcade game, Defenders' image on it.

'Good to see you again, Inspector,' Neil said, shaking Joseph's hand. 'And you are?' he asked Megan.

'DC Anderson,' she replied.

'Then it's a pleasure to meet you.' His gaze flicked to the laptop under Joseph's arm. 'Is that the computer you mentioned?'

Joseph nodded. 'As I said on the phone, the first of three that will be coming your way. But I do realise it might not even be possible for someone even with your talents, to dig up anything useful. But if there is something our people have missed, we need it recovered sooner than later.'

'Well, we won't know until we try. So please come join me in my kingdom, and I'll see what I can do for you.' Neil stepped aside and ushered them into the house.

Joseph took in the well-ordered hallway with dried flower arrangements and the shopping trolley parked just inside the front door.

'Is that my Amazon delivery?' an old woman with a wrinkly face asked as she appeared in the doorway.

'No, just some friends who need my help with something,' Neil replied.

The lady gave Joseph and Megan a look up and down. 'You don't look like students to me.'

'That would be because we're not, but we do need Neil's help with a very important matter,' Megan replied.

The woman's eyes narrowed. 'He's not in any sort of trouble, is he? You do have the whiff of police about you.'

Must be the aftershave I'm wearing, Joseph thought to himself. Out loud, he said, 'No, it's nothing like that. We actually need Neil's expertise in computers to help us on a case we're investigating.' The DI showed the laptop to the old lady just to prove the point.

'I see,' she replied, not looking at all convinced before turning her attention to the student. 'If you're all heading up to your room, Neil, please keep that dreadful noise from that tech music down.'

'Techno music,' he corrected her. 'And I promise we'll be as quiet as church mice up there.'

'Good, because you know how it gives me a headache.' Then the woman spotted the detectives still had their shoes on. 'You can both take those off before you head upstairs as well. I don't want mud on my carpets.'

Joseph glanced down at their spotless shoes, and then at the threadbare carpet on the stairs. But he knew from experience to pick his battles with someone like this.

'Of course,' he said with his best winning smile, slipping his suede boots off as Megan did the same with her shoes.

The old woman made a huffing sound, then turned and disappeared back into the room she'd materialised out of.

With Neil leading the way, the detectives headed up the stairs.

'Apologies about getting the third degree from Edith,' Neil said.

'No need to worry, I know from experience what some landladies can be like,' Joseph replied.

'Oh, she's not my landlady. She's my gran. Despite her fierce exterior, Edith's actually got a heart of gold. She must have, to let me live here rent-free. Just as well with the rental prices in Oxford.'

'Tell me about it,' Megan replied.

On reaching the first landing, the detectives followed the student up a second, narrower staircase into a converted attic space.

It was obvious to Joseph the moment they entered it that, unlike the rest of the house, this was very much Neil's domain. There were so many vinyl LPs filling racks of shelving it would have given a decent record shop a run for its money. There was also a bed and a well-worn sofa, along with a gaming console under a ridiculously large TV.

But the focus of the room, and what made it abundantly clear what the programmer's real passion was, were several bench desks joined together and filled with keyboards and hard drives. There were also six screens mounted on a complicated rack system. Most of the displays were filled with what looked like lines of code to Joseph's untrained eye. One was different, showing a live feed from the doorbell camera the DI had spotted when they'd first entered the house.

However, it was the computer glowing like an alien mothership that had landed on one of the desks that really stole the show. It blazed with blue neon lights mounted inside a transparent case and illuminating the most complicated motherboard Joseph had seen in his life. It was exactly the sort of thing he would have expected someone with this student's talents to own.

'Okay, let's have a look at her,' Neil said, holding out his hand as he sat down on an expensive-looking designer office chair in front of his bank of monitors.

Joseph handed the laptop to him. The programmer connected it with a cable to his computer as the detectives took up seats on either side of him.

One boot-up sequence later, Neil had the laptop's display mirrored to one of the larger monitors.

'Okay, what am I looking for here?' Neil asked, fingers poised over his keyboard like a pianist getting ready to play.

'We're trying to find any video files that may have been accessed on the internet from this machine.'

'No problem. I can simply check the browser history to see what he watched, then look for them online, but surely your people have already tried that?'

Joseph shook his head. 'No, the online video files seem to have been deleted, so there's no way to access them now.'

'Okay, there may be some remnants in this laptop's browser's cache. Have you got the domain name so I can look for any entries pointing towards it?'

Megan nodded as she opened her notebook. 'Yes, it's DamienStorme.com.'

'Okay, that should be enough to get me started.'

The programmer started to type on his keyboard, also glowing with multicoloured neon lights, at a rate that would have given most people a nosebleed. Within moments, text was scrolling up one of the screens as Neil scanned it. Then he stopped, a wide smile on his face.

'Ah, there you are.' He doubled-clicked a file, and the screen filled with a long string of random letters and numbers.

'Okay, it looks like this is a fragment of the original file in the cache. Unfortunately, it's been broken because it's been partly overwritten. But if you give me a sec, I should be able to fix at least a fraction of it.'

Neil's fingers flew over the keyboard again, adding lines of code to the start and end of the file. Then the programmer hit enter, and a still frame from the video appeared on his largest screen.

Joseph took in the still frame of a bald man, possibly in his early forties, with piercing green eyes, gazing directly into the camera. Behind him was a bank of frozen clouds in a blue sky.

'That's Damien Storme—I recognise him from his photo on the back of the book,' Megan said.

Joseph nodded. 'Looks like you're on the right track, Neil. Can you play the video for us?'

'Yes, but I've only been able to retrieve a short fragment of it, but I can show you what I have.' He hit play.

Immediately, gentle rhythmic electronic music started playing through a set of expensive floor-standing hi-fi speakers, filling the room. The clouds started to billow and form in slow motion. There was also a kaleidoscopic geometrical pattern superimposed over the top of the backdrop, almost like a watermark. It was spinning and changing in a hypnotic pattern.

'Imagine yourself walking along a beautiful path,' Damien said. 'Each step you take makes you feel lighter, freer. You notice the vibrant energy within you, awakening with every breath—' The video came to an abrupt stop as the image broke up into squares with missing gaps.

'Is that it?' Joseph asked.

'I'm afraid so,' Neil replied.

'Is there any chance you could recover any more of it?' Megan said.

'No, and to be honest, we were lucky to even retrieve this

fragment. I don't suppose whoever owned this laptop had any sort of backup system?'

'Not that we're aware of,' Megan said. 'The same also goes for the other two laptops, which are also being sent over from St Aldates the moment they arrive.'

Neil sat back in his office chair and rubbed the back of his neck. 'There is only one thing else I can do. I could look at his website server and try to gain access to any file systems stored on it. Even if the rest of this online video was deleted, I would still stand a reasonable chance of being able to retrieve it from the server storage system it was kept on.'

'Not without a warrant, you can't,' Joseph said. 'Even if we turned a blind eye, any evidence you might uncover would be inadmissible in court.'

'Don't worry, I wouldn't as a point of principle, as I'm meant to be one of the good guys. But get me a warrant, and I'll happily hack away on your behalf.'

'Unfortunately, we're nowhere near that point yet, as it's still early days in this investigation,' Megan replied.

'Okay, but if things change, you know where to find me.'

Joseph nodded. 'Thanks for trying anyway, Neil. But on the plus side, this at least confirms that Simon did actually watch one of these hypnosis videos.'

'So what do we do now?' Megan asked.

'If I can get the okay from Chris, it looks like the time has come to go and give this Damien Storm a visit and see what he has to say for himself.'

The DC nodded before returning her attention to Neil. 'Would it be possible to take a copy of that file? I'd like to take another look at it later, just in case we missed something.'

'Of course,' the programmer replied. He took a USB stick from a large collection in one of his desk drawers and copied the file over, before presenting it to Megan with a smile.

'Okay, where does this Damien Storme character live anyway?' Joseph asked.

Before Megan had a chance to reply, Neil had already tapped at the keyboard and pulled up an address.

'He has one of those posh flats in St Luke's Manor.' He scanned down the screen. 'And here's an interesting fact for you. Apparently, St Luke's was originally called Largemore, a former mental asylum before it was converted into luxury flats by the developers.'

'No wonder they wanted to change the name—not exactly the association the developers might have wanted while trying to sell the flats,' Megan replied.

'Aye...' Joseph said distractedly as his brain raced ahead. Could Damien really be behind all these deaths? He turned to Neil. 'Okay, we better get going. Thanks for all your help.'

'Anytime, and I'll check through those other laptops when they arrive. But as I said, just get me that warrant and I'll be happy to hack Mr Storme's server for you.'

'Let's not get ahead of ourselves. We'll see what he has to say for himself first, hey?'

Neil grinned at him. 'Of course.'

A few minutes later, when the detectives were back outside on the street, Megan turned to Joseph.

'A former mental hospital and at least three people who suffered some sort of breakdown. That can't be a coincidence, can it?'

'Exactly, and there's that word again—coincidence. Mind you, if this Damien Storme character really is hypnotising people into taking their own lives, he hasn't exactly done a lot to cover his tracks, or even be very subtle about it.'

'Which may mean he's entirely innocent. Either way, I'm still looking forward to meeting him. You do realise the guy is a minor celebrity?'

Joseph narrowed his eyes. 'You're not going to go all starstruck on me again, are you, like you did that time with Anna Millington, that sitcom actor we had to interview during the Jimmy Harper investigation?'

'No promises, but if you didn't notice, he is rather good-looking.'

'If you go for that whole bald-headed look, I suppose so. But you would be the better judge of that than me.'

'Trust me, I am,' Megan replied, grinning at him.

CHAPTER NINE

The electric wrought-iron gates swung open so slowly that Joseph wondered why anyone ever bothered installing them. If this was someone's idea of luxury, they could keep it. When the gates had finally finished their tortoise crawl, he finally drove through them onto the short drive towards St Luke's Manor.

'I had no idea this was even hidden away here,' Megan said, taking in the golden stone building, flanked by octagonal towers on either side of it.

'As luxury flats go, it certainly screams money, and I can see why the developers chose this place,' Joseph replied, as he swept the car around the circular turning area lined with ornamental flower beds, before stopping in front of the main entrance.

'It's definitely hard to believe it was ever a mental asylum.'

'Aye, I think that's very much by intention. Padded rooms and bars on the windows wouldn't exactly have as much sales appeal.'

'Unless you're into that sort of thing,' Megan said almost straight-faced, before bursting into a grin.

'Alright, Ian,' Joseph replied with an eye roll.

Megan snorted as the DI turned off the engine.

As they both got out, her eyes swept over the TR4, as she gave it an approving look. 'You know this car does look rather at home parked here in front of a manor house. Maybe you should consider upgrading your lodgings and live here instead.'

Joseph shook his head. 'You obviously labour under some delusion about what I earn. Besides, I'd rather live on board Tús Nua any day of the week.' But even as the DI spoke, he couldn't help thinking that if Kate got wind of an apartment being available here, she might have a very different opinion. As it was, he knew for sure it was going to be an uphill battle for Kate to persuade him to leave his floating home anytime soon.

The two detectives headed up the steps towards the entrance and headed into a lobby area with polished marble walls and columns. There was also a suitably impressive wooden staircase. Brass plaques were everywhere, with arrows pointing towards the numerous flats scattered throughout the building.

Megan was already studying the ones at the foot of the staircase. 'According to the address Neil found for us, Damien Storme lives in one of the penthouse flats.'

Joseph raised his eyebrows a fraction. 'Of course, he does.'

They headed up the ornate staircase, and the DI took in the tasteful black-and-white photographs of Oxford's finest architecture, including, of course, the Radcliffe Camera. The general feeling of the place was as far removed as Joseph could imagine from what it must have once been like.

It was certainly quite a leap of the imagination to think this building once echoed with the screams of this establishment's more troubled clientele. In contrast, there was an atmosphere of tranquillity and peacefulness now in the building. It seemed the tasteful pastel tones and interior designer touches of black and white photos on the walls had laid to rest any ghosts of the past.

When the detectives reached the top landing, they followed the signage, and walked along a wide-panelled corridor towards a large wooden door at the end.

Joseph took in the CCTV camera mounted above it, a red light indicating it was active.

Megan pressed the doorbell and a few seconds later, the speaker below it clicked to life.

'Hello, how can I help you?' a woman replied in a smooth, rich voice.

'We're here to see Damien Storme,' Megan replied.

'And you are?'

'Detective Inspector Stone and Detective Constable Anderson,' Joseph replied, looking up at the camera as he and Megan flashed their warrant cards towards it.

'If you don't mind me asking, what's this about?' the woman asked.

'It's probably better for you to invite us in, rather than for us to discuss this on the doorstep where the neighbours might overhear our conversation.'

'Okay, just give me a moment.'

A handful of seconds later, the door was opened by a pretty blonde middle-aged woman with dark eyes, who was holding out a hand. 'I'm Catherine, Damien's personal assistant. Sorry for the interrogation on the doorstep, but we have to be careful of random fans turning up here.'

'You get a lot of those, then?' Megan asked.

'Yes, some of whom pretty much fall into the stalker category. Thankfully, they are all harmless and seem happy enough with a signed copy of one of his books, before I send them on their way. Anyway, if you would like to follow me through, I'll park you in the waiting room.'

'Thank you,' Joseph replied, looking at the woman. He had

the feeling he'd met her somewhere before. 'Sorry, do I know you?'

Catherine peered at him and then shook her head. 'Sorry, I've never seen you before, but I do have one of those faces that people seem to confuse. I'm forever getting stopped in the street and asked if I'm Gwyneth Paltrow.'

'Lucky you,' Megan said, as they were ushered through into a bright pastel-painted room.

Joseph took in the large curving white sofa that faced an enormous TV, which almost filled one wall. On it, slow-motion footage of waves breaking on a tropical beach was playing with gentle rhythmic music. There were also numerous backlit framed theatre posters arranged on the walls, Damien's face on all of them.

Catherine gestured towards a selection of herbal tea bags, a hot water dispenser, and a pile of healthy snack bars that Megan's food radar had already locked onto. 'Please help yourself,' the woman said, turning on a diffuser which glowed green and started to fill the room with a very pleasant-smelling mist of jasmine.

Joseph took in the magazines arranged on a coffee table, most of which were about well-being and mental health.

'This place feels a bit like a spa reception area,' Megan replied, also noticing them.

Catherine nodded as she turned a ring on her finger. 'It's all intended to relax the clients. It helps make them far more open to suggestion during their hypnotism sessions.' Then she brushed first Joseph's and then Megan's shoulders with the gentlest of touches, before gesturing towards the sofa. 'Damien shouldn't be too long, so please make yourself at home in the meantime and make yourselves comfortable.' With a smile, the assistant turned on her heel and headed out of the door.

'Tactile, isn't she?' Megan said.

'Well, some people are very touchy-feely,' Joseph replied.

Once Megan had raided the snacks, taking one for later, she tucked into a raisin and nut one, as they settled onto the sofa. As none of the magazines seemed like Joseph's sort of thing, his attention inevitably settled on the TV screen because it was almost impossible to ignore, thanks to the sheer size of the bloody thing.

As he gazed at it, he noticed a faint geometrical kaleidoscopic pattern superimposed over the whole video, just like they'd seen in the broken-link video. The whole effect was mesmerising and Joseph found himself stifling a yawn. It was certainly one of the most restful videos he'd ever seen in his life. With every passing second, he felt his body physically relax down to the core of his bones, the music and jasmine scent, only amplifying the effect.

It was only when he felt his shoulder being gently shaken and his eyes snapped open, he realised he'd fallen asleep. Megan, next to him, was also blinking as though she'd just woken up as well.

Catherine withdrew her hand from Joseph's shoulder, giving him a wide smile. 'I see Damien's waiting room has worked its usual magic.'

Joseph blinked again at her as his mind tried to surface. 'Sorry, I must have drifted off for a moment there.'

'Me too,' Megan said, the half-eaten snack bar still clutched in her hand.

'Don't worry, everybody does it,' Catherine replied. 'Anyway, if you'd like to follow me, Damien is free to see you now.'

The two detectives stood, mentally shaking off the effects of the sleep, and followed the assistant out of the waiting room and along a corridor.

After the bright waiting area, Joseph had expected the rest of the flat to have a similar design. Instead, the corridor, lit by glowing Edison-style orange filament bulbs, had an illustrated design of a dark jungle scene, complete with nocturnal animals looking out. Whether that was some sort of visual metaphor for journeying into the subconscious, the DI had no idea.

Catherine ushered them into an octagonal-shaped room where all the window blinds had been drawn. The walls, painted black, almost felt like they were sucking the light away. That helped to enhance the soft glow of several coloured three-dimensional star-shaped glass lamps hanging from the ceiling. There was also another large screen TV, this time showing a field of slow undulating wheat blowing in a gentle breeze. Once again, Joseph noticed another faint animated kaleidoscopic geometrical pattern superimposed over it.

A bald man with sharp cheekbones and the most penetrating green eyes Joseph had ever seen headed across the room to meet them. 'I believe you need to talk to me about something?'

'It's regarding an ongoing investigation,' Joseph replied, recognising the man as Damien Storme from the photo on the back of his books.

A troubled look filled the mentalist's face. 'I see.' He turned to Catherine. 'Can you please advise Mrs Newell that there will be a slight delay in starting her session today?'

'I've already contacted her.'

Damien shot her a grateful look. 'I honestly don't know what I would do without you.'

'Me neither,' Catherine replied, smiling at him. Then she nodded towards the detectives, before heading out of the room and closing the door quietly behind her.

'Is this where you see your clients?' Megan asked, taking in the room around them.

Damien smiled. 'I suppose you were expecting to see a

psychiatrist's couch, or better still, a collection of gold watches on chains for me to hypnotise my clients with?'

Megan raised her shoulders. 'Something like that.'

'Well, if you're not already familiar with my work, you can probably already tell I take a far more modern approach to hypnotism.'

Joseph nodded, wondering if Simon and the others might have sat in this very room at some point. 'So you see a lot of patients here then?' he asked.

'I really don't like to use the words patients, as I see it more as a collaborative journey. Friends would be a more accurate term, and my objective is always to help them get past whatever issue they are struggling with. But to answer your question, I don't take many patients on. Those I do tend to be people who I believe I can genuinely help and particularly those who have tried everything else without success.'

'And you use hypnosis to help them do that?' Megan asked.

'Partly, but it's also about giving people the opportunity to talk in a safe place without any judgement. This is somewhere they can afford to let their guard down, which is essential when we're talking about hypnosis. It's all about building a foundation of trust between myself and the people who come to see me.'

'So what about your hypnosis books, which seem to have been very successful?' Megan asked.

'I see that as a way to bring my special brand of help to the masses, especially those who can't afford, or maybe don't want to see, a professional psychologist for a private consultation. I like to think of myself as a philanthropist, helping to make people's lives better where I can. Anyway, enough about my professional life. You obviously came here for a reason. So how is it exactly that I can help you? Unless you're about to tell me you both need a hypnosis treatment?'

'Nothing like that,' Joseph replied. 'Actually, it's something of a sensitive situation we're hoping you may be able to cast some light on.'

Damien steepled his fingers together. 'Really? How so?'

'There have been three suicides recently where a common factor linking them has recently come to light.'

'Which is?' Damien asked.

'They all seem to have been reading your self-help books just before they died. We're actively exploring the possibility that this might have been linked to their actions in some way.'

Damien stared at the DI. 'Sorry, but how could you have possibly jumped to that conclusion just because they were reading one of my books?'

'I'm sure you understand we have to explore all possibilities, however unlikely,' Megan quickly added.

The hypnotist frowned and his expression became wary. 'I can assure you that you're barking up the wrong tree. I put all sorts of measures and checks into my books.'

Joseph peered at the man. 'That's very reassuring to hear, but can you explain to us why the included courses in the books all have links to webpages that no longer work?'

Damien looked genuinely surprised at hearing that. 'Really? Are you absolutely certain?'

'Yes we are, and we also had a computer expert look at it who says that the online files have been deleted from your web server,' Megan added.

'That doesn't sound at all right.' Damien stood and headed over to a bookcase filled with copies of his own books and took one down about improving self-confidence. He flicked the book to its back page where there was a QR code and then handed it to Megan. 'If you try that one you will see that the link is working perfectly.'

The DC took her phone out and within seconds had a video course up on her phone and running. This one had a beautiful sunrise rising over a lake as spa-like music played in the background. Then Damien appeared on the screen and started to speak.

'Welcome to my self-confidence guidance course. Please take a moment to find a quiet, comfortable place where you can fully relax and focus on yourself. This is your time—a time to let go of distractions and reconnect with your inner strength and sense of control. Let your gaze soften, and take a deep breath in... and slowly exhale. With each breath, feel your body begin to relax, your mind becoming calm and still. And as you sink into this feeling of calm, know that you are taking control—control of your thoughts, control of your emotions, and control of your choices.'

Damien reached over and hit stop on the phone's screen. 'As you can see, the video is very much live online. If you check any of my books from my collection, I can assure you that you will find that they're all working perfectly.'

'Then how do you explain the broken links in the books of the suicide victims?' Joseph asked.

Damien's forehead ridged. 'I can't. But I do know someone who might be able to assist you. I hire the services of an IT consultant, Gregory Richards and his company Nexus Online Solutions, to maintain my website and online video courses. If anyone can explain why those links may no longer work, it will be Greg. Anyway, I'm certainly going to be chasing this up as a matter of urgency, as the last thing I want is a customer buying a book only to find that the video links no longer work.'

'In that case, we'd like to talk to Gregory as well,' Joseph said.

'Really, you think that's necessary?'

'I'm sure you understand we need to follow up every lead,' Megan replied.

Damien nodded, lines spidering out from the corner of his

eyes. 'Of course you do.' He headed over to a mahogany desk and took an old-school Filofax out of a drawer. A moment later, he returned with an address written down on a notecard, which he handed over to the DC.

'Here you are, Greg's phone number and address. Give him a ring, and I'm sure he'll be able to put your mind at rest.'

'I think that's all we need for now,' Joseph said. 'Thank you for all your help. We'll be in touch if we need anything else.'

'Always pleased to assist, but before you go...' Damien headed back to the desk and picked up a couple of tickets from a stack on it and returned with them, handing them to Joseph and Megan. 'Please accept these. They're for my last mentalist show at the New Theatre in Oxford at the end of this week. I've decided to finally call it a day with my stage shows, so I can concentrate more on my writing, as well as my clients.'

'The tickets are very kind, but we can't accept any gifts,' Joseph replied.

'Nonsense, it's not as though I'm offering you both a bribe,' Damien said with a broad smile.

Joseph slowly nodded. 'In that case, maybe we will.'

Megan positively beamed at the mentalist. 'I've always wanted to see one of your shows. I've heard great things about them.'

'I look forward to seeing you both there. Maybe I can even persuade you to join me for a drink afterwards if you're off duty?'

'That sounds great,' Megan replied before Joseph could get a word in.

'Then I look forward to it.' Damien reached out and, rather than shake the DC's hand, took it in his and kissed it with a small bow.

Joseph was surprised at how lit-up Megan looked at that. Thankfully, Damien restrained himself with the DI, giving him a firm handshake. 'I'm always here to help if you need to see me again.'

'Thank you. We'll keep that in mind,' Joseph replied.

The mentalist smiled as he pressed a buzzer on the wall.

A moment later, Catherine reappeared, a couple of books under her arm. 'I'll show you out,' she said with a wide smile.

As the detectives followed her down the corridor towards the front door, the assistant turned to them, giving them each a book. Megan's book was about boosting self-confidence. The other that she gave to Joseph was about sleeping better, which, if the DI was honest, was something he frequently struggled with. The pressures of the job and all that.

'Please accept these with our best wishes,' Catherine said.

Joseph shook his head. 'As I just said to your boss, we really shouldn't be accepting gifts.'

Catherine fiddled with her ring again. 'Oh, don't worry, these were free samples from the printers. You'll probably find yourself flicking through them later—maybe just out of curiosity—but once you start, you won't want to put them down. It's funny how the right words just seem to draw you in, isn't it?'

'I suppose accepting them can't do any harm,' Joseph said.

Megan quickly nodded, and then her face lit up as she opened the front cover. 'He's signed it as well.'

'Anything for a fan of Damien's,' Catherine said, smiling at her.

'Then thank him from both of us,' the DC replied.

'I certainly will,' Catherine replied, opening the front door for them.

As soon as they'd left the flat, Joseph turned to his colleague. 'What was that performance about just now?'

'What do you mean?' Megan asked with her most innocent expression.

'You positively fluttered your eyelashes at the man when he

kissed your hand, and then went all misty-eyed when you got a signed copy of his book.'

'Well, he is very good-looking, and that voice of his is like velvety chocolate. I could listen to him talk all day.'

Joseph rolled his eyes at his colleague. 'If you say so. Okay, that aside, you better give this Gregory Richards a ring and try to get a meeting arranged ASAP. I'm keen to see what he has to say about these broken video links. Anyway, what do you think? Is Damien behind all these deaths?'

'My instinct is that he really had no idea about those broken video links,' the DC replied. 'So if that's true, maybe we'll find a completely innocent explanation for them when we speak to this Gregory character.'

Joseph exhaled slowly and nodded. 'I suppose best case, we've wasted our time chasing shadows.'

'And the worst case?'

'Let's cross that bridge if and when we ever get to it,' Joseph replied as they reached the stairs and headed down them. He felt uneasy, and he wasn't sure why. He also had a hint of headache, which didn't help matters. Something didn't quite stack up here, but so far he couldn't put his finger on what it was exactly.

CHAPTER TEN

JOSEPH AND MEGAN stood outside the building Damien had given the address for. The former sawmill in Blenheim had been converted into a suite of plush modern offices, which housed Nexus Online Solutions. Megan pressed the buzzer.

The DI gave his colleague a sideways look as they waited. 'I still can't believe you passed up the opportunity for a Maccy D's on the way over here. Are you sure you're feeling alright?'

She shrugged. 'I didn't feel hungry, that's all.'

Joseph tucked his chin in. 'Who are you and what have you done with Megan Anderson?'

The DC raised her eyebrows at him, as a voice came from a speaker panel mounted just below a security camera.

'How can I help you?' a woman's voice asked.

'We're here to see Gregory Richards,' Megan replied.

'Have you got an appointment?'

'No, but he's going to want to see us anyway,' Joseph replied, flashing his warrant card at the camera.

'Oh, I see,' the woman said. 'I'll buzz you in. If you could just wait in the lobby, I'll come down to meet you.'

A few seconds later, the detectives were standing in the

lobby as a woman with dark hair and round glasses, a sort of female version of Harry Potter, headed down the glass-panelled stairs towards them.

Her hand was already outstretched as she reached the bottom. 'Hi, I'm Stacey Ellis, one of the coders here demoted to covering the phones whilst our receptionist is off sick. Can I ask what this is all about?'

'I'm afraid this is a private matter we can only talk directly to Gregory about,' Joseph replied.

Stacey grimaced. 'Sorry, I didn't mean to pry. It's just not exactly an everyday occurrence, having the police turn up at our doorstep. Anyway, if you follow me, I'll take you straight up to his office to see him.'

The coder led the way back up the staircase and then through a large open office. It was filled with men and women sitting at desks, some with headphones on, all working on computers. There was a general atmosphere of intense concentration pervading the room, the only sound was the rapid tapping on keyboards as the detectives walked through.

Joseph's gaze was caught by one of the workers' screens with a time-lapse video player of a mountain range with clouds flowing between them like water. 'Is that one of Damien Storme's hypnosis videos?' he asked.

Stacey gave him a surprised look. 'I'm afraid we can't talk about work we do for our clients because of the NDAs we sign.'

'Mr Storme told us your firm does work for him,' the DC replied.

'Is that why you're here, then?' Stacey asked.

Joseph jumped in. 'As I said, this is a private matter.'

Stacey grimaced. 'Sorry, me and my big nose.'

They headed past a glass-enclosed room filled with racks of equipment with blinking blue and green lights.

Stacy gestured to it as they passed it. 'That's our state-of-the-art server room where we host the websites and online resources for our clients.'

'Looks expensive,' Joseph said.

'Oh, it is,' Stacey replied as she headed past the room to a door and knocked on it.

'Come in,' a man's voice called out.

'I'll leave you to it and I promise not to listen at the door with a glass,' Stacey replied with a grin.

Joseph raised his eyebrows at her, before following Megan through into the small office.

A man with thinning blond hair, wearing an open-collared shirt, sat at a large desk behind a curved monitor. He stood up as they entered, his hand outstretched.

'Gregory Richards,' the man said, shaking their hands. 'I believe you wanted to see me about something, Detectives.'

'Yes, it relates to a website you run for one of your clients. They sent us over to talk to you,' Joseph replied.

Gregory shot them a knowing look. 'Then you better make yourselves comfortable. Can I get you a coffee?' He gestured towards the gleaming machine in the corner, taking up pride of place on a table. 'A present from a coffee shop chain we do some work for. I love any excuse to use it.'

'Then I don't mind if I do,' Joseph said. 'A black Americano if it's no problem.'

'Of course, and you?' He turned his attention to Megan.

'No, I'm fine, thanks,' the DC replied.

Joseph wasn't sure he'd ever heard his colleague turn down a beverage. First passing up a Maccy D's and now this. Perhaps Megan was getting sick or something.

Gregory nodded, before setting to work on the coffee. A suitable amount of hissing and steam venting later from the silver beast, Joseph had a rather excellent cup of black nectar in his hand. It was just the right strength to oil the DI's tonsils and sharpen his mind. A professional barista would have been proud of this man's efforts.

'So you're here to ask some questions about the broken links for some of Damien Storme's videos?' Gregory asked as he sat back down behind his desk with an espresso, downing it in one gulp.

'Sorry, you already know why we're here, then?' Megan asked.

'Yes, Damien rang me to say that you were on your way over to talk to me.'

Joseph exchanged a look with Megan. Was the hypnotist just being helpful, or was there a more shady reason?

The DI gave the man a measured look. 'That's right. So, can you explain what happened with the broken video links?'

'I can assure you there's a very innocent explanation. The videos briefly went offline because one of our servers used to host Damien's website, as well as storing his video archives, crashed. We quickly restored the system from a backup, but some of the links had to be manually fixed, which took us a while to work through by hand, and even now a few are still broken.'

Megan tilted her head slightly to one side. 'You host the website from these premises rather than use one of the usual Cloud service providers, like Google or Amazon?'

Joseph glanced at his colleague, impressed that the DC seemed to know about this sort of thing.

'Yes, that's right. Among the other services we provide, we also can also supply a secure hosting service for clients who want to make sure their sites can't easily be hacked and need to be kept more secure. It's the sort of thing the MOD does to maintain the security of their data. Anyway, you can imagine my embarrassment when one of our RAID drive arrays, including the mirroring disks, all failed at once. Stacey, who you've just met, thinks it was down to a power surge. Anyway, I've already apologised to Damien for the outage. Thankfully, he was very magnanimous about it, realising that even with the best systems, these things occasionally happen.'

'So, am I right in thinking you also produce the content of the hypnosis videos for Damien's courses as well?' Joseph asked. 'I noticed one of your programmers working on one just now in the room next door.'

'Yes, we do most of the content creation as well, and all according to his unique specifications. Damien's exacting attention to detail also extends to the audio side of things.'

'Anything specific?' Megan asked.

'Without going into too much detail, because of client confidentiality, which is something of a watchword around here, Damien was keen for us to make full use of stereo in his recordings, and that is why he encourages people to wear headphones during his courses.'

'Stereo isn't exactly tricky, is it?' Joseph asked.

'It's a bit challenging. We have to create a soundtrack to encourage Theta and Alpha waves in the brain. We use what's known as a binaural beat technique. It creates two slightly different frequencies in each ear—a hundred hertz in the left and ninety-six hertz in the right. The brain perceives the difference between the two sounds as a four-hertz beat, helping to induce a deep, relaxed state. This helps guide a listener towards entering the Theta state of consciousness. The slow-motion video we use encourages the brain to enter a similar meditative state as well.'

'And the geometrical patterns? What about that?'

'They're also designed to help the brain focus and enter a relaxed state. Damien takes a very active interest in those and actually has an editor he uses to design the patterns which we then overlay onto the videos.'

'So what about subliminal messages? Any of those slipped into the videos?' Megan asked.

Gregory raised his hands. 'I can assure you there's nothing like that in them. But now I have to ask, why all these questions about Damien's videos? Has something happened, because, if so, I need to be made aware so I can contact our public liability insurance company?'

Joseph considered Gregory for a moment, weighing up in his mind whether to tell the man what had happened. Then again, nothing ventured, nothing gained.

'We're investigating whether there's a connection between a number of people who watched Damien Storme's self-hypnosis videos and their suicides.'

Gregory gawped at him. 'Bloody hell, you're saying you think there's a connection?'

'We're not sure yet. But that's exactly what we're trying to ascertain.'

Gregory sat back in his office chair, staring at his empty espresso cup as though willing it to magically refill itself. 'I suppose that could be possible if they were dealing with major emotional issues, making them more susceptible to taking their own lives.'

'I suppose that could be one explanation,' Joseph replied, deciding to bite his tongue about the link to the Dawson case. As far as he was concerned, the fewer members of the public who knew about that, the better. But there was another thing that Gregory might be able to cast some light on.

'There is one other common factor that may be of significance, and that's that each of these people had also been watching the videos with the broken video links.'

A troubled look filled Gregory's face. 'That is puzzling.' Then he nodded. 'Okay, I'm going to personally investigate this matter further. If I find anything even vaguely suspicious, I promise you I'll be in touch straight away.'

'We'd certainly really appreciate it,' Joseph replied, handing the man his card. 'Anyway, I think that's all we have for now.'

'Actually, I'd like to ask one final question before we go,' Megan said. 'What's your opinion of Damien Storme?'

'He's a good man and an excellent client, who's never given me any cause for concern—until now.'

'That's very helpful to know,' Joseph replied, nodding to Megan. It was always good to get a character reference for someone in danger of becoming a chief suspect in an investigation. 'Anyway, we've taken up enough of your valuable time.'

A short while later, the two detectives were walking back to the TR4. To Joseph's eye, the vehicle certainly held its own among the far newer and far more expensive cars in the car park. Gregory was obviously a man who paid his team well.

'So what do you think?' Joseph asked Megan as they reached the car.

'That Gregory was telling the truth regarding the broken links being down to one of their servers going offline,' Megan replied. 'But having said that, hearing all that business about manipulating people's Theta and Alpha waves sounds an awful lot like brainwashing to me.'

'That wasn't lost on me either. And isn't it just the sort of thing that might be used to manipulate someone into doing something they would never dream of?'

'So you're saying there really might be a link between the self-hypnosis videos and all these deaths, then?' Megan asked.

'Possibly, but we're certainly not there yet for a case that the CPS has any hope of winning. Don't forget we haven't found anything suspicious in those videos. The other glaring problem is that we're also lacking a clear motive for why Damien would want to kill anyone connected to the Dawson case.'

'Then let's hope Ian and Sue have had some success looking into Damien's background,' Megan said. Then she darted towards the driver's door of the TR4, giving Joseph her best attempt at a puppy dog-eyed look as she held out her hand.

Joseph narrowed his eyes at her. 'You're not seriously suggesting I'm going to let you drive Chris's car, are you?'

'Actually, the boss did say it was okay when I spoke to him about it.'

'I see. Going behind my back, were you?'

A mischievous smile filled her face. 'Something like that.'

Joseph was unable to suppress a smile but more aimed at Chris than the DC. It seemed as though the DCI had come up with a cunning plan to win Megan's affections. A set of keys to a sports car was certainly as good a way as any for a woman who was a self-proclaimed petrolhead.

He gave Megan the look as he tossed the keys to her. 'Please, just take it easy. And if you bend it, you pay for it.'

She waved a dismissive hand at him. 'Trust me, that will never happen.' Then with a grin wide enough to rival the Cheshire Cat's, she leapt into the driver's seat before the DI could change his mind.

Megan looked positively lit up as she turned the key and the engine of the Triumph burbled into life. 'Now that's what I call music,' she said, her grin somehow growing even wider than before.

CHAPTER ELEVEN

WHEN JOSEPH and Megan walked into the incident room, Ian and Sue were bent over their keyboards, hard at work. But it was the woman with long grey hair and wearing a trouser suit, standing with Chris at the evidence board, that drew the DI's attention. Although it had been years since he had last seen her, Joseph could already feel his mood heading south. Neither of them had exactly ever been a fan of the other.

Chris turned towards Joseph and Megan as they deposited their things onto their desks. 'How did you both get on with Damien Storme?'

'No real surprise, but he denies any link between his hypnosis videos and the suicides,' Joseph said, doing his best to ignore the woman now staring at him over the top of her glasses.

'And what about the broken links in the back of his books?'

'We spoke to a man called Gregory Richards. He runs the company that maintains Damien's website and videos,' Megan said. 'He said they had a server crash which temporarily took those videos offline, before their links were manually fixed. But he promised to look into it further to see if he could discover anything.'

The woman gave Chris a triumphant look. 'So, there you go, DCI Faulkner. That supports my theory that hypnosis is unlikely to have played any part in any of this.'

Chris gave the woman a perplexed look, before gesturing towards Joseph and Megan. 'Let me introduce Doctor Nicky Hunt, a forensic psychologist who I've brought in to consult on the case. I specifically asked for her because she was also involved in the original Samuel Dawson investigation.'

'Oh, I remember Doctor Hunt very well,' Joseph replied. But there had always been something about this woman that had rubbed him up the wrong way—like using sandpaper as toilet paper on his arse. The best the DI could say of the—po-faced, know-it-all, stuck-up—woman was that allegedly she was on the side of the police, although he wasn't really sure about that.

The psychologist narrowed her eyes at him, suggesting she was feeling something similar. 'DI Stone, what a delight after all these years,' she said with zero sincerity.

'Indeed,' Joseph replied with about as much warmth as a body in a mortuary.

Then Doctor Hunt's gaze settled on Megan and she, unlike the DI, was rewarded with a hint of a smile. 'DC Anderson, I've been hearing a lot of good things about you from DCI Faulkner.'

'Good to hear,' Megan replied, giving Chris a what on Earth have you been saying about me look.

He just shrugged in the way of a response as Doctor Hunt gestured towards the names of the potential victims on the board.

'As I was just telling your SIO, and as you can both probably already gather, in my professional opinion, I'm highly sceptical that hypnotism could have played any part in these people's deaths,' she said.

'Why's that exactly?' Joseph asked.

Doctor Hunt adjusted her glasses as she gave him her best withering stare.

'Look, I understand the allure of blaming hypnosis, or even brainwashing for these suicides—it's dramatic, almost theatrical. But I'm afraid that scientifically, that theory really doesn't hold water. You see, hypnosis isn't some magical tool that can override a person's moral compass or even their survival instincts. It's a state of focused attention, yes, but it relies heavily on the willingness of the subject. The idea that DCI Simon Hart could have been persuaded to shoot his colleague and then walk out in front of a bus because of hypnotism, goes against everything we know about human psychology. Don't forget, we're all wired with a very strong self-preservation instinct.'

'You don't think there's any room for exceptions to that?' Megan asked.

'I suppose if someone was already in an emotionally vulnerable state, then there might be a faint possibility someone could pull it off.'

'And all the people we have down as potential victims, don't exactly fall into that category.'

Doctor Hunt gave the DC an impressed look. 'Exactly. As I was telling DCI Faulkner, I really think you're heading up a dead end by suggesting hypnosis could have been any sort of factor.'

Chris rubbed the back of his neck. 'It does sound as though it's looking less likely by the second.' He nodded towards Joseph. 'And now hearing there was an innocent explanation for those broken video links, might just kill off this theory altogether.'

But as Joseph's gaze settled on the photo of Simon on the board, he wasn't ready to give up on it yet. If nothing else, he owed it to the memory of the man. There'd always been a strength of character to Simon that made the very notion he would have willingly done any of this impossible to believe. No, there had to be something else at play here that, so far, they'd missed.

The DI met the psychologist's gaze head-on. She looked like she was going to enjoy debating this point and trying to cut him down to size. And who was Joseph to deny her that opportunity?

He lifted his chin a fraction towards Doctor Hunt. 'But surely, under the right circumstances, somebody might be persuaded to do something they would never normally dream of doing?'

Sue and Ian, who'd been listening in, nodded.

'Like the Stanford University Prison experiment Geoff Goldsmith was inspired by,' Sue suggested. 'He certainly used it effectively enough against the people he tried to persuade to murder each other.'

'Ah, you're referring to the Hidden Hand Club murder investigation,' Doctor Hunt said. 'I was consulted about that by the CPS as they were putting their prosecution case together. I have to say it was a really fascinating use of behavioural psychology to manipulate his victims.'

Joseph gave her a triumphant, told you so, look. 'There you go then, and that's exactly my point. The same could be true here. I knew Simon Hart, and I can categorically tell you the only way that he could have acted that way, was if he'd been coerced into doing it.'

The psychologist folded her arms. 'I understand you had a personal connection to DCI Hart, DI Stone, but I'm afraid that maybe your judgement is clouded here. You see, the Stanford University Prison experiment worked because people were effectively isolated from their normal social networks, with a constant reinforcement of the new rules. That was also the case with the Hidden Hand Club, where Goldsmith used similar techniques to manipulate his players into doing something that would normally have been unthinkable for them.'

'I sense a but coming?' Chris said.

'Exactly.' Doctor Hunt gestured towards the photos on the board. 'All these people in this latest case were living their normal, everyday lives, with access to outside opinions and influence. Real brainwashing—or coercive control—requires time, isolation, and an awful lot of psychological pressure. And just to be utterly clear about this, you can't just hypnotise someone over coffee and make them jump off a building the next moment. It simply doesn't work that way.'

Joseph could understand the force of the woman's argument, but something inside him still refused to write it off just yet. There was another angle that couldn't so easily be ignored.

'Okay, even if I accept that, we can't overlook the fact that all these people were connected to the Dawson investigation. Tell me that's not significant.'

The psychologist's lips puckered as though she'd just sucked on a very sour lemon. 'Maybe it's simply a coincidence and nothing more. To me, it sounds like you're far too willing to base your case on something fantastical, rather than embrace a far more pragmatic and likely explanation.'

Chris looked between the DI and psychologist, finally picking up on the open hostility between them. He didn't exactly jump in between them to stop it from turning into a fistfight, but he did the next best thing by trying to defuse the building thunderstorm.

'So, in your professional opinion, we should consider writing off hypnosis as a real possibility, Doctor Hunt?' he said.

The forensic psychologist's shoulders dropped from where they had risen around her neck. 'Yes, that would be my recommendation. Also, without any real motive, I think you may be in danger of chasing shadows here. I mean, have you even found a connection between Storme and the Samuel Dawson investigation?'

Chris turned his attention to Ian and Sue. 'Did you manage to unearth anything so far?'

Ian shook his head. 'There's nothing, I'm afraid, boss, other than Storme did a psychology degree at UCL.'

Sue nodded. 'It's a small world among psychology professionals, and maybe Storme knew Dawson from some conference he attended, but if so, we couldn't find anything to support that.'

Doctor Hunt made a scoffing sound. 'Storme, a professional, hardly. That man squandered his training when he pedalled his talents to become a mentalist. Anyway, with a distinct lack of any supporting evidence, I would strongly advise you to either look elsewhere, or to drop this case entirely. It will be the latter course of action I'll be advising DSU Walker to take when I see him.'

Joseph couldn't help but feel a sense of satisfaction at seeing the fleeting look of irritation cross Chris's face at having the big man card being dangled over him.

'I'd be grateful if you could complete your written psychological analysis of each of the victims first. Dotting the Is and crossing the Ts, and all that. Then we can decide what our next step will be, and not before.'

Doctor Hunt gave the SIO an amused look. 'We'll see. Anyway, I have another appointment I need to head off to. If you have any more questions, you know where to find me.'

'We do,' Chris said, his jaw muscles tensing as though he was chewing on broken glass.

Doctor Hunt nodded to him and the other detectives, with the notable exception of Joseph, before heading out of the room.

'Flipping heck, what a woman,' Ian said.

'Aye, tell me about it,' Joseph replied.

Even Chris was shaking his head. 'Talk about winning

friends and influencing people. You'd think a psychologist might be a bit more skilled at that.'

'So what's the verdict, boss?' Ian asked.

The SIO sighed. 'Sadly, I think we're rapidly running out of options if the hypnosis angle really is dead in the water.'

Joseph shook his head. 'We're not there yet. There's still a chance that Gregory Richards might turn up something.'

'If he does, then great, but if he doesn't, then maybe Doctor Hunt is right about where this investigation is headed.'

Megan caught Joseph's eye and frowned. But the DI also knew that was the truth of it. Unless they had a breakthrough and soon, he doubted, even with the personal angle, Derrick would keep the investigation going any longer than he had to. Police resources and budgets only stretched so far.

The DI took in the slightly deflated looks on the faces of everyone else in the room. Yes, right now, it really did feel like they were clutching at straws. But there again, the DI had always prided himself on looking at every angle of a case, however unlikely, and this time wouldn't be any different, whatever the crow-face of a forensic psychologist might think.

Dylan, sporting an amused look, stood on the towpath next to his boat, watching the squirrel he'd nicknamed Raffles, hanging off the bird feeder. Tux sat guard on the ground beneath, watching as well. He chattered every so often in frustration, but ever hopeful in case the beast fell off and into his waiting jaws.

Joseph leant his bike against Tús Nua, and couldn't help but notice the squirrel's obvious annoyance. Trying to gnaw its way through the bars of the caged feeder, its tail twitched as the metal refused to yield to his safe-cracking efforts.

'What's going on here?' the DI asked.

'Exactly what it looks like,' Dylan replied with more than a note of satisfaction. 'After trying four different feeders, I've finally discovered one which is actually Raffles-proof.'

Joseph cast an eye over the jail-like bars encircling an inner feeder where the sunflower kernels were stored. With a glower towards its audience, the squirrel finally gave up and leapt onto a neighbouring tree, before using the aerial network of branches to speed away.

Tux turned to the humans and did the equivalent of a cat shrug.

'And good riddance to you,' Dylan called out to Raffles and his departing tail.

'I wouldn't get too confident just yet,' Joseph replied. 'Knowing that beast's skills, he'll be off to borrow an oxyacetylene blowtorch to cut through those bars.'

Dylan chuckled. 'Knowing my luck, probably true. Anyway, how's the investigation into Damien Storme going?'

'I'm afraid it's very much stalled right now. And the cherry on top is that Doctor Hunt, the forensic psychologist and right royal pain in the arse, who worked on the Dawson case, got involved. She just threw cold water on the idea that hypnosis could be used to get someone to do anything against their will.'

'Hmmm,' the professor replied.

Joseph gave his friend a look. 'You disagree?'

'Well, far be it from me to cast doubt on an area where Doctor Hunt is a far greater expert, but I think that might also be her blind spot. She wouldn't be the first specialist to have something of an issue with hypnosis and what she probably considers a pseudo-science of psychology.'

'And you don't?'

'All I know is, you should never write something off just because it's improbable. Besides, that's not the same thing as saying something's impossible.'

'That's actually a very good point and also very Sherlock Holmes of you.'

'I'll take that as a compliment. But before you lose too much heart about this case, I have the name of someone I think you should talk to. She is actually something of an expert when it comes to hypnosis and what exactly is possible.'

That immediately piqued Joseph's interest. 'Go on.'

'Well, I've been asking around and it turns out that in Magdalen College they run an Experimental Psychology course.'

'And what's that when it's at home?'

'It is a specialist degree where they utilise controlled experiments to research how people think, feel, and behave. Instead of just guessing or coming up with theories, it actually tests those theories in real-life situations or a lab.'

'So you're suggesting they might know how someone could manipulate someone else into killing themselves?' the DI asked.

'Exactly, and this is where it gets really interesting for your case, because hypnosis is one of the areas specifically studied. Iris was telling me that researchers there test how it affects things like memory, pain perception, and decision-making. They run experiments to see if hypnosis can help people remember things more clearly, reduce pain, or even change how they react to suggestions. By using brain scans and behavioural tests, they are able to see what's really happening in a person's mind when they enter a hypnotic state.'

Joseph's eyes widened. 'Okay, I need to meet whoever runs this course as a matter of urgency, before our investigation is prematurely shut down.'

Dylan nodded. 'Don't worry about that. Iris has already used one of her contacts to set up a meeting tomorrow morning at eleven with Doctor Clara Winslow. She's one of the senior tutors on the Experimental Psychology course. If anyone can help you, according to Iris, it will be Clara.'

'You're both superstars.'

'Actually, on this occasion, you should really thank Iris. She did most of the legwork. She's become so invested in this case after I took her into my confidence, that she's going to be at the meeting as well. She even suggested she and I get tickets to Damien Storme's final theatrical show at the New Theatre later this week. Iris thought we might be able to pick up something from it that might be useful for your investigation.'

'Then thank you again, but you're saying this isn't just a pretence, so you two can finally go out on a date?'

Dylan made a huffing sound, not meeting his friend's eyes and blushing slightly as he gave the barest nod.

'Then about bloody time, and I expect you to bring your A-game to your wooing,' Joseph said. 'And that starts with cooking for the woman. Do that, and Iris will be putty in your hands, as you pointed out so correctly with the gumbo I cooked Kate, although in fairness, she was putty before she'd even taken a bite.'

Dylan gave him a searching look. 'You really believe this could work with Iris?'

'Just trust me on this.'

The professor slowly nodded. 'Okay, maybe I will.' Then he gave a sharp nod. 'Yes, I definitely will. I think I need to talk this through with you. Speaking of which, I'm trying out a new gin that arrived today. It's from the Isle of Harris and is made with sugar kelp. Apparently, that's perfectly balanced with the bitter orange peel and liquorice root they use in the botanicals.'

'Why am I not surprised that you're a member of a gin club?'

'Would you expect anything less? Anyway, what do you say to a quick glass?'

'To be honest, you had me at gin,' Joseph replied, smiling.

Joseph's phone rang. As soon as he saw his daughter's name on the screen, he took the call straight away.

'And how's my golden girl doing?' he asked.

'Great. I'm ringing to ask if you would like to join John and me at that rooftop fusion sushi restaurant in Oxford tonight. Mum's already said yes.'

'Of course. What's the occasion?'

'I have big news, but I'll tell you when we see you,' Ellie replied.

'In that case, I'll see you there.' Joseph's mind was already rushing ahead to what this might be about.

'Okay, the table's booked for eight p.m. See you soon. Love you.'

'Love you too,' Joseph replied, but the line had already clicked off.

Dylan's gaze narrowed on his friend as he put his phone away. 'Is everything alright?'

'I'm not sure, but so help me if John has got her pregnant—'

Dylan held his hands. 'Whoa there. Don't get ahead of yourself now. This isn't the first time you've jumped to that particular conclusion. Reserve judgement until you hear what Ellie has to say.'

Joseph blew out a puff of breath. 'You're right. But I'll have to take a rain check on trying that gin for now. Although, if Ellie does tell me she and John are having a child, maybe have it on standby for when I get back.'

Dylan nodded. 'Understood, but I'm sure it will all be fine. Ellie has a sensible head on her shoulders.'

Heading to his boat to get changed, Joseph just wished he could believe that.

CHAPTER TWELVE

Joseph sat with Kate across the table from Ellie and her boyfriend, John, a serving police officer who had chosen to work in St Aldates. At the start of his daughter's relationship with the PC, the DI had given the man the third degree. In hindsight, he realised he'd fallen into the classic trap of no one is good enough for my daughter. Slowly but surely, as time passed, John had become family.

It turned out the restaurant the young couple had chosen specialised in a fusion of Danish and Japanese grilled skewers and sushi.

Not that Joseph had much headspace to actually concentrate on the food he was putting into his mouth. The problem was their daughter had insisted they eat first, before they revealed their big news. Thanks to that, his mind was caught in a loop, having rushed ahead to the punchline that he and Kate would soon be grandparents. He had already rehearsed in his head a dozen versions of his speech, but they all started with— you're both far too young to be starting a family.

Ellie's voice cut through his internal monologue. 'Dad, what do you think of the food?'

He looked up from the piece of California roll he'd raised halfway to his mouth with his chopsticks.

'Yes, it's grand.'

'I'm so glad you like it.'

Kate shot him a smile. 'I think you may have to bring Dylan up here at some point. This place will be right up his street.'

'It's certainly one of our favourites, although because it's a bit pricey, we reserve it for special occasions,' John said with a slight frown.

Upon hearing that, Joseph thought, Oh Jesus H. Christ.

'Then you must let us pay,' Kate said, smiling at the young officer.

'Aye, absolutely right,' the DI added.

John shook his head. 'No, we wouldn't dream of it.'

Joseph immediately spotted the grimace he briefly flicked towards Ellie. That well and truly was the straw that broke the camel's back.

The DI put his chopsticks down and peered at the young couple. 'Come on, please put us out of our misery already.' He only just managed to stop himself from adding, So when's it due?

When Ellie gave John an uncertain look, Joseph felt like his bone marrow was slowly being replaced with lead.

'Okay, but I want you both to remain calm,' his daughter replied.

Joseph started to wonder if there was a paper bag anywhere in this expensive establishment he could borrow to breathe into.

Initially, he thought Kate was holding it together better than he was, but when she reached across to take his hand, her grip was strong enough to bend iron.

'So what's this all about, Ellie?' Kate asked with the lightest of tones, as though she wasn't about to snap Joseph's fingers in two.

When their daughter looked beseechingly at her boyfriend, Joseph mentally braced himself for the bombshell the couple was about to drop on them.

'Don't look at me,' John said. 'I've said my piece to you about this already, but at the end of the day, this is your decision, Ellie.' Then he looked across the table at Joseph and Kate. 'Having said that, I'm hoping you may be able to talk some sense into her.'

It was Kate's turn to look properly rattled. 'Okay, Ellie, whatever it is, we're here for you.' She raised her eyebrows expectantly at Joseph.

'Aye, of course we are,' he replied, drawing in air through his nose to try and stave off the threatening hyperventilation.

For a brief moment, he was reminded of the time Ellie had managed to kick a football through the patio window as a young child. She'd arrived in the kitchen, staring down at the floor, not able to meet her parents' eyes as she'd told them what she'd done. That was pretty much the same aura Ellie was now radiating as she gazed down at her plate, albeit a twenty-two-year-old version, about to confess to something.

'Well, it's like this.' Ellie drew in a deep breath before raising her head. 'I want to give up college.'

Joseph felt like the planet had stopped spinning on its axis. Okay, their daughter might not be pregnant, but somehow this actually felt worse—giving up when she was so close to the finish line.

Kate, who looked as taken aback as Joseph felt, was the first to rally. 'Okay, but we've been here before, Ellie, when you had a wobble over your course.'

'Are those students giving you a hard time again?' Joseph said, recalling the last time she'd voiced giving up. 'If so, my promise still stands. I'll happily find a reason to lock them up in a cell.'

Ellie smiled at her dad. 'Thank you, but no need for the handcuffs. That's all ancient history now. But rest assured, it's nothing like that. This time it's actually for a really good reason.' She met Joseph's gaze head-on. 'I want to follow in your and John's footsteps and join the police force.'

In a parallel world where his daughter hadn't been in the final year of her Master of Public Policy degree, Joseph would have been flattered, enthusiastic even, if she wanted to follow in her old man's footsteps. But in this world, the one that they all actually lived in, and where Ellie had dedicated so many years of her life to her degree at the Blavatnik School of Government, it felt like a major misstep.

'But why would you want to throw away everything you worked so hard for?' he blurted out before he could stop himself.

John nodded. 'That's pretty much what I said.'

Joseph felt relieved to hear that his daughter's boyfriend wasn't exactly on board with this, either.

'Because I'm not sure my current degree is really what I want to do with my life. Dad, you've always been an inspiration to me, making a real difference in the world with your dedication and commitment. And I've seen how much John has enjoyed police work as well. Think about it. The force has been part of my life for as long as I can remember. So this just seems like such a natural step for me to take. To be honest, I don't know why I didn't think of it before now.'

'It's not all sunshine and roses, you know,' Joseph replied. 'Some days it's the hardest job in the world, and grinds your soul into dirt.'

Ellie shot him a challenging look. 'And on the good days?'

'Okay, yes, then it's the best job in the world. But those moments are often few and far between. John, you'll back me up on this, won't you?'

'Yes, a hundred percent. And as I keep telling Ellie, it's not like she can't make a real difference by going into an area like politics.'

Ellie ignored her boyfriend and instead turned to Kate. 'Mum, please tell me you understand?'

'Yes, I can understand the appeal, and if this is what you really want, I'll support you.'

'Kate—' Joseph started to say, but he was silenced by her raised palm.

'Hear me out,' she continued. 'Ellie, you're so close to finishing your degree. I really think you should complete it. How many months have you got left; four at most?'

'Yes, but I've already looked into the Police Constable Degree Apprenticeship, and their recruiting drive is next month for the Thames Valley Police. I know I want to do this, so seriously, why wait?'

'Because you'll keep your options open by graduating first,' Kate replied.

'And, although I can understand your enthusiasm to get going right away, why rush into it?' Joseph added.

John reached over and rested his hand on Ellie's. 'Once again, echoing exactly what I've been telling you.'

The DI felt a surge of gratitude towards the man.

But his daughter's expression hardened as she pulled her hand away and sat back in her seat. 'So is no one sitting around this table going to support me in this?'

'We're not saying that,' Kate quickly replied. 'But maybe you need to take a bit more time to think this through. I think I can speak for everyone when I say we'll be here for you, whatever you decide.'

Joseph nodded. 'We are. Just take a brief pause before you make such a big decision. That's all we're asking.'

Ellie let out a long sigh. 'Okay, okay. Not that it's going to change anything, but if it will make you all happy, I'll wait a month before I do anything about it. That'll be just before the deadline for the apprenticeship course expires.'

That wasn't exactly what Joseph had wanted to hear. A stay of execution until after her degree would have been best. But he also knew his daughter was strong-willed, so even a slight delay in this life-changing decision was a major concession on her part.

'Good, and that will give us all time to think about it a bit more,' Kate said.

'You mean, so you can try and talk me round?' Ellie asked.

Kate gave her a straight look. 'Well, obviously.'

Ellie held her eye, and then, of all things, laughed. Just like that, the tension that had been building like a thunderstorm evaporated, and everyone was all smiles again.

'Okay, now that's all sorted, let's get on with eating this sushi before it goes cold,' Joseph said.

'It was already cold, Dad,' Ellie said, grinning at him.

He winked at her. 'You know what I mean.'

She laughed. 'Anyway, what's this I hear about you and Mum buying a place together in North Oxford that backs onto the canal?'

'Sorry, what?' Joseph said, turning his attention to Kate.

'Well, it's good to have dreams, isn't it?' Kate said, smiling at him. 'You could even keep Tús Nua moored up at the bottom of our garden.'

'Unless we win the lottery, because of the eye-watering money those places go for, I can't see that happening anytime soon.'

'But even you have to admit the idea has a lot of appeal?'

'To be honest, as long as we're together, we could be in a tin shack, and I'd be just as happy.'

Kate gave him a look that made his heart skip several beats. 'And right there is the reason why I fell in love with you the first time round. You are, and will always be, an Irish romantic at heart.'

Joseph smiled. 'Guilty as charged.'

John looked between them. 'So, let me get this right, you're seriously considering moving in together?'

'Let's just say, conversations have been heading that way,' Kate replied. 'Although I'm not sure if Joseph will be ready to be prised away from Tús Nua anytime soon.'

Joseph spread his hands. 'It's just I've set down roots there, that's all.'

Kate gave him an unreadable look and nodded. 'Of course, you have.'

The DI gave her a small smile, before looking at his family gathered around him. 'So what does anyone say to another round of sake as none of us is driving?'

'Why not?' Kate said, smiling at him.

Just like that, even though their daughter might be on the cusp of making a decision he was worried that she would come to regret, everything felt right with the world again. Tonight they would laugh, and whatever Ellie decided, they would cope with in the future.

Joseph and Kate walked hand in hand as they headed away from the restaurant, that small, simple act enough to make Joseph's heart swell. Being back together was all about the small moments like this.

'Well, that was certainly an interesting night,' Kate said.

'Isn't that the truth,' Joseph replied. 'I just hope we manage to talk Ellie round.'

'I don't know about you, but I'm prepared to use every trick in the book to get her to delay her decision about joining the police until after she's graduated—' Kate stopped mid-sentence and dropped Joseph's hand as though she'd just become aware she'd picked up a scolding hot pan.

Then Joseph saw the reason why.

Derrick was heading towards them, a Sainsbury Indian takeaway meal for one, dangling from his hand. He stared at the two of them, his initial look of bewilderment morphing into one of anger.

Kate shot Joseph a beseeching look. 'What do we do?'

'Run?' the DI replied, only half joking.

That didn't so much as raise a smile from her as Derrick drew closer. Some men might have walked past, pretending they hadn't seen anything. But not someone wired like the DSU, and who seemed to thrive on confrontation.

Derrick glowered at Kate as he reached them. 'Okay, now I finally understand why you really left me, so you could get back together with your lover boy here.'

Kate was already holding up her hands. 'Look, it's nothing like that. Joseph and I got back together after you and I separated, and not before.'

'As if I'm going to believe that when you two have always been an item, even when you're not. And you.' Derrick turned to scowl at Joseph. 'Talk about stabbing a man in the back. Not to mention Amy. What's she going to say when she discovers you've been carrying on with Kate and having an affair?'

Joseph grimaced. 'She won't say anything because we broke up a few months back.'

Derrick stared at him. 'Oh, I see. Now I get the picture. You've been deliberately keeping that from me because you knew I'd quickly work out what that really meant. The moment Kate dropped me, I bet you wasted no time sniffing around her like a dog after a bone. Or was it even before?'

Joseph felt a spike of irritation. 'It was nothing like that.'

Kate reached out for Derrick's shoulder. 'We certainly didn't mean to hurt you, and I just hate that you found out this way.'

Derrick flinched away from her touch. 'But here we bloody are anyway. This is the worst sort of betrayal, Kate. I might expect it from Joseph, but not you.'

Before Joseph could get a word in, Kate unleashed at the DSU with both barrels.

'You need to get over yourself, Derrick. If you want to know the one who is responsible for our breakup, you need to take a long, hard look in the bloody mirror.'

The DSU ground his teeth together, his eyes slitting. 'I know full well about my own shortcomings, but maybe you should be the one looking in that fucking mirror!'

Joseph could feel the heat building in his chest, but he also knew he needed to keep a lid on it. If he started to unleash the years of pettiness that Derrick had focused on him, the downright spite, and the need to put him down whenever the big man had a chance, he might not be able to stop. As justified as the DI was in telling the arsewipe exactly what he thought of him, that would end up helping no one. Right now, a cool head was called for.

So instead, he gave the superintendent a measured look. 'You can't talk to Kate like that,' he simply said.

'Can't I? The last time I looked, we were still technically married,' Derrick replied.

Kate's nostrils flared. 'That's neither here nor there. But as you bring that up, I think it's time we got divorced, don't you?'

The colour literally drained from the DSU's face. 'But Kate—'

She stopped him dead with a sharp head shake. 'No, we both know that's where we are, with or without Joseph in my life.' Then Kate softened her tone. 'Look, it's time that we're both honest with ourselves. I've already moved on, and you should, too.'

Derrick opened his mouth to say something, but then closed it again. Instead, he just shook his head and walked off into the night, head down.

When Joseph turned to look at Kate, he wasn't surprised to see tears running down her face.

'Are you okay?' he asked gently.

'No, of course I'm bloody not. That's why I'm going to stay the night with you.'

'Aye.' He took her hand again.

As they started to walk away in the opposite direction that the superintendent had taken, Joseph was already considering what the fallout at work would be. But one thing he was already crystal clear on. Tonight, he'd made a real enemy of Derrick, someone who would no doubt go out of his way to make his working life a living hell.

CHAPTER THIRTEEN

WHEN JOSEPH ARRIVED at work the following day, Megan was wearing headphones and staring intently at her screen. Even though he nodded towards her, the DC didn't blink, or look up from her screen until he placed a cup of coffee from the mobile barista van, the Roasted Bean, down in front of her.

'Thank you,' she said distractedly, her gaze returning to her screen.

'Anytime. What are you watching?'

The DC hit a key and swivelled the screen towards him to show him a paused video. Damien Storme was standing before a beach scene, with another of the geometrical patterns superimposed over the scene behind him.

'You're watching one of Storme's self-hypnosis videos, then?' Joseph asked.

'Yes, this one I picked up from Blackwell's.'

Joseph took in the title, Willpower Unleashed: A Hypnotic Guide to Self-Control.

'Interesting choice of subject matter,' he said, raising his eyebrows at her.

'I wanted to compare it to the books his assistant gave us, to see if I could spot any differences from the video fragment Neil recovered from Hart's laptop.'

'And was there?'

'Nothing I could see, and I've watched both at least a dozen times now. I've also compared it to the signed book Damien's assistant gave me, but can't see any differences. I did wonder if Damien might have slipped in some subliminal message into that superimposed geometrical pattern, but even going through them frame by frame, I found absolutely nothing.'

'So in other words you're telling me we've well and truly barking up the wrong tree here?'

'If there was ever a tree to bark up in the first place,' Chris said, materialising behind them with nothing less than a bag of Ben's Cookies from the Covered Market in his hand. 'I'm afraid I come bearing bad news. Derrick has set a deadline for the end of the week for us to wrap things up one way or another. Hence these cookies to celebrate or commiserate—you decide which.'

'To be fair to the superintendent, what choice did he have in light of a very distinct lack of evidence?' Megan said.

No doubt the foul mood he was in last night didn't help either, Joseph thought to himself. But for the benefit of the others out loud, he said, 'Actually, I wouldn't be too quick to throw in the towel just yet.'

They both turned to him.

'Why's that?' Chris asked. 'Have you managed to dig something up?'

'Not yet, but I might've found someone who can point us in the right direction. Thanks to my neighbour. He and his friend, Professor Evans, have set up a meeting with a Doctor Clara Winslow. She's a lead tutor on the Experimental Psychology Degree course at Magdalene College. Apparently, one of the things they specialise in researching is hypnotism.'

'And you think this woman may be able to cast some light on

whether it's even possible for someone to use hypnotism to get someone to carry out suicide or murder?' Chris asked.

'That's what I'm hoping to find out. Even if she shoots the theory down as quickly as Doctor Hunt did, at least it means it's been corroborated by an independent expert.'

'Then I very much look forward to hearing about your meeting. In the meantime...' He proffered the bag of Ben's Cookies first to Joseph, who happily helped himself to a hazelnut and chocolate one. But when the SIO presented the bag to Megan, she shook her head.

'No, I'm good,' she said.

Few things in life left Joseph speechless, but this was definitely one of them. He gawped at his colleague, not sure if he had heard her correctly. But it was Chris who got there ahead of him.

'Are you sure you're feeling okay, Megan?'

'I just don't fancy one.'

The SIO pulled a face. 'Seriously, since when do you turn your nose up at a free snack or any sort of food for that matter?'

Irritation flashed in Megan's eyes. 'Look, I can turn down a biscuit without being interrogated about it, okay?'

Chris held up his hands. 'Whoa there, just making an observation.'

'Well, don't,' Megan replied with a fierce look that was completely out of character for her, especially when talking to the boss. Then she returned her attention to the monitor and pressed play on the video again. It seemed the normally sunny disposition of the DC was taking a short break today.

The SIO raised his eyebrows a fraction at Joseph, then gestured with his chin towards the door. Joseph nodded. A few moments later, they were both standing together outside in the corridor.

'What's got into her?' Chris asked the moment the door was closed behind them.

'No idea, but then again, we're all allowed an off day every so often.'

The SIO remained silent for a moment. 'Look, maybe she's picked up on the fact that I'm interested in her.'

'You didn't go ahead and ask her out, did you?'

'Of course not. But maybe she picked up on the vibe coming off me. Maybe that's why she snapped at me like that just now.'

'That doesn't sound like Megan at all. Even if she did pick up on something, even if she wasn't interested, she certainly wouldn't hold any sort of grudge towards you. I've seen the way she handles Doctor Jacobs, who's a full-paid-up member of her fan club. She's the model of tact with him, and certainly has never had a go. So I wouldn't read too much into this. Maybe she's just coming down with something. That said, would you like me to have a word with her?'

Chris quickly shook his head. 'God, no. If she realises I've been speaking to you about this, it will only make matters worse. Just leave it.'

Before Joseph could give Chris the talk, the boss was already heading down the corridor like a man with the weight of the world on his shoulders.

With a shake of the head, Joseph headed back into the incident room to see if Megan had calmed down, and God forbid, might even fancy a cookie now.

Doctor Clara Winslow's study in Magdalene College was everything that Joseph had imagined it would be. Its walls were lined with dark wooden panels, its carpet was so well-worn it looked like it had seen countless footsteps over the years, and there were oil paintings of former tutors everywhere. It was as though this room was stuck in some sort of time warp from the 1950s, or perhaps even more accurately, straight out of an episode of Inspector Morse.

Clara looked at Joseph, Megan, as well as Iris, who'd joined them for the meeting as promised. 'Can I interest either of you in a mint tea?' the psychologist asked. 'I rather live on the stuff.'

'Sorry, I'm more of a coffee man,' Joseph replied.

'Nothing harder tucked away in that desk of yours?' Iris asked.

'Sadly not,' Clara replied with a smile.

'Then a mint tea it is.'

'Not for me, thank you,' Megan added, who had been uncharacteristically quiet on the journey over to the college.

Joseph was starting to get the definite impression the DC's nose was so out of joint that it might as well be sticking out the side of her head.

'Each of us to our own poisons,' Clara replied as she filled a cup from the freshly boiled kettle and dropped a green tea bag in it. Once that was done, she settled herself behind her desk. 'So Iris was telling me you wanted to pick my brain about hypnotism as it relates to a case you're currently investigating?'

'Yes, I was hoping you might be able to shine a light on the subject for the detectives,' Iris said. 'To start with, what can you tell us about hypnosis?'

'Well, the quick overview is it can shift a person's consciousness into different states,' Clara replied. 'For example, we might study how hypnosis changes what people see or feel, or how it's been used—sometimes controversially—to bring back memories. But we don't just take it at face value, either. We focus on the actual evidence and the ethics behind it, rather than teaching people how to do it, although that is an area that I do actually specialise in.'

'So what about someone using it to persuade someone to kill, or even commit suicide?' Joseph asked.

Clara's eyebrows shot upwards. 'Now there's a question. From a psychological perspective, there's no strong evidence that hypnosis alone can compel someone to do something that goes against their moral compass. It can increase suggestibility, but ethical research shows it works best with actions that align with the person's existing values or beliefs.'

'That sounds like you're writing it off,' Iris said.

Much to Joseph's surprise, Clara shook her head.

'I didn't actually say that. It may be unlikely, but it's not beyond the realm of possibility, either. In an extreme case—say when hypnosis combined with psychological manipulation, or even exploitation of someone's specific vulnerable state—people can be influenced in very harmful ways. But that goes far beyond hypnosis into the broader realm of psychological control and abuse of trust. Cases like that would rely on a mix of persuasion techniques, emotional leverage, and sometimes traumatic conditioning, rather than hypnosis alone acting as a kind of'—the tutor made air quotes—'mind control.'

'So you're suggesting a skilled psychologist might be able to pull it off?' Joseph asked.

'I suppose I am. But please understand, it's not hypnosis itself that's inherently dangerous, but used in the hands of someone skilled enough to manipulate a subject's fears or desires, it could become a lethal tool.'

Joseph slowly nodded. Unlike Doctor Hunt, it sounded like Doctor Winslow was far more open to the idea of hypnosis being used as a tool by a murderer. He noticed Megan grimace as she squeezed the bridge of her nose.

'Are you okay?' he asked her.

'I've got something of a headache coming on. Anyway, don't mind me.'

Joseph felt relieved to hear that. It could certainly help to explain her recent behaviour.

He returned his attention to Clara. 'So am I right in thinking someone would have to be very suggestible for someone to be able to manipulate them into taking their own life?'

'Normally, yes.'

Joseph sat up straighter. 'There's an exception?'

'Well, there are ways to make anyone more open to suggestion, such as the use of specific drugs, for example. It's actually something we've researched.'

'That sounds very interesting,' Iris said.

Clara quickly held up her hands. 'Before we all get too carried away with this line of thinking, I feel duty-bound to point out it would still be very tricky to pull off. Even if a psychologist was using drugs to make someone more suggestible, they would need plenty of time with that person to fully condition them to do the things you're suggesting.'

'How long are we talking here exactly—days, weeks, months?' Joseph asked, casting a look over at Megan, who was looking greener by the second.

'Probably a few days over a number of sessions, the more the better, to persuade a person to do something they would never normally dream of. However, tell someone black is white for long enough, and throw enough spurious evidence in to support that, and eventually, they will come to believe you. But I'm intrigued to know who it is you're investigating because the world of psychology is quite a small one, and I might be able to throw some light on whoever they are.'

Joseph realised there was no point in holding back, not least because he was keen to hear Clara's insights on the man. 'This is obviously of a highly confidential nature as this is part of an ongoing investigation, but we are specifically looking at the mentalist, Damien Storme. Apparently, he graduated from UCL with a psychology degree.'

'Well, I suppose that's one way of making a living,' Clara replied with a smile. 'But why do you think he might be involved?'

Joseph pushed Damien's self-hypnosis book across the table. 'All of the victims watched hypnosis videos by Storme. We're trying to work out if there's something in these books, which effectively allows him to brainwash his victims. Not that we can find any evidence of that in his books. We may, of course, just be on a flight of fantasy with this, but it would be good to get your professional opinion. Megan here has also looked at another of his books from Blackwell's, but couldn't find anything incriminating in those, either.'

'Then we'll have a look in one of our labs to see if we can find anything hidden in it, or just as likely not.'

'That would be a great help either way. Thank you.'

'Anytime, but if we're talking about someone who is a mentalist, there is one thing you should be aware of. They are often very highly skilled at slipping keywords into sentences using subtle reinforcements, such as physical touch, tugging their earlobe or something similar, or even just eye contact. This combination of a verbal cue and a physical action helps anchor the keyword in the listener's mind. It's a classic psychological technique to create associations or trigger memories. The person wouldn't even be aware that anything was happening to them.'

'That's a chilling thought,' Iris said.

'Particularly when we're talking about it not just being used with a willing subject, or just to entertain an audience. Anyway, I'm afraid I have a tutorial with a student, so you're going to have to excuse me. But if we find anything of interest, I'll be in touch.'

A short while later, Joseph, Megan, and Iris were heading out of Magdalene College together.

Megan suddenly made a retching sound and bent over.

'Goodness, you're really not well,' Iris said, rubbing her back.

'I think it might have been a dodgy kebab I ate last night,' Megan replied. 'I better get back to St Aldates in double-quick time.'

'Then go ahead. I'll see you back there,' Joseph said. 'But to be honest, based on the look of you, I think you'd be better off heading straight home.'

'No, I can push through this,' Megan said with a backward wave as she hurried away.

'That woman is too dedicated for her own good,' Joseph said as they watched her go.

'Indeed,' Iris replied as she turned to him. 'But I'm glad we're alone for a moment because I need to ask you something about Dylan.'

Joseph took in the woman's slight frown. 'There's nothing wrong, is there?'

'No, nothing like that. I just want to make sure I'm not getting my wires crossed. You see, we've arranged to go to the theatre this Friday evening. It's actually to see Damien Storme's mentalist show to help with your research into this case.'

'Yes, he told me all about that. But what do you mean about getting your wires crossed?'

Iris looked around to check no one was close by and then leant in, dropping her voice to a whisper. 'To cut to the heart of the matter, I'm not certain if it's meant to be a date or not. Either way, I want to be sure, because I've certainly been waiting long enough for him to get round to doing it. But Dylan being Dylan. Well, you know...' She looked beseechingly into the DI's eyes.

'Aye, I do. Anyway, you didn't hear this from me, but...' Joseph raised both thumbs at her.

'Really? So you're saying he's actually interested?'

'Very much so, and from what I gather, he has been for a long time.'

'Then about bloody time he actually asked me out, that silly man,' Iris said, smiling. 'And if this isn't the perfect excuse for a new outfit, I don't know what is. On that note, I better go and get prepared for this momentous event.'

'You do know Friday is still three days away?'

'These things take time, my dear man.' With a wave, Iris turned and headed away in the general direction of the shops.

With a smile, the DI headed in the opposite direction back to St Aldates. After talking to Clara, and unlike the impression he'd got from Doctor Hunt, he certainly felt fresh hope there might be something to the whole hypnosis angle after all.

CHAPTER FOURTEEN

WHEN JOSEPH RETURNED to the incident room, he wasn't surprised that there wasn't any sign of Megan.

Chris headed over and nodded towards her vacant desk. 'I took one look at her and sent her home.'

'Good. I don't think the cleaners would have thanked you for having to mop her vomit from the walls.'

'They're not the only ones,' Ian said, looking up from his screen. 'I doubt I could have faced my pilchard sandwiches if Megan had started hurling everywhere.'

'The smell of your often-pongy lunch would almost certainly have been enough to finish her off,' Sue said.

Joseph chuckled as he hooked his jacket over the back of his seat. 'So did Megan manage to get you up to speed on what we learnt from Doctor Winslow at Magdalene College?'

'She didn't have a chance to, before she went tearing out of here,' Sue replied.

'Not surprising, really. Well, the upshot is Clara was a lot less dismissive about hypnotism being used as a weapon to murder someone than our own Doctor Hunt. But she did say hypnotism was unlikely to have been effective if only used by itself. But this is where it gets really interesting. She told us that if used in the hands of a skilled psychologist, given enough time, they might have been able to condition someone deeply enough to be able to pull off something like this.'

'Such as Damien Storm, you mean?' Chris asked.

'She certainly didn't rule him out. We also left a copy of one of his books with her so they could study it in their labs to see if they could unearth anything.'

'That certainly shines a more positive light over this investigation,' Sue said.

'Maybe, but by itself, I doubt it's enough to convince Derrick to extend the investigation beyond Friday,' Chris replied. 'That's why we need to find something of substance, and quickly.'

'What are you thinking?' Joseph asked.

The SIO headed to the board and tapped Damien Storme's name written under chief suspect, and then a list of motives, including revenge. 'If Storme really is our man, this is the key piece of information we're still missing. If we discover that, then just maybe we start to have the foundations of a real case we can build against him. But here's the thing we're up against. If Storme really does have the ability to manipulate others into doing his dirty work, he is also able to keep his distance from any actual murders. That's why we need to take an even harder look into Storme's background.

'Ian and Sue, I want you to take a second look in case we missed anything.' Then he turned to Joseph. 'I need to bring you up to speed about another development.' He gestured towards the door.

The DI followed the SIO out of the room, suspecting he knew what this was about. Soon, the two of them were ensconced in a meeting room, with the door closed firmly behind them.

'So, if this is about Megan...' Joseph said.

'That's not why I needed a word. One of my colleagues from the NCA, who has been monitoring a Serbian drug gang operating out of the UK in a separate investigation, sent me a video that you're going to want to watch.'

'Is it connected to the Night Watchmen?'

The SIO nodded as he wirelessly connected his tablet to the screen on the wall and pressed play. 'This was captured by one of our spy cameras we hid in a building we knew the gang was using to distribute their product.'

Joseph watched the screen, taking in the high-resolution video of the inside of a warehouse. There was a clear area in the middle where a group of men were sitting around a long table. They all appeared to be listening to a woman speaking. With a shock, the DI realised with a start who he was looking at.

'That's Chief Superintendent Kennan,' he said.

'In one, and she's talking to this Serbian gang headed up by none other than Dragan Marković.'

'Fecking hell, even I've heard of him, and that man is as ruthless as they come. Isn't he the guy who loves to dismember people with a machete if they just cross him?'

'That's the man, and everyone is too terrified to testify against him. That's why the NCA has had Marković under surveillance in the hope of trying to build up some hard evidence against him. Thanks to that, we were able to capture exactly what happened in this meeting last night.'

'I'm guessing, nothing good.'

'Exactly. It marks a major escalation in just how far the Night Watchmen are prepared to go.' Chris turned up the volume so they could hear what was being said.

'You're a man of vision, Dragan,' Chief Superintendent Kennan was saying to the gang leader. 'I've heard the stories of how you built your operation from nothing. Bricks of ambition, held together by loyalty from your men recruited from a young age.'

Marković took a slow drag from his cigarette, letting the smoke curl around his face before responding. 'Flattery is a weak currency in this business, lady. If that's all you come to offer me, then you've wasted your time.'

Kennan's smile didn't reach her eyes. 'Hardly. I'm here because my colleagues and I recognise what you've built, and are offering you a chance to make it untouchable. This is about taking your operation to the next level by expanding your reach and making your supply chain impenetrable. Work with us, and you can have all those things.'

The man's eyes became as cold as steel. 'Us? You mean your crew of bent coppers and henchmen in your pay? Forgive me if I don't leap at the chance to let the wolves into my house.'

The chief superintendent crossed her arms. 'We're not wolves. We're the shepherds who see the bigger picture. You keep things messy, Marković, and you make enemies. Sooner or later, the law will catch up with you. But by being allied with us, no one will touch your operation—not the law, not your rivals. You'll be above it all.'

The gang leader chuckled, shaking his head, his men joining in and trading amused looks.

'Bold words, lady,' he said. 'But I don't need your protection. People have learnt that the hard way and know better than to challenge me and my men.'

Chris hit pause. 'So what do you think so far?'

'That you now have clear evidence that Kennan had a sit-down with this gang so she could try to recruit them into the Night Watchmen. Pretty damning, if you ask me.'

The SIO nodded. 'Exactly, and with this video evidence alone, it gives us enough to take the superintendent down.'

But Joseph could read between the lines and had already picked up on the lines radiating around the boss's eyes. 'And the but is?'

'Unfortunately, it's a massive one. But we'll get to that in a moment. For now, just keep watching.' He pressed play again.

On the video, Kennan stared across the table at Marković. 'You think your kingdom is untouchable? You've been lucky so far, but anyone's luck can run out. We're offering you longevity for your business. A partnership where everyone wins. Or would you rather gamble it all by rejecting our offer?'

The Serbian gang leader leaned forward, his voice subzero. 'Let me make this perfectly clear, lady. I built this empire with my own hands. My risks, my blood. I don't share it with anyone. Especially someone who works for the fucking police.'

Kennan shook her head, and then with a smirk, stood. 'You know, Marković, I thought you were smarter than this. I thought you'd see the potential in this alliance with our organisation. But it seems your ego's louder than your instincts.'

Marković rose as well, towering over the superintendent. 'And I thought you were clever enough to understand that men like me don't take orders. Not from anyone.'

'Then have it your way and let your bloated ego get in the way of a shrewd business opportunity. But make no mistake, you and your men will pay the price for this stupidity.' She turned and started to walk towards the door.

The gang leader shouted at her departing back. 'Is that a threat, Kennan?'

The chief superintendent paused, her hand on the door handle, turning slightly. 'No, Marković, it's a promise.'

Joseph blew his cheeks out. 'Well, that's certainly not good.'

'Oh, trust me, it's about to get much worse,' Chris replied. 'If you were in any doubt about how ruthless our chief superintendent is, just keep watching.'

The gang leader was joking with his men, who were all shaking their heads.

Then, the door burst open with a bang and a small dark canister was lobbed inside, landing between the gang members. Before they could move, it exploded in a blinding burst of brilliance that briefly whited out the video camera. When the view cleared again, the men were lying on the floor, some clutching their ears.

'Was that a fecking flash-bang?' Joseph asked.

'Yes, and you can probably already guess what's about to happen,' Chris replied.

Joseph gave the SIO a grim nod as he watched as Marković, the first of his gang to recover, staggered to his feet, pulling a pistol from beneath his jacket.

At that moment, men in body armour and wearing black balaclavas burst through the doorway. The way they handled themselves told Joseph they'd all had serious tactical training. He also recognised the weapons in their hands as MP5 submachine guns, the signature weapon that the Night Watchmen loved to use against rival gangs. It felt like he was watching an action movie play out. The only problem was this had happened in real life.

The men began spraying fire into the prone men, their victims' bodies shuddering as the bullets struck them. Marković alone managed to stand, bringing his pistol up and shooting one of the advancing men, hitting him squarely in the chest. The man staggered backwards, but his body armour absorbed most of the impact.

It was too little, too late.

The man's colleagues turned their weapons on the Serbian gang leader. He twitched as plumes of blood erupted from his body, struck by countless bullets. Marković dropped to one knee, but somehow still found the strength to raise his pistol, as one of the armed men advanced towards him. With a well-aimed kick, the weapon flew from the gang leader's hand. Then, the Night Watchmen's man unholstered his Glock and pointed it at Marković's head.

'Fuck you all!' the gang leader bellowed, baring his teeth.

The man fired at point-blank range. The back of Dragan's head exploded, his snarl frozen in place, and he toppled sideways to the ground.

As the video ended, Joseph glanced at the timestamp. 'Feck. One minute was all it took them to murder the whole gang.'

Chris gave Joseph a grim look. 'Just shows how ruthless they really are.'

'So what happens now? You arrest Kennan and the other corrupt coppers on their payroll?'

Chris shook his head. 'That's the problem I alluded to earlier. You see, my bosses are determined to bring down the Night Watchmen once and for all by identifying the kingpin that Kennan is working for. Intelligence is starting to close in on a specific politician we believe may be behind it all, although so far we don't have a name. But when we have that, the NCA will finally make their move.'

'Are you seriously saying that we can't touch Kennan, even with this footage?'

'I'm afraid so.'

Joseph scowled. 'So let me get this absolutely clear—in the meantime, the bodies keep piling up?'

The SIO just nodded, his expression drawn.

'Fecking hell. Okay, I understand the desire to take down the person at the top, but if they don't act now, there could be a hell of a lot more blood on their hands.'

Chris gave him a tight-lipped look. 'I didn't say I agreed with this strategy, Joseph. Far from it. But the ones further up the pay scale aren't prepared to risk what they see as a golden opportunity to bring this organisation down once and for all. They're worried that if they don't get the ring leader, they'll be leaving the door open for them to regroup and start again.

'After all, that's exactly what happened after the Jimmy Harper case, where the NCA were able to shut down most of the Night Watchmen's shell companies, but they still survived. This time round, they don't want a repeat of what they see as a mistake by acting too soon. But before you say anything, trust me, I've tried arguing against this strategy, but I appear to be the lone voice at the NCA.'

'So, in other words, since it's criminals killing criminals, the powers that be at the NCA feel they can afford to wait a bit longer. Is that about the measure of it?'

'I didn't say that.'

Joseph met the SIO's gaze head-on. 'You didn't need to.'

Chris's forehead ridged. 'Look, I know how much you're invested in this, especially as you and your family were threatened.'

'Invested is one way of fecking putting it. Wanting to throttle those Night Watchmen gobshites with my bare hands is another.'

'Trust me, I feel the same way.'

Joseph sighed. 'Aye, I know. So I have to ask, have you dug up any more dirt on Amy?'

'Not at the moment, and I wanted to ask, has she tried to talk to you again?'

'It's all been strictly work-related—otherwise, she's given me a wide berth that I'm more than happy about.'

'What about Kate and Ellie, not to mention Derrick? No more threats to them you know about?'

'All quiet on that front, too. Mind you, it's only a matter of time before Kate starts asking tricky questions again about the Night Watchmen. But to be honest, I think now Ellie's life is no longer in danger, even though Kate might not admit it even to herself, I think she's happy to leave them well alone for now.'

'Good, then try to keep things that way as best you can. The same goes for Derrick. If he suggests so much as trying to tackle the Night Watchmen, steer him well away from doing anything stupid.'

'I doubt he's going to be in much of a mood to listen to me about anything from now on.'

'Why's that?' Chris asked.

'Because I ran into him in town last night when I was with Kate. Let's just say it didn't go well.'

'Bloody hell, so he worked out you two were an item again?'

'Aye, and now I fully expect him to make my life a living hell. Derrick is absolutely a man to hold a grudge, and for a very long time.'

'Then I'll try my best to protect you from any crap he decides to throw your way.'

'I'd certainly appreciate that. But the good news, at least for now, is that Kennan and her cronies seem happy to leave us all alone.'

'That's only because they probably believe they have you where they want you. But that could change at a moment's notice, and if it does, you must let me know at once.'

'Don't worry about that. But my guess is, based on that video, Kennan has her hands more than full organising all of these gangland hits.'

Chris grimaced. 'Yes, I suppose she does. Still, we can't afford to get complacent. Things have a way of shifting for the worse when you least expect it.'

'Don't worry, I know that better than anybody. But you

should also watch yourself, Chris. If Kennan gets even a hint of who you really are...' Joseph deliberately let his words trail away.

'Unfortunately, that's the risk I deal with every day in my job. Anyway, if only to distract ourselves, let's make the most of what little time we have left on the Damien Storme case.'

'Oh, I hear you,' Joseph said, as the two men stood and headed back towards the incident room.

CHAPTER FIFTEEN

'What did you think of the ramen noodles I bought for us?' Kate asked as they sat eating at the table inside Tús Nua, with Tux curled up on her lap.

'Grand, but I have to say, I've got a lot of love for those steamed bao buns. That filling is fantastic. But I'm suspicious of your motives here. What are you after, my mind, or is it my body like usual?'

A small smile curled the corners of her face. 'Well, I suppose there is always that, but do I have to have a reason to spoil you?'

'Of course not, but...' Joseph narrowed his eyes a fraction.

Kate gave him her best I've been busted grimace. 'You know me far too well. Anyway...' She dug her hand into her bag and withdrew a folder with what Joseph recognised as a logo of one of the more upmarket estate agents in Oxford. He suddenly had a strong hunch about what this meal was really all about. Those suspicions were confirmed when Kate took out a selection of glossy flyers of properties for sale, from small flats to houses on the outskirts of the city.

'Ah, so you're on a mission to soften me up into buying that home together?'

'Of course, I am. You didn't think I would just let it drop, did you? Anyway, there are some really lovely properties I'd like you to take a look at.'

Joseph sighed. 'If it will make you happy, then I'll cast an eye over them.'

Fine lines spidered out from the corners of her eyes. 'This isn't just about my happiness, Joseph. This needs to feel right for you as well. I'm not going to try to impose a decision this big on you.'

'I know, it's just...' He waved a hand around at the cabin.

'That you love living here on board Tús Nua, and all she represents. Yes, I get it, I really do. But some of these properties come with parking so you can keep your TR4 there, rather than leave it at work.'

'To be clear, it's still Chris's car. But yes, I'll grant you, that would be more convenient. But if I did that, then I'd end up being tempted to use the TR4 every day rather than my bike. And that would be the beginning of the end. Before I knew it, I'd have a potbelly and end up snarled in the commuter traffic like everyone else, watching my life ebb away in traffic jams. Better to have the wind blowing through my hair as I speed down the back streets of Oxford.'

Kate snorted. 'Wind blowing through your hair now, is it?'

'You know what I mean.'

She nodded. 'I do, but trust an Irishman to go all lyrical on me. Just please do me a small favour and try to keep an open mind when you look through those properties.'

'I'll try to do my best,' Joseph replied, realising that it would be something of an uphill battle. Leaving his life on the canals of Oxford would break several of his heartstrings. 'Anyway, property searches aside, have you had any more thoughts about our precious daughter?'

'I can't help but feel she's in danger of making a massive mistake.'

'Aye. But I also know Ellie well enough to know that she won't be told what to do. She has to work this out for herself.'

'Maybe she gets a little bit of that stubbornness from both of us,' Kate said.

'No doubt. I don't know what you think, but I was wondering if Dylan might have a word with her, especially as Ellie sees him as an honorary grandfather.'

Kate nodded. 'He's certainly someone she's turned to in the past, so there's a good chance she might actually listen to him. Anyway, I'm glad you said that, as I've already spoken to him.'

'Oh, it's like that, is it?' He smiled at her.

'Trust me, it wasn't planned. Dylan just happened to be outside when I arrived, so I grabbed the opportunity to have a quick word with him. Anyway, after talking it through, he said he might have an idea about how to change Ellie's mind.'

'How so exactly?' Joseph asked.

'All he would say is that he needed to talk to someone first.'

'Well, that man has more contacts when it comes to Oxford than a pint has bubbles. That aside, talking of Dylan, did he happen to mention to you that he's finally plucked up the courage to ask Iris out on a date?'

Kate's eyes widened. 'Seriously?'

'Yes, although he may have had some prompting from yours truly for him to get on with it.'

'Then good on you. I think those two could be really good for each other.'

'I agree, although Dylan has also pretty much perfected his bachelor life on the water here. Having said that, he's also been carrying a torch for Iris for decades now. I certainly couldn't stand by and watch him let the love of his life slip away.'

'You and that old romantic heart of yours.'

Joseph pulled a face at her. 'Shush now, or you blow my cynical old man cover.'

'Definitely not cynical, or old for that matter. But you are definitely one of a kind, Joseph Stone.'

'I think there's a compliment hidden in there somewhere?'

Kate smiled at him as his phone went off.

When Joseph glanced at the display, he saw it was an unknown number, but he took the call, anyway.

'Hi, DI Stone here,' he said. That was normally enough to make a scam caller immediately slam the phone down at the other end. But that didn't happen this time.

'Hi, it's Gregory Richards. You visited my business, Nexus Online Solutions, earlier this week to ask about Damien Storme's website and his hypnosis videos.'

'Ah yes, you were going to look into the videos with the broken links for us.'

'I think I may have found something you're going to want to see. Can you come over right now? This is very important.'

'Of course,' Joseph replied, mouthing sorry to Kate. 'Give me twenty minutes, and I'll be with you.'

'Good, then I'll see you soon.'

After Joseph put the phone down, he turned to Kate. 'It looks like work is going to pull me away yet again from the love of my life.'

'Such as it ever was.' She gave him a sad smile. 'Is this something to do with Damien Storme by any chance?'

'Indeed, and just when it was looking like we were on the verge of closing down the investigation, this sounds like it might be our first real lead.'

'Then I'll keep my fingers crossed for you. Are you going to take Megan with you?'

'No, she went down with what might have been food

poisoning earlier today. It's best to let her get her beauty sleep. Besides, this isn't anything I can't handle by myself.'

'Then you better get to it, although there is absolutely no way I'm going to leave without taking some of this delicious ramen with me to finish later.'

Joseph shook his head. 'Where's the rush? Finish it here. Besides, why don't you stay the night again? After all, I shouldn't be too long.'

A mischievous grin filled her face. 'In other words, so I can keep the bed warm for you?'

'I didn't say that, but if you're offering.'

Kate made a mock swipe at his head. 'And to think I was calling you an old romantic just now? Now get going, because the sooner you do, the sooner you can get back to me.'

'Now there's a very good point,' Joseph said as he stood, bending down to kiss her.

Tux looked up, and he made sure to fuss the side of his head. The cat leaned into his hand and let out a contented purr.

As the DI grabbed his jacket and headed out of the door, he glanced back at the woman who he loved with his whole being. Yes, he really was one of the luckiest men in the world.

Joseph pulled up in the car park outside the Old Watermill business park in the TR4 he'd grabbed from work. There was a single car outside, an electric Porsche Taycan that certainly looked expensive enough to belong to the man who ran Nexus Online Solutions.

A single window in one of the upstairs rooms glowed in the darkness, which Joseph was fairly certain was Gregory's office.

As the DI headed towards the outside door ready to press the intercom button, he spotted the crazed glass around the door lock. On closer inspection, he noticed the metal frame had been bent inward. The lock had been forced. The DI took out his phone, calling the number Gregory had rung him from earlier. He let the number ring until it finally went to voicemail.

'Gregory, it's DI Stone here. Ring me the moment you get this.'

When Joseph saw no flicker of anyone's shadow moving behind the blinds of the upstairs windows, he headed back to the TR4 and grabbed his baton from the glove compartment. As the DI walked back to the front door, he slipped on some latex gloves. He might be on estranged terms with Amy, but he still didn't want to risk the SOCO's wrath by contaminating any fingerprints if someone had broken in.

The DI nudged the door with his foot, and it swung open to reveal the shattered lock. He stepped through into the darkened hallway, taking his torch out and flicking it on.

'Police, if there's anyone here, make yourself known,' he called out. Only silence answered him. His instinct was growing louder by the second that something was seriously off here. Joseph, knowing he should have done so before stepping over the threshold, belatedly pulled out his phone and dialled.

'St Aldates Police Station,' a man's voice answered that the DI recognised as belonging to Gary, one of the duty sergeants.

'Hi, it's Joseph here. Is there a patrol car anywhere in the vicinity of Blenheim? I'm looking at a possible break-in and could do with some backup, just in case.'

'Yes, I have PC John Thorpe in the area. Do you want me to send him over?'

'Please, but tell him I'm heading in, as I'm worried someone might have been hurt.'

'Will do.'

After giving Gary the address, the line clicked off. The DI's mind was racing as he walked towards the stairs. It couldn't be a coincidence there'd been a break-in, just after he'd received that cryptic phone call from Gregory. If this had something to do with those broken video links, had Storme already taken steps to remove any trace of those original video files?

Joseph began to creep up the stairs, trying Gregory's mobile again as he reached the landing. This time he heard the faint answering echo of a ringtone coming from somewhere ahead of him. The DI began to move quickly towards the source of the sound and wasn't surprised when he arrived at the door of Gregory's office.

Then he noticed the distinct whiff of nose-stinging petrol and turned towards the open door to the server room. A discarded fuel can had been thrown onto the floor, the racks all glistening with liquid. It looked like they'd also all been smashed with a fire extinguisher, still partly buried in one.

Feck! Joseph thought. If this wasn't someone trying to hide incriminating evidence, he didn't know what was.

The DI turned back to the partly closed door as the ringing mobile on the other side of it went quiet as the voicemail kicked in again.

'Gregory, are you here?' Joseph called out, a deep sense of unease growing inside him when no one answered. Just how far might Damien Storme be prepared to go to cover up his secrets?

Joseph flicked his baton out to its full length. He balanced it backwards over his shoulder so he could swing it at a moment's notice. Then he edged forward towards the door and shoved it with his elbow to swing it open. The air caught in the DI's throat as he took in the scene before him. Gregory was slumped forward onto his desk, blood pooling over the documents beneath his chest.

The DI rushed forward, pulling the man up as he got ready to take his pulse. But his hand froze as he took in the multiple stab wounds in the man's chest and face, and his lifeless, wide, staring eyes.

Joseph heard the softest footfall behind him. Adrenaline thrummed through his system as he whirled around. But it wasn't Damien Storme standing there as he'd been expecting, but Stacey Ellis, the coder he and Megan had met earlier that week. The woman rushed at him, a kitchen knife in her raised hand, mouth twisted with wild fury.

The DI whirled his baton, striking the weapon from Stacey's hand and sending it flying, just as blue lights lit up the outside of the building. The cavalry had arrived, but maybe too late to help save him. Joseph had no time to alert John to what was happening inside, because the woman was scrabbling towards where the knife had disappeared under the desk, like a crazed animal desperate to kill.

He raised his baton again. 'Just fecking stop already!' he bellowed.

Stacey ignored him, her hand reaching towards the handle of the knife. The DI knew right then that this woman wasn't about to listen to reason. With all his weight behind it, he swung his baton down, smashing it hard across her shoulders.

A whimper escaped from Stacey's mouth as she rolled onto her back. Too late, Joseph spotted the knife in her hand again, but before he could move to disarm her, in a fast, brutal movement, Stacey drew the knife across her own throat. The shocking wound gaped open as her head tilted back and blood spurted out.

'Sweet Jesus,' Joseph said, as he heard running footsteps and John burst into the room.

The DI dropped to the woman's side, desperately clamping his hands over the wound, trying to staunch the flow of blood that bubbled up between his fingers.

The hardness in the woman's eyes was suddenly replaced

by one of bewilderment as she stared up at him. Her mouth opened and closed but only a gurgling sound came out as she arched her back. Then her eyes glazed as her life slipped away and her body stilled.

He sat back onto his haunches, mentally trying to process the sudden gut-churning turn of events where this woman had just taken her own life after murdering her boss.

'Joseph, are you okay?' John asked gently.

'No, I'm fecking not,' the DI snapped before he could stop himself. 'Sorry, that was aimed at the universe in general, not you.'

'Don't worry, I understand,' the PC replied, as he took in the two dead bodies.

'You better call in reinforcements,' Joseph said.

'Already done. They're on their way. I'll call Amy and her team, too.'

'Good, the sooner they get here, the better,' Joseph said, trying to order his own thoughts. The first question already spinning around his mind was: what had driven Stacey, a woman who seemed absolutely fine when he'd first met her, into this state of utter madness? The second, and just as pressing question, was whether Damien Storme had anything to do with it.

CHAPTER SIXTEEN

I‍t had been a long night for Joseph that had sucked his energy away to the depth of his bone marrow. Now, in a white protective forensic suit, he was grabbing a breather as he stood outside the Nexus Online Solutions building. If someone had offered him a cigarette right then, even though he didn't smoke, he might have been tempted to accept it.

Daylight was just beginning to creep through the branches of the woodland surrounding the business park, a dawn that neither Gregory Richards nor Stacey Ellis would get to see. Inside, the SOC team, led by Amy, was hard at work, picking over the murder scene for any clues and hoping to discover the motivation behind these brutal deaths.

Despite his exhaustion, the DI's mind was still racing from the events of the previous night. But the one thought kept overriding all the others. That was the look on Stacey Ellis's face as she'd gone for him with the knife. In that moment, the woman had looked like an absolute psychopath who'd lost control. Also, based on all those stab wounds, the ferocity of her attack against Gregory was one of the most brutal murders he'd ever witnessed. The intensity alone suggested she utterly loathed the man. But could hypnotism really be responsible for pushing her that far into the realm of madness?

Chris, also suited and booted in white coveralls, headed over with two coffees in hand, one of which he handed to Joseph.

'You better get this down you before you fall asleep on your feet,' the SIO said.

Joseph took a sip. The black nectar immediately hit the spot and helped push back his fatigue a fraction, both mentally and physically.

'Ah, that's better,' he said.

The SIO peered at him. 'You know you really don't need to stay. Your crime scene report can wait until later today. In the meantime, why don't you get yourself home for some rest? I'll update you when I have any news from Amy and her team.'

'If it's all the same, boss, I'll stay. I won't be able to get any sleep until I know what we're dealing with here.'

'Fair enough, but the moment we do, you head home and get some rest. And just so we're clear here, that's an order, not a request.'

'Aye.' Joseph didn't even have the energy to give his boss a mock salute. 'Anything of interest so far?'

Chris was about to answer when Amy materialised in the doorway behind him.

'Okay, we're about to wrap things up,' she said.

Her gaze met Joseph's and, as he often witnessed now, he saw the hurt in her eyes before her professional mask slipped back into place. For someone who had played him so well, her performance was almost believable.

'If you'd like to follow me, I'll get you both up to speed with what we've found,' she continued.

Joseph gulped down the last of his coffee before following the others back into the building.

Chris stopped and pointed at the lock.

'I was wondering if you had any thoughts of why the lock was forced, when presumably Stacey had a key?'

'We found the key in her bag,' Amy confirmed. 'However, the security camera footage that should have shown her entering the building had already been deleted. The computer logs showed that happened just before you arrived, Joseph.'

The DI met the SOCO's gaze, which was pure business, and he nodded. 'That doesn't surprise me. Ellis was probably trying to make it look like a break-in so that we would think Gregory had disturbed the intruder before being killed. What her little plan didn't factor in was me arriving to spoil the party.'

'That's a theory the forensic evidence supports as well,' Amy replied. 'My team found a crowbar in the back of Ellis's car that matches the dent marks in the doorframe. As for the rest, you better follow me back up to the victim's office.'

Joseph had already prepared himself by popping a fresh Silvermint into his mouth before he entered the murder scene. As he entered the room, his gaze was inevitably drawn to the grizzly sight of the two bodies. Alison Rogers, one of the other SOCOs, was taking close-up photos of every stab wound on Gregory's body.

Megan would have been in her element if she'd been here, not batting an eyelid and asking all the right questions. Unfortunately, she was still out of action with what was obviously an epic bout of food poisoning. Joseph might feel exhausted, but on his way home, he fully intended to go to drop off some electrolytes for her from the all-night chemists.

'I suppose the first thing to ask is whether you can confirm if Ellis was the one who definitely murdered her boss?' Chris asked.

'That's exactly what it looks like from the forensic evidence,' Amy replied.

'Which is?' Joseph asked.

'The blood splatter patterns on Ellis's clothing, discounting her own blood from her neck wound, indicate proximity to the victim as she stabbed him. This was an upfront and personal attack. Also, the entry points match the width of the same kitchen knife that she used to attack you with, Joseph, before turning it on herself.' Amy then gestured to the carpet nearest the door, where an evidence marker and a ruler had been placed.

Joseph and Chris took in the blood splatters on the carpet.

'It looks like this is where the initial attack began,' Amy continued. Then she gestured to similar blood marks heading towards the desk. 'We can tell from these that Ellis continued to stab him multiple times as she drove him backwards. We've also found multiple wounds in his arms and hands where the victim tried to defend himself. Then, based on further splatter patterns on the desk, Ellis continued to stab him another thirty times before he collapsed into the position you found him when you first entered, Joseph.'

The DI nodded, but his imagination was already playing out the final moments of this man's life—hearing someone outside when he thought he was alone in the office—heading to the door only to be met by Ellis with a knife in her hand—before he could stop her, the woman driving the blade into her boss. The shock Gregory must have felt of seeing someone he knew and trusted attack him like that, as he'd stumbled backwards. The disbelief, the confusion, the terror knowing he was going to die in those final awful terrified moments of his life.

Joseph could see it all so clearly in his mind's eye.

'Not that there was very much doubt, but you're basically confirming that this was a frenzied attack?' Chris asked.

'By any measure,' Amy replied. 'We'll obviously be waiting for DNA and fibre analysis to help confirm what this initial evidence is telling us, but I think I'm confident enough to be able to tell you that there's little doubt in my mind that Stacey Ellis murdered the victim, then took her own life.'

'And the time of the victim's death was?' Chris asked.

'Based on algor mortis, he died somewhere between eight forty-five and nine forty-five p.m.'

'That makes sense,' Joseph said. 'I received the phone call from Gregory around eight-thirty. That means Ellis must have let herself into the office shortly afterwards. But what about the destruction of the server rack? Have you been able to link that to Ellis as well, Amy?'

Amy gestured to the fellow SOCO. 'Alison already did.'

The blond-haired forensic officer looked up and nodded. 'I was able to lift a full set of prints from both of Ellis's hands that match ones I've also taken from the extinguisher and the petrol can,' she said with a slight hint of a Northern accent. 'There's little doubt she was the one who destroyed it.'

'In that case, is there any indication of a motive, including the destruction of the server?' Chris asked.

'Nothing yet, although we'll obviously be examining any phone or computer she might own,' Alison replied.

'Well, based on the fact Gregory was looking into those broken video links and wanted to show me what he'd found in person, there has to be something incriminating Damien Storme,' Joseph said.

Chris's lips thinned. 'You're suggesting he managed to hypnotise Ellis into doing all of this?'

'All I'm saying is, it's one hell of a coincidence if he didn't, especially based on the timing of Gregory's death after his phone call to me. I have no doubt that if I hadn't disturbed Ellis, she would have burned the servers as well, to make sure they were utterly destroyed.'

'I'm afraid anything concrete regarding her motive or whether she was coerced will have to wait until we've had time to go through all of her devices and do a thorough search of her home,' Chris said.

'We can also do the same for Gregory Richards,' Amy said.

Chris nodded. 'And what about the server rack? Her attack on it has to be significant, and as Joseph suggests. I can't help but think it's connected to what Gregory discovered.'

'I wouldn't hold out much hope. Our murderer did a very thorough job of destroying those drives. I doubt the digital forensic team will have much joy recovering any data from them.'

Joseph rubbed the back of his neck. 'In that case, would you have any objection to hiring Neil Tanner again, Amy? If anyone can work a miracle, it's that man.'

'None at all, especially as that will leave our people free to concentrate on analysing the victim's devices to see if they can dig up anything,' the SOCO replied.

Chris gave an approving nod. 'You'll certainly get no argument from me. Neil more than proved his credentials during the Goldsmith investigation.'

'Then leave it to me, and I'll get the server rack parcelled up and couriered over to him,' Amy replied. 'Anyway, that's all I have for you right now.'

The SIO turned his gaze to Joseph. 'In that case, I think it's time for you to head off home.'

The DI nodded, barely stifling a yawn. Then, with a nod to the others, he headed for the door.

'Are you okay?' Kate asked the moment she laid eyes on Joseph as he entered the cabin of Tús Nua.

'To be honest, several steps beyond shattered,' Joseph

replied, slipping his jacket off and dropping the chemist's bag down on the counter.

'No, I mean about that bloody woman trying to attack you with a knife.'

Joseph took a moment to work out how Kate could know about that, until his mind finally caught up. 'I see the family grapevine has been working overtime as usual.'

'Yes, Ellie rang first thing after John told her what had happened.' Kate reached out and pulled Joseph into her arms. 'I don't know what I would do if I lost you when we only just found each other again.'

'Look, I'm okay,' he said, kissing the side of her head.

Kate pulled away and scrutinised his face. 'Thankfully, I can see that for myself now.' She blew out her cheeks. 'I've been worried sick since Ellie rang me.'

'But surely if it came via John, you knew I was okay?'

Kate flapped her hands in her face. 'Yes, but still.'

'Aye, you do love to worry about me.'

A smile curled the corners of her mouth. 'I always have, and always will. And there I was feeling so relaxed after a wonderful night's sleep on your boat.'

'Ah, so Tús Nua is starting to seduce you with her wily charms, then?'

'Let's just say, I'm starting to see some of the attraction to boat life.'

'But not a fully signed-up convert yet, then?'

'I wouldn't go as far as that. I mean, there's hardly room to swing a cat.' She glanced down at Tux, who was looking at her with what amounted to a steely gaze. 'With apologies to the current company, of course.'

He smiled. 'It's bijou, that's all, and with buckets of charm to go with it.'

'If you're thinking of becoming an estate agent anytime soon, I wouldn't bother if that's the extent of your sales pitch.'

Joseph snorted. 'I'll keep that in mind. Anyway, away with you now. This man needs his sleep. And if you're still here, I might be in danger of not getting any.' A slow grin filled his face.

'Bloody hell, you're insatiable.'

'Well, it takes two to tango in bed.'

Kate laughed. 'Now, there's a mental image.' She glanced at the open chemist's bag on the counter and frowned. 'Why do you need electrolytes? You're not feeling sick, are you?'

'Don't worry, those aren't for me. Megan's been off ill from work with suspected food poisoning. I popped round to her flat in Iffley to see how she was doing and drop those electrolytes off for her, but she wasn't there even though her car was. When I rang her she didn't pick up, either.'

'Maybe she's staying with a boyfriend or was just fast asleep.'

'Well, I know for a fact she isn't dating anyone, but I suppose she could be staying with friends or family.'

'As long as she has someone to hold her hair as she pukes into a toilet bowl, I'm sure she'll be fine,' Kate said.

'So now it's your turn to conjure up quite the lovely image there.'

Kate grinned at him. 'Anytime. That aside, I wouldn't worry too much about Megan. She's more than capable of looking after herself. I'm sure she'll check in the moment she's feeling better.'

'Aye, you're right, of course.'

Kate nodded. 'Anyway, I must love and leave you, before you tempt me into that bed tango that you mentioned.'

'Then maybe tonight for that performance?' Joseph winked at her.

Kate chuckled, and kissed him on the cheek, before dancing away out of his reach. She headed for the door, followed by Tux, his tail erect like he was a cat on a mission to put the world to rights.

The moment the DI was alone, the sense of mental and physical exhaustion finally swept over him. That was accompanied by a pounding headache. Wincing, he headed for the bathroom to grab some paracetamol. The moment his head hit the pillow, rather than simply fall asleep, he passed out.

CHAPTER SEVENTEEN

THE WHITE LIGHT in the room was blinding, swallowing everything in its sterile glare around Joseph. That was, apart from the hypnotic and pulsing geometrical pattern hanging in the air before him. The DI's pulse pounded in his ears as he tried to shield his eyes, to look away, to do anything. But his limbs felt like stone, his body frozen to the spot.

The shapes in the pattern twisted and folded in impossible ways, their movements burrowing into his mind. He knew he needed to stop looking, but his gaze stayed locked onto the moving kaleidoscope as his brow prickled with sweat.

'Do you understand what I want you to do?' Storme's disembodied voice said.

'I understand,' he replied.

Joseph's heart lurched. No! his brain screamed inside his skull as he fought to turn his head away, to resist, to do something—but nothing happened.

'You're doing very well,' Storme's voice continued. 'And from now on, you won't question my directions. You will do exactly what I say.'

'Exactly what you say,' the other version of Joseph echoed.

Even as it was said, the DI's stomach churned. Fight it and fecking move! he thought, willing his body to break free. But all he could do was watch, paralysed and trapped within his own body.

The geometrical pattern shifted more quickly, warping like liquid glass, and a single word emerged from the chaotic depths —Chrysalis. The word pulsed, beating in time with the DI's hammering heart.

What the hell does that even mean? he thought.

Then, Damien Storme's face appeared before the DI, too close, his eyes sharp, lips curled into a smile. 'Embrace the void,' he whispered, his voice melodic.

Joseph's breath hitched. No, no, no! The DI tried to scream, but his mouth wouldn't open.

Then, of all things, he heard a sound that didn't belong there —a faint bark.

He strained his ears trying to locate the source of the sound in the white nothingness. Then another bark, this time closer, and cutting through the fog in his mind.

'Joseph, are you in there?' Dylan's voice called out from a distance.

The blinding light fractured as the DI blinked his eyes open. Then the world around him shifted, and he was suddenly back in Tús Nua's cabin, where sunlight slipped through the gaps in the curtains.

It was just a dream, just a stupid dream, he thought.

The rap of knuckles came from the cabin door. 'Joseph, are you alright?' Dylan's voice called out again.

The heaviness pulled at Joseph's legs as he swung them off the bed, like a swimmer weighted by gravity after emerging from a pool. He grabbed his dressing gown and headed to the cabin door, trying to shake the grogginess still threading through his brain.

When the DI swung the door open, Tux darted in and headed straight over to his food bowl.

Joseph raised his gaze to see Dylan looking in at him, flanked by White Fang and Max.

'Sorry, I was asleep,' he said.

'I thought that might be the case, but I just wanted to check in on you because it is nearly six p.m.' Dylan replied.

'What?' The DI turned to stare at the wall clock, confirming what his friend had just told him. 'Jesus, I need to get to work.'

Dylan's eyebrows drew together. 'A long night, hence the lie-in?'

'Yes, but not intentionally. And I just had the strangest vivid dreams. Damien had hypnotised me, and I couldn't move. Then there was a single word, Chrysalis, in one of those geometrical patterns we've seen in Storme's videos. I know it never happened, but it honestly felt so real. Thank God it was just a nightmare.'

'Well, you be pleased to hear I can confirm Damien was nowhere near your boat,' Dylan replied, giving his friend a concerned look.

'That's a relief. But I suppose when I think about it, I've been immersing myself in his world of hypnosis. So it's not surprising some of it has spilled over into my dreams. It certainly wouldn't be the first time that's happened with a case.'

'That makes a lot of sense, but I have to say the word Chrysalis is certainly an interesting choice for your subconscious to conjure up.'

Joseph gave his friend an intrigued look. 'In what way?'

'Because that word suggests transformation, or even a period of change. Maybe a deep part of your mind is trying to tell you that you're on the cusp of a breakthrough with your investigation.'

'I certainly hope so, especially after what happened last night.'

Dylan peered at him. 'Which was?'

'Gregory Richards, that man who runs the company that hosts Damien Storme's website, rang asking me to meet up with him. But when I turned up at his business, one of his programmers, Stacey Ellis, had already killed him, and then she turned her knife on me.'

The professor's eyes grew round with shock. 'But you're okay, at least based on the fact you're not in a hospital?'

'Yes, although the same can't be said for Ellis. Before I could stop her, she slit her own throat right in front of me.'

Dylan's face paled. 'Hang on, doesn't that sound a lot like what happened with your friend, DCI Hart?'

'Exactly. And that's where it gets into territory that has to be significant. Gregory was looking into those broken video links for me. He found something and wanted me to see it in a hurry.'

'So you think he dug up something that might connect Damien Storme directly to the murders?'

Joseph shrugged. 'Well, it seems like too great a—and here's that fecking word yet again—coincidence, for it not to be. That's why I need to get into work sharpish to find out what additional evidence Amy and her forensic team may have turned up.'

'Actually, I do need to talk to you, if you have a few moments before you go. I've had something of a brainwave regarding Ellie's future.'

'In that case, you better come in and brief me as I get ready.'

As Dylan nodded, Tux miaowed and did the cat equivalent of pointing to his empty food bowl by dipping his head towards it.

'Message received and understood, little fella,' the DI said, taking down the very expensive dry cat food from the cupboard.

White Fang and Max licked their lips. Shaking his head, the DI handed the dog treat bag to Dylan, who smiled.

After having showered and feeling a bit more human after the troubling dream, Joseph was currently having a shouted conversation through the door with the professor as he quickly got dressed.

'The good news is that by taking into account Ellie's newfound passion for police work, I think I may have managed to kill two birds with one stone,' the professor said.

'How so exactly?' Joseph replied as he buttoned up his shirt.

'I tried to find an area where someone with a degree from the Blavatnik School of Government would be welcome with open arms, but would also have some relevance to the police. That's when I came across something I think would suit her right down to the ground. Have you ever heard of the Centre for Criminology based here in Oxford?'

'It rings a bell from somewhere, but remind me?' Joseph replied, as he slipped on his cycling jacket.

'It's one of the leading academic crime centres in the world. For example, they work with policymakers to produce research that contributes to a better understanding of crime and justice. As part of that, and this is where it gets really interesting for Ellie, they also work directly with the police, especially the TVP.'

'Hang on, that's where I know them from. Aren't they involved in the Integrated Offender Management scheme? They deal with high-risk repeat offenders, trying to help steer them away from a life of crime?'

'That's them.'

Joseph nodded, enthusiasm for Dylan's idea quickly gaining

traction in his own mind. 'Yes, I remember a case with a man called Tom Blatchard. He was a twenty-seven-year-old repeat offender in and out of prison for burglary and drugs. He was flagged by the IOM scheme, and instead of just monitoring him, their team got him proper help—stable housing, drug rehab, job training, and a mentor to help guide him. At first, Tom didn't trust anyone, but with police and IOM support workers encouraging him, he stuck with it. Within months, he passed a construction course, landed a job, and the burglaries stopped. A year later, I'll never forget him telling me that for the first time, he felt like he had a future. And that was all thanks to the men and women in the IOM.'

'So you think working with them might appeal to Ellie, then?' Dylan asked.

A smile filled the DI's face as he slipped his bag over his shoulder. 'Absolutely. It will speak to her heart, a job that makes a real difference. That's why she wanted to join the police in the first place. So I think working with this criminology centre will be right up her street.'

'In that case, you'll be pleased to hear I've already taken the liberty of speaking with the centre's director, Doctor Stuart Hargreave. When I told him all about Ellie, he was very open to the idea and said she could join them as a research assistant, once she graduates, of course.'

'You really don't muck around, do you?' Joseph replied with a smile, as he opened the bedroom door to see Dylan sitting in the galley kitchen with the dogs at his feet, and Tux on his lap.

'No, when I'm a man on a mission, especially when it comes to looking out for your family, I don't,' the professor replied. 'Anyway, I'll leave it up to you to discuss this with Kate to see what she thinks.'

'Trust me, she'll be fully on board with it, especially as this might mean Ellie would remain in Oxford, rather than having to move away with some government job or other.'

'Then let's hope Ellie will be just as enthusiastic when you both tell her all about it.'

Joseph raised his palms. 'Hang on, and I'm not trying to duck my parental responsibilities here, but I think it would be a lot better coming from you. Something tells me she will listen to you in a way that she might not listen to me, or even Kate for that matter.'

Dylan nodded. 'Then consider it done. I do have rather a good track record about turning students around who were on the verge of throwing away their degrees.'

'Then you're the man for the job, especially as Ellie adores you. So once again, thank you, my friend. I honestly don't know what my family would do without you.'

The professor smiled at him. 'The feeling's entirely mutual. Anyway, you need to get going. As regards Damien Storme, Iris and I will keep digging, so do please keep me posted about the investigation.'

'Will do.' Joseph patted his friend on the shoulder, and tussled the side of Tux's head, before heading to the door.

But once outside, as the DI started to unlock his bike, his thoughts returned to his dream. What exactly was his subconscious trying to tell him, and why specifically did he still have a knot of anxiety in his gut? With that thought stuck in his mind, he swung his leg over his bike and set off for St Aldates, now also wondering what, if anything, the team had discovered in his absence.

CHAPTER EIGHTEEN

'Hello stranger, did you enjoy your beauty sleep then?' Ian asked the moment Joseph walked into the incident room.

'I didn't so much sleep as pass out, and with a mind-bending dream thrown in as well.'

'Too much cheese before bed?' Sue asked, looking over from her desk.

'I wish, but no such luck. No, it was a regular nightmare and one where I couldn't move a muscle.'

Ian's ears pricked up at hearing that. 'You sure this wasn't some sort of bondage fantasy?' he asked, a perfectly serious expression on his face.

Sue frowned at him. 'Dear God, I sometimes worry about where your mind goes so quickly.'

Ian grinned back at her.

It was then Joseph noticed there was still no sign of Megan's bag next to her desk. 'Isn't Megan in?'

'No, but with a bout of food poisoning, it can take days to get over it,' Sue said.

'Yes, she sent an email this morning to say she was still ill,' Chris said, joining them. 'But putting our DC's health to one side for a moment, we better get you up to speed about today's events.'

'Which were?' the DI asked, shrugging off his jacket.

'Amy and her team have already come back with some pretty conclusive evidence about what Stacey Ellis's motive was for murdering Gregory Richards. From her phone, they managed to recover a series of voice recordings. When you listen to them, it quickly becomes obvious what her motive was.'

'Based on your expression, nothing to do with Storme then?'

'Correct, and that's why you need to hear this for yourself.'

The SIO headed over to his computer, pulled up a file, and pressed play. Joseph immediately recognised Ellis's voice as she began to speak.

'Gregory... I don't even know if I'll ever let you hear this, but I have to say it somewhere to get this out of my system. That night... it wasn't just a mistake for me. It was everything. I felt something I haven't felt in years, and I know you did too. You don't have to say it—I saw it in your eyes. Please don't pretend it didn't happen.'

The recording finished, and the SIO was already pulling up a second file.

'So you're saying Ellis had a one-night stand with her boss?' Joseph asked.

'That's what it sounds like to us,' Sue said. 'We already spoke to Gregory's widow about it, which was one hell of a difficult conversation.'

'A grieving widow being asked if her husband was having an affair. Yes, I can imagine that was like stepping barefoot through a field of thistles.'

'Absolutely bloody right it was,' Ian replied. 'Anyway, she was adamant that her husband wouldn't ever have done anything like that.' He held up his hands. 'And I know what you're going to say, she wouldn't be the first one to have been misled by their partner.'

'Maybe, but we also can't rule out the possibility that Ellis may have been a fantasist,' Joseph replied.

'That could be true, but even if this one-night stand actually did happen, it seems Ellis's feelings for Gregory weren't exactly reciprocated,' Chris said. 'If you listen to this next recording, you'll see what I mean.' The SIO hit play again.

'You're avoiding me, aren't you?' Ellis's voice said, this time her tone tense. 'I've been waiting for you to say something, anything. But it's like I don't exist anymore. Is it her? Is it your wife? Gregory, you don't have to stay stuck in that hollow life with that woman. I could give you so much more. Why can't you see that?'

Joseph nodded as the recording ended. 'Right, so this tells us Stacey definitely became obsessed with her boss.'

'Precisely, and this next recording makes it clear what her state of mind was tipping towards.' Chris said.

'I saw you with her today,' Stacey said, her voice dripping with anger. 'Holding her hand, laughing like everything's fine. How can you lie to yourself like that? How can you act like I don't exist? You're mine, Gregory. She'll never love you like I do. Never. You don't belong with her, you belong with me. You know that.'

As the recording ended, it was becoming very clear to Joseph what his colleagues were thinking, because it was the only logical conclusion. 'She really does sound several degrees beyond deranged,' he admitted.

'Well, this final recording really underlines just how far down that path she was by the end,' Chris replied, pressing play once more.

'I understand now, you're scared,' Ellie said, her voice now eerily calm. 'You're too afraid to leave her, and that's why you're pretending I don't matter. But it's alright—I've figured it out. If I can't have you here, then I'll take you somewhere no one can steal you away from me. We'll be together, Gregory, forever. Just you and me.'

Chris turned to Joseph. 'And now we know where that somewhere was. United in death. When Amy's team searched her home, it turns out Ellis was a regular churchgoer, so probably believed in some sort of afterlife. And before you think we're putting too much weight on that final entry on her phone, Amy also discovered a suicide note in her flat.'

As compelling as this new evidence seemed, something inside Joseph still wasn't sure. 'I'm afraid this doesn't smell right, boss. Those entries make her sound like a forlorn teenager. But the woman Megan and I met at Nexus Solutions didn't seem to have any sort of crush on Gregory. Quite the opposite in fact. She certainly didn't come across as his biggest fan.'

'Maybe she was just very good at hiding how she actually felt,' Sue said.

'Possibly, but aren't we in danger of ignoring the elephant in the room? Namely, Gregory just happened to call me in to discuss what he'd discovered about those broken links, but before I could get there, he was murdered in cold blood. Doesn't that timing strike any of you as at least odd? Also, there are the similarities to all the other deaths around the Dawson investigation. In every case, they acted extremely out of character by either taking their own life or murdering someone else.'

'Those are all valid points,' Chris replied. 'But if you are still suggesting that Storme is the puppet master behind all of this, there's one major problem with that theory, as I currently see it. Despite all our efforts to find one, what possible motive would Storme have to do anything like this? Despite our continued digging, he appears to have no connection at all to Samuel Dawson.'

Joseph frowned. 'Yes, I hear you. But just because there isn't an obvious connection to the Dawson case, that may only be because we haven't found it yet. I still feel that he has to be behind all these deaths, including now Gregory and Stacey's, and the common link is hypnotism.'

'You do know you are starting to sound obsessed,' Chris said.

'He is. I can certainly already hear the CPS laughing when you try to present that to them,' Derrick's voice said.

The team turned to see the superintendent standing in the doorway and glowering at Joseph.

If the DI was under any illusion that some time to reflect might have softened the big man's attitude towards him after the run-in with him and Kate, that was swept away by his next comment.

'So stop wasting everyone's time with another of your stupid pet bloody theories, Stone. Also, what the hell do you call this time to arrive at work? Where have you been all fucking day?'

'It's not a problem,' Chris quickly said, as Ian and Sue traded a look. 'Joseph pulled an all-nighter at the crime scene and I gave him permission to take the day off to catch up with some sleep.'

Joseph was certainly grateful for the SIO covering for him, especially as he'd given no permission of the sort. But the DI could also fight his own battles. 'Don't worry, I'll make up the time by working late.'

'Too bloody right you will,' Derrick replied with a stare hard enough to break rocks. 'I don't want slackers on my team and if you can't cope with the pace, you know exactly what you can do. I'd certainly be happy to accept your resignation anytime you want to hand it over to me.'

It took considerable willpower for Joseph not to tell the big man where he could shove a resignation letter. Thankfully, before the conversation could escalate any further, Derrick turned and stalked out of the room.

'What the hell did you do to piss him off so much?' Ian asked.

'Probably by just breathing in his general vicinity,' Joseph replied, quickly steering the conversation away from the truth.

Chris gave him a knowing look, and Joseph just shrugged.

'As I was saying about my stupid pet bloody theory...' the DI continued, raising a smile from everyone, 'this isn't the first time we've been here with a case. Remember how good Geoff Goldsmith was at manipulating players of his Hidden Hand game into trying to murder each other? That was all about psychological control, so couldn't this be a more extreme case of that? After all, we are talking about a mentalist who's built his career on reading people and even coercing them into doing something without them necessarily realising it. If true, Storme is an infinitely more dangerous individual than Goldsmith could've ever hoped to be.'

Sue frowned. 'I hear what you're saying, but I'm still not sure. It all still sounds a bit too out there.'

'Oh, I know. To be honest, I'm finding it hard to believe, as well. But before we all write it off as a flight of fancy, I'm keen to find out how Neil Tanner is doing. Has he managed to salvage any useful information from that destroyed server rack? Maybe that's where we'll discover a clue that will finally unlock this case.'

'I wouldn't put too much hope there,' Chris said. 'Amy said that server rack looked seriously beaten up.'

'I've still got faith in the man,' Joseph replied. 'And seeing as I have to make up that overtime, would you have any objection to me checking in with him tonight to see how he's getting on?'

'You're really not about to drop this hypnosis theory anytime soon, are you?'

Joseph raked his hand through his hair with a slow smile. 'You better believe it, boss. I would certainly still like to get Storme in the interview room to see if we could squeeze the truth out of him.'

'Unfortunately, without any hard evidence, we've not reached that point yet. His solicitor will simply advise him to say "no comment" and that will be the end of it. But without any other current leads, feel free to chase Neil up.'

'Then I'm on it,' Joseph replied, grabbing his jacket.

CHAPTER NINETEEN

JOSEPH HEADED past Keble College in the growing darkness, one of the more striking Oxford colleges. That was saying something when there were so many in the city vying for that particular crown. The DI had always thought the Victorian Gothic design, with its striking red, yellow, and white patterned brickwork certainly made it a worthy contender. But today his destination was another college just beyond it, namely the Department of Materials, where Neil Tanner had arranged to meet him. That building stood in stark contrast to Keble. It wasn't unlike a number of unloved concrete buildings from the 60s or 70s scattered throughout the city, all slabs of grey that never caught the eye in a good way.

After Joseph had done the usual and waved his warrant card at the man behind the desk, a very helpful security guard led him to one of the labs inside the Hume-Rothery Building. If he was under any doubt that serious scientific research was carried out within the tired exterior, that was swept away when he stepped into the lab.

It positively shone with all the state-of-the-art equipment packed into it, including robotic arms and other esoteric items of equipment, all operated by students and tutors in the obligatory white coats. The only disappointment was a distinct lack of test tubes and Bunsen burners like back in the day for his school's chemistry and physics lab. That, in Joseph's humble opinion, would have properly completed the look.

Neil Tanner spotted the DI enter, and waved him over.

The student was standing next to a pretty, short, dark-haired Asian woman. She appeared to Joseph's untrained eye to be using what looked like an oversized, high-tech microscope. The whole thing was mounted on a large metal bench that looked sturdy enough to be earthquake-proof. On it was what the DI was reasonably sure was a hard drive. Some sort of needle connected to the machine hovered just above it. The top of the disk had been removed to expose a cracked, mirror-like circular disc. Nearby on a monitor, a pattern of dots, resembling an abstract landscape with valleys and hills, scrolled across the screen.

'That thing looks expensive,' Joseph said, gesturing towards the device as he reached Neil.

'Yes, MFNs don't exactly come cheap.'

'A what?'

'That stands for magnetic force microscopy machine,' the woman replied with a bright smile.

Joseph frowned. 'Okay, still none the wiser here. Can you please explain in layman's terms why you're using it on what I'm guessing is one of the broken hard drives from the Nexus Solutions server rack?'

'Correct,' Neil replied. 'And the reason we're here rather than back in a computer lab is because I needed a very specialised microscope to get anywhere with it. Thanks to the platter being fractured, it wasn't just a case of me hooking it up to a computer and reading the contents. If it had been, your digital forensics team would have easily been all over it.'

'You're seriously telling me that by pointing a microscope at the hard drive, you can see the files stored on it?'

'In a manner of speaking, we can,' Neil replied. 'But maybe I should let an expert in materials science explain it.' Neil turned to the Asian woman. 'Do you want to do the honours, Yume?'

She gave him a beaming smile. 'No problem.' She spun on her chair to face Joseph. 'So basically, an MFM is really just an advanced microscope. But instead of looking at the surface of something, it actually maps the magnetic fields. Think of it like a metal detector, but for tiny, nanoscale magnetic fields.'

Joseph scraped his hand through his hair. 'And this is the simple explanation?'

Yume grinned and grabbed a whiteboard marker. She sketched a quick diagram of a needle hovering over a squiggly line. 'The tiny needle you can see almost touching the hard drive's platter is coated in a magnetic material. When it gets really close to the surface, like a hair's width away, it can feel the magnetic forces. Those forces make the needle move, and we measure those movements to create an image.'

The DI nodded. 'Okay, I think I understand. Like a vinyl record moving the needle on a turntable and translating that to sound.'

Yume beamed at him. 'Exactly.'

'Okay, but what are you hoping to detect with that thing? I assume it's not music.'

She grinned and pointed to the shiny, fractured circular surface of the platter.

'Data is stored magnetically on these tracks, kind of like a record, like you said, but instead of grooves, it uses magnetic fields. If someone smashes the drive, it makes it hard to read with normal methods, but the MFM doesn't care about that. It maps the magnetic fields directly, right down to the nanoscale.'

Joseph's brow knotted. 'So even if the surface is damaged—'

Neil jumped in. 'You've got it. As long as parts of the magnetic structure are intact, Yume can use the MFM to pick up what's left. It'll show us the patterns of magnetic forces, which I can decode to recover bits of the data. Think of it like piecing together a shredded document.'

Yume tapped the monitor where the landscape scan was displayed. 'It's not fast though, and it's not always perfect. But if someone thought smashing a hard drive would destroy the evidence, an MFM scan could prove them wrong. If there's data left, even fragments, we can pull it out. It's a bit like reading the ghost of the hard drive.'

'That sounds dangerously like a scientific version of clairvoyance,' Joseph replied. 'That aside, what exactly have you been able to recover so far?'

Yume waved her hands towards Neil, like an assistant towards a magician. 'Over to you, gorgeous.'

A crooked smile filled Neil's face, then he refocused his attention on Joseph. 'Thanks to Yume and her fancy MFM here, we now have a magnetic map of what was left on this particular hard drive. You can see part of it in the image displayed on the screen.'

Joseph peered closer at the valleys and hills. 'And you're telling me you managed to pull a video file out of that lot?'

Neil nodded. 'Not the whole thing, but certainly enough to be useful. That map on the screen is basically how data is stored, the zeros and ones of binary code. It's not very pretty or organised, especially on a broken hard drive, but it's all still there in fragments.'

'Even so, how do you turn any of this into something useful?' Joseph asked, feeling more out of his depth by the second.

Neil tapped the keyboard of his laptop, bringing up a grid of numbers on the screen. 'I've taken that raw magnetic data and fed it into a reconstruction program I've called DataPhantom. It's designed to piece together corrupted files, kind of like solving a jigsaw puzzle when you've only got half the pieces and no picture on the box. Thankfully, the program doesn't care about scratches or gaps—it just works with whatever's left.'

The DI squinted at the rows of numerals on the screen. 'So, this is the video?'

Neil shook his head. 'Not quite, at least at this point, because it's still raw data at this stage. It's gibberish until I clean it up with DataPhantom. Think of it as a digital archaeologist. It roots through corrupted or fragmented data, hunts for patterns, and stitches everything back together. It runs algorithms to identify file structures. Basically, it looks for patterns that tell it where the video data starts and ends. Then it reconstructs the bits of any file found. I concentrated this first search with it on any files that were recently deleted on the server.'

'In other words, the broken links that were pointing at missing videos?' Joseph asked.

'Exactly, and I think I may have struck gold in the first fragment I've been able to retrieve.'

A sense of anticipation filled Joseph. 'Then please put me out of my misery.'

'Okay, but just so you're warned, it's not perfect, and there's plenty of digital breakup in the video. But so far we've managed to recover about twenty seconds of footage. We also believe it's the video DCI Simon Hart watched about giving up smoking, making it relevant. So here we go...'

Yume did an imaginary air drum roll as Neil hit play.

Joseph leaned in towards the screen, his jaw tightening as the video began to play. Whatever was on that hard drive, could it be the missing piece of evidence they'd been looking for?

Damien Storme's face appeared in the video with a woodland scene behind him, and the now familiar geometrical pattern superimposed over it. The video flickered erratically, the hypnotic spirals of blue and green glitching into broken-up holes, before settling back into their rhythmic flow.

Storme was speaking, his voice interrupted by bursts of static. 'Close your...now, and picture a world... cigarettes...you can control...break the hold...your life. With each... you feel... stronger, free...'

The hypnotic patterns seemed to pulse harder with each fragmented word, the video glitching again as the screen froze on Storm's piercing gaze, his eyes almost seeming to bore into Joseph's eyes despite the distortion.

Neil turned to Joseph. 'I'm afraid that's all we have, although it does definitely correspond to the broken link of the video we know DCI Hart watched based on the file fragment we found on his laptop. There do seem to be some minor changes in the background pattern compared to the new revised linked videos we looked at. Apart from that, it looks identical.'

Joseph felt a surge of disappointment because absolutely nothing had jumped out at him whilst watching the video. 'So apart from the corruption, there's nothing obvious about why this particular file was deleted from the server?'

'Not that we can tell you,' Yume said.

Any sense that this might be a breakthrough started to fade within Joseph. 'I suppose I better watch it again for myself, just to make sure. I'll also send it over to Doctor Clara Winslow, a tutor on the Experimental Psychology degree, to look at. She's already got one of their labs looking at another video.'

'The more eyes on this, the better,' Neil replied.

'And I can set you up on a computer in the corner if you like, whilst we carry on here, Detective,' Yume added.

'That would be grand,' Joseph replied, already imagining Chris's reaction when he broke the bad news to him, that so far at least this was yet another dead end.

Joseph had watched that same fragment of video for what felt like the hundredth time. But for the life of him, he couldn't spot anything out of the ordinary. The only surprise was that by the end, his brain had done a very good job of filling in all the missing words. Also, the very notion of anyone wanting to smoke a cigarette now made him physically ill. No wonder he had a splitting headache.

But the more the DI thought about it, the more he realised maybe all his efforts hadn't been in vain after all. At the very least, it helped to confirm that there really was something in this hypnosis idea after all, at least when used on a willing subject like Simon, who wanted to give up smoking. The problem was that it was still a very long way indeed from someone persuading a victim to harm themselves or anyone else for that matter. His only hope was that either Neil or Yume would turn up something more damning for Damien Storme. Alternatively, maybe Clara and her team would come up with something good. Then there was always the wildcard of the rest of the team spotting something in the broken link video file he'd missed.

The DI walked back along Parks Road, lost in thought and barely aware of his surroundings. But in the hour he'd been in the Materials lab, from what had been a bright spring evening, a heavy fog had rolled in, transforming the streets and buildings of Oxford into a tapestry of grey and black. There was an otherworldliness to it, the people walking past becoming nothing more than indistinct shadows in the gloom.

The chill seemed to be deepening, burrowing into the DI's skull, and making the pain in his head sharper with every step.

He rubbed at his temple as his vision blurred for a moment, before spotting another figure heading his way. But unlike the hazy outlines of everyone else in the swirling fog, this person was impossibly clear and very solid.

Joseph squinted, and then his heart stuttered as he recognised the man—Daryl Manning, dressed in his mechanic's coveralls. But that was impossible because Manning was dead, killed at the hands of the Night Watchmen. He'd seen it with his own eyes. So what the hell was this? Somebody who just happened to look like him?

But the figure stalked straight towards him, slow and deliberate. There was no mistaking the angular, weasel-like face or those dark, intense eyes. A surge of ice ran through Joseph's veins as the man stopped a few paces away and pointed directly at him.

Manning's voice was impossibly loud in the sudden silence of the street, everyone else having vanished. 'My death is your fault, Stone,' the apparition said.

The DI stumbled back, clutching his head as the pressure inside it increased. 'I didn't know they would kill you,' he tried to explain.

Manning took another step forward, his finger still aimed at Joseph like a weapon, eyes burning with malice. 'But they did, and now you owe me.'

Joseph's vision swam, the pain inside his skull unbearable, almost like it might crack open. The DI squeezed his eyes shut, trying to make this madness stop. When he risked opening them again, the ghost was gone. Pedestrians hurried past, casting wary looks at the man who'd just been clutching his head and evidently talking to someone who wasn't there.

What the hell just happened? Joseph managed to think. Then his phone chirped. Fumbling with the mobile, he took it out and managed to focus on the message from Chris.

'Could you do me a favour and check in on Megan? I tried

to ring her, and she's not picking up. I just want to know she's okay.'

Despite the confusion currently clouding Joseph's mind, this was one thing he could focus on, one thing he could do. 'Leave it to me, boss,' he texted back.

As Joseph pocketed the phone, he tried to work out what had just happened. Could the madness he'd just experienced have something to do with the video fragment he'd watched? It seemed too great a coincidence otherwise.

But even as his headache started to lift, a chilling thought struck him. What if Megan had been triggered by watching those videos as well, hence her no-show at work?

The DI increased his pace, worrying more about his colleague than himself, and terrified about what he might discover when he reached her flat.

CHAPTER TWENTY

The cool, misty air on his cycle over to Megan's home in Iffley had helped clear Joseph's mind after what had happened, even though he still wasn't sure about the what himself. The DI had felt fine before he'd watched the video. It was the only explanation for seeing Manning's spectre that made any sense. Unless he was actually losing his mind or he really had just seen the man's fecking ghost.

Even though Joseph liked to think of himself as a rational man, he couldn't help but shiver at that particular thought. But as he cycled up Iffley Hill along a broad, tree-lined street in the growing darkness, he mentally shook his head at himself. No, this had to be linked to watching that fragment of Storme's hypnosis video. And if so, Joseph was starting to realise just how dangerous the mentalist really was.

He turned onto the long driveway of the large Victorian house. It was filled with the cars of the tenants who lived in the converted flats. Megan's Mini Cooper was parked among the other vehicles, just as it had been the last time he'd been here with the electrolytes.

The DI leant his bike against the wall and glanced up at the first-floor flat where Megan lived. The curtains were drawn with no chink of light between them, suggesting she was either asleep or not there at all. Alternatively, and this was what he'd been increasingly worrying about on the way over: what if he was already too late, and just like Storme's other victims, she was dead up there?

Joseph's heart clenched, and he rushed to the front door. He leant hard on the buzzer for Megan's flat. When there wasn't any answer, and because time might be of the essence, the DI had two options as he saw it. Flash his warrant card, which he wasn't sure that Megan would thank him for if he caused a fuss with her neighbours. For all he knew, she might be perfectly fine but keeping her head down. But there was a second option, which would almost certainly save time because he wouldn't need to explain himself. Checking the front door was definitely locked, he went for option two and pressed all the door buzzers. One by one, voices started to answer.

'Food delivery,' Joseph said to all of them.

He ignored all the wrong address, mate, type responses, but felt a surge of relief when someone pressed the door release button. As soon as the front door started buzzing, he pushed it open before the lock could slide back into place again.

A lone man looked down from the stairwell at him.

'Delivery for Megan Anderson?' the DI immediately said.

'Oh right, you want flat eight, up here on the first floor. I didn't think Megan was in because I haven't seen her for a few days.' Then the man took in the distinct lack of any sort of delivery box in Joseph's arms. Thankfully, he chose not to challenge the DI. Instead, he gestured to Megan's door, turned, and headed back into his own flat.

The knot of anxiety had really taken hold now as Joseph ran up the stairs two at a time. The moment he arrived at her door, he knocked hard on it.

'Megan, are you in there?' Once again, there was no response.

Joseph grabbed his mobile and dialled her number. He heard a mobile ringing somewhere in her flat on the other side of the door.

Barely resisting the urge to kick the door down, he glanced over his shoulder to check no one was watching, and took a small pouch out of his pocket. He slipped out the lock pick kit he'd bought. The DI had picked up a few off-curriculum skills over the years as a policeman, and this was one of them thanks to a criminal who'd once boasted just how easily he could get through nearly any lock. A few YouTube videos and a kit from Amazon later, the DI was all set for the job in hand.

Joseph inserted the tension tool into the bottom of the lock, and pushed it slightly sideways. Meanwhile, he used a hooked lock pick to push each pin into position. He was all too aware this wasn't a good look for any detective if one of the neighbours decided to put in an appearance at that precise moment, but by that point, he really didn't care. His imagination was already serving up a vivid mental image of Megan, her lips cracked, lying dead on the floor with her throat opened up.

When the last pin of the lock clicked into place, and with a prayer of thanks slung in the direction of the big man upstairs, Joseph opened the door and rushed in.

To his relief, the smell of a decaying corpse was thankfully missing. The second thing he registered was the silence that enveloped the flat.

Joseph turned and flicked on the light switch. As the room was illuminated, he took in the cosy but small living room. It had a squishy teal sofa, covered with a soft throw and several cushions that looked well-loved. On the wall behind it, there was a cluster of framed photographs. He studied the one of Megan in her police uniform as a young cadet, and then another of her as a lass kneeling in a garden, her arms wrapped around a grinning golden Labrador with its tongue lolling to one side. There was one of two people in their sixties, presumably her parents based on how much Megan looked like the woman, all caught mid-laughter at something.

In front of the sofa was a battered wooden coffee table with a stack of dog-eared crime novels. There was also a mug of tea with congealed milk on top. A quick check confirmed to the DI what he already suspected—cold.

'Megan, are you here?' Joseph called out.

Still nothing.

The DI tried ringing her again, and her phone's answering warble came from the next room. He headed through, mentally bracing himself for the worst.

Megan's phone glowed in the darkness on its charging stand next to a made-up bed. When he didn't see her body curled up in it, Joseph sucked in a big relieved lungful of air. Okay, perhaps he'd just let his imagination get the better of him. A quick sweep through the rest of the flat confirmed the DC really wasn't there. But far from feeling reassured, Joseph was already dialling Chris.

'Hi, Joseph,' the SIO said, finally picking up after ten rings.

'I'm at Megan's and she's not here. She left her mobile here as well, which isn't like her, and her car is out front. Look, I've got nothing to base this on, but I've a bad feeling about this, especially after one of her neighbours confirmed he hasn't seen her for three days. My worry is, she's been affected by one of those videos.'

'Okay, then we better not take any chances,' Chris replied. 'I'm going to put the word out, and we better start checking the hospital's admissions just in case.'

'You can leave that to me, boss,' Joseph replied. 'If you hadn't guessed, this is already personal for me.'

'For both of us,' Chris corrected.

'Aye, of course it is. I also need to brief you when I see you about a video fragment that Neil managed to retrieve.' Joseph had already decided it was better to keep quiet about his ghostly visitation until he could discuss it face-to-face with his boss. 'There might be something in it, but I can't be sure.'

'Okay, then I'll wait to be fully briefed by you. In the meantime, let's just hope there's a simple explanation for Megan not being there.'

'That's what I'm praying for, boss,' Joseph replied, before ending the call.

CHAPTER TWENTY-ONE

Joseph felt run ragged by the time the following morning had arrived. It turned out that trying to find out if Megan had been admitted to any of the Oxford hospitals had swallowed most of his night. After waiting ages for someone to pick up the phone when he'd tried calling, the DI had ended up slamming the phone down. Instead, he'd visited each of the hospitals in person. Once there, and thanks to a certain amount of tenacity on his part, he'd finally been able to confirm Megan hadn't been seen by any of the A&E departments across the city.

With no sleep to top up his batteries, Joseph was back at his desk, having broken the bad news to Chris, who'd just arrived back at the station.

'So where the hell is she?' the SIO asked.

'I honestly don't know, and I'm starting to get seriously worried,' the DI replied. 'Now I've got this bloody idea in my head that she's been hypnotised into doing something stupid, I can't get it out of my mind, especially after what happened to me.'

Chris peered at him. 'Sorry, what happened to you?'

'Well, I don't want you to think I need a Fit for Duty mental check or anything, but I had a moment yesterday evening that made me question my own sanity.'

'Go on,' Chris replied, sitting down at the desk next to the DI's in the incident room.

'First of all, full disclosure here as this could be of relevance to Damien Storme's investigation. Neil Tanner and a friend of his used some very high-end kit in one of the Oxford labs to retrieve a longer fragment of a video file from one of Nexus Solution's hard drives. It turns out the deleted video is almost identical in every way to what we've already seen in the commercially available ones. But there's one key difference—a variation in the geometrical pattern Storme likes to use in the backgrounds of his videos. Apart from that, none of us could see any real difference.'

'So in other words, apart from a change in backdrop, you drew a blank?' Chris asked.

'Not quite...' Joseph paused, trying to frame this so he didn't sound like an outright lunatic. 'As I said, I don't want you to end up thinking I'm not up to being on duty, but I left the lab with a splitting headache that came out of nowhere. Then I saw something...'

'Out with it,' Chris said, frowning at the DI.

The DI mentally braced himself for his boss's incredulous reaction. 'Look, I know how crazy this will sound, but I had a visitation from Daryl Manning's ghost on Parks Lane Road. And if that isn't enough for you, it gets better. He actually told me I was responsible for his death.'

Chris sat back. 'Okay, anyone else, and I'd be sending them home for some R & R, with a session booked in for a psychological assessment.'

'Aye, I would too, in your position. But here's the thing, this all happened after I watched the video clip, the same one Simon was exposed to, and the same but smaller fragment Megan also watched.'

'So you're seriously suggesting this clip triggered what happened to you?'

'It's the only thing that makes any sense to me.'

'And what about Neil and this other person who must have seen the video, weren't they affected?'

'No. I rang them first thing to check.'

'In that case, I assume you have this video with you. I need to take a look at it for myself.'

'Aye, I do.'

A few minutes later, and with some technical help from Chris, Joseph had the retrieved file displayed on the large screen on the wall.

When the SIO started the video, the DI couldn't help but avert his eyes. Then, having watched it twice, Chris hit pause in the middle of the third run and turned to Joseph with a frown. 'Well, if there's something in there to trigger what happened to you, I'm damned if I can see it.'

'Exactly, so the question is, if it did trigger this reaction in me, then how? Just please tell me you've got no hint of headache having watched that thing?'

'Nothing at all, and no ghost visitations, either, if you were wondering.' The SIO raised an eyebrow.

'Okay, okay, then it sounds like you better sign me up for that sanity check.'

Chris was already shaking his head. 'No, I think you're as mentally sound as anyone I know. If you saw something, especially due to the timing after watching this video, then I think there has to be a connection, even if we can't, quite literally, see it yet.'

Joseph felt a wave of relief at hearing the validation from his boss. 'That's good to hear, and hopefully, we'll hear back from

Doctor Winslow with some more information. But my... experience, if you will, has only added to my worry about Megan. Out of all of us, she watched these Damien Storme videos more than anyone else. If they did influence her, has she been programmed to behave as his other victims did?'

Chris's forehead ridged. 'Okay, you're getting me more worried by the second.'

Ian and Sue walked in, bacon baps in hand.

'Still no sign of Megan, then?' Ian said, spotting her empty desk as he shrugged his coat off. Then he flicked his tie over his shoulder, before settling down to the serious business of eating his breakfast.

'No, and we have reason to be concerned about her whereabouts and even her state of mind,' Chris replied. 'That's why I want you to notify all forces in the area.'

Joseph thought of the photos in Megan's flat. 'We should also contact her parents just in case she's with them.'

'Good idea...' Chris's words trailed away as he stared at something behind Joseph.

The DI turned to see that Megan had just walked in, a bright smile on her face. 'So what have I missed?' she asked.

For a moment, everyone was too surprised to say anything, but it was Joseph who first found his voice. 'Where the feck have you been, Megan? You've had us all worried sick.'

The smile fell away from the DC's face. 'You were, but why?'

'Because of those fecking videos you've been watching, especially after you didn't answer your phone,' Joseph said.

Megan shot him a confused look. 'But I just left that at home.'

'As an officer, you always need to keep your mobile close to hand, no excuses,' Chris said, his tone tinged with steel. 'I need a quiet word.'

Megan nodded, and looking bewildered, followed the SIO out of the room.

Ian shook his head. 'Bloody hell, she's in for a roasting now.'

'No, it'll be just a gentle rap across the knuckles for not being reachable,' Joseph said. 'But he and I were really worried about her.'

Sue nodded distractedly, her gaze fixed on the screen on the wall as she ate her bacon bap. 'Since when did Damien Storme start using Magic Eye images in his videos?'

'Come again,' Joseph said, giving her a confused look.

'You know, they were all the rage at one point. I've always had a knack for seeing them really quickly. If you look at them in the right way, or I should say focus your eyes beyond the picture, a hidden 3D image pops out.'

Joseph stared at her, and then at the screen. 'Yes, I remember those things, but it always took me ages to get them. Why, what is it you're seeing now?'

Sue shrugged. 'Just a single word, Chrysalis, whatever that means? It's buried in that pattern in the background.'

Joseph gaped at her as the implication slammed into him. First, his dream about Damien saying that exact same word to him, then the even stranger encounter with the spectral version of Daryl Manning less than a day later. This all had to be linked to this word, hiding in plain sight, in the hypnosis video. The one thing he knew for sure was, this investigation was anything but over. It was actually only just warming up.

CHAPTER TWENTY-TWO

JOSEPH WAS PAINFULLY aware of Megan's continuing silence as they headed out on foot again back to Magdalene College. After the latest revelation about the hidden word Chrysalis in the deleted video, they were on their way to meet up with Doctor Winslow to get her professional opinion about what that might actually mean and the significance of it.

After a minute had become five, and the DC still hadn't said a word, Joseph finally cracked. 'Will you talk to me already, rather than wandering around with the expression of someone chewing a fecking wasp?' When that didn't elicit so much as a smile, the DI cast a concerned look towards his colleague.

'Okay, what did Chris say to make you look so pissed off?' he asked.

At last, Megan, who'd been giving her colleague the silent treatment since leaving St Aldates, threw her hands up in the air. 'If you really want to know, he laid into me. Our esteemed SIO gave me this massive lecture that I'd been totally irresponsible not having my mobile on me, even though I sent in an email to explain I was ill.'

Joseph pulled a face. 'Well...'

Megan glowered at the DI. 'Oh great, I thought you might have my back on this, Joseph.'

'And I do, when you're right. But I'm afraid, on this occasion...' The DI shrugged.

'Bloody hell, so someone can't feel so ill that they don't know which way is up, and forget their phone, without getting reprimanded for it?'

'Chris was about to organise a search party for you, including bending Derrick's ear to send out a helicopter.'

Megan stopped dead and turned to stare at him. 'Seriously?'

The DI couldn't stop his grin from breaking out.

At last, like a glimmer of sunlight on this grey day of March, a smile also broke out on his colleague's face.

Megan mock-punched his arm before shaking her head. 'I still think Chris overreacted. Honestly, you should have heard the way he talked to me.'

Joseph shrugged. 'It's only because he cares, Megan.'

She rounded on him. 'What's that meant to mean?'

The DI realised this wasn't the time and place, and he certainly wasn't the one to reveal that Chris had feelings for her. So instead, he went for a diversionary tactic.

'That he was almost as worried about you as I was. When you didn't pick up your phone, I was starting to imagine the worst. I even thought it was something to do with those fecking hypnosis videos.'

Megan grimaced. 'Okay, nothing like that. It was nothing more than a lapse on my part. I was so ill I was a bit out of it, then my Dad swooped in to take me back to the family home in the New Forest to recover. But of course, you know I left my phone behind, because Chris told me you let yourself into my flat.'

Joseph immediately felt uncomfortable about where this conversation was headed. 'Aye.'

'And he assumed you got a key from a neighbour. Care to explain how you managed to gain entry when there was no sign of the lock being forced?'

'May be better if you don't know.'

Megan scowled at him. 'In other words, you broke into my flat, what, by picking the lock?'

'Look, I was really worried, so shoot me already.'

The DC's face softened. 'I suppose if I could pick locks, I might have done the same in your place. Just please don't make a habit of it.'

'As long as you promise not to go dark on me again.'

She met his gaze and nodded. 'I promise. So am I forgiven for being a thoughtless idiot by not contacting you?'

Joseph held his thumb and forefinger a fraction apart. 'Almost,' he said.

Megan grinned at him as they approached the entrance to Magdalene College and waved their warrant cards at the porter sitting at the entrance desk.

After getting Doctor Winslow up to speed on recent events, the psychologist gazed at the frozen frame from the paused video on her monitor. 'Well, I have to give credit to Storme. This is certainly an ingenious way to hide a trigger word in plain sight,' she said. 'Even our lab techs didn't spot it.'

'A trigger word?' Joseph asked.

Clara leaned forward, elbows on her desk. 'A trigger word is a specific word or phrase embedded into the subconscious, often through hypnosis or psychological conditioning. When the subject hears it—consciously or unconsciously—it activates a programmed response. Think of it like a key fitting into a lock, and then unlocking a predetermined action or state of mind.'

She tapped her fingertips together. 'In a clinical hypnosis, trigger words can be used therapeutically—to induce relaxation, manage pain, or break unhealthy habits. But in more, let's say for the sake of argument, manipulative settings, they can be used to control behaviour, bypassing rational thought altogether. The person might not even be aware of why they're doing something. They just feel compelled to act.'

Joseph traded a surprised look with Megan. 'So, you're saying someone could be made to act against their will when they see or hear one of these trigger words?'

Clara grimaced. 'It's not quite that simple. A trigger word by itself doesn't create an entirely new desire or override free will in the way you're suggesting. But when combined with an individual's programming, it can tap into existing thoughts, emotions, or behaviours—things already lurking in the subconscious. It can then amplify them and bring them to the surface. It could even, with the right preparation, push someone towards an action they might not otherwise have considered. For example, if someone had some inner guilt or anger, it could even be redirected towards a particular person.'

Joseph stared at her. 'That sounds like exactly what we've been seeing with these murders, but what about the suicides?'

'Those feelings of a past hurt or resentment could also be deliberately misdirected towards the person themselves, and maybe even to the point they felt they couldn't carry on. In that context, a trigger word received at the right moment could heighten that emotion and make them act on it in a way they wouldn't have. But there is one caveat here about turning a normal, peaceful person into a killer. If that instinct wasn't already there—that could be tricky. But there again, I suppose that with enough conditioning, maybe even that's possible.'

Megan frowned. 'So, it's more about nudging someone

towards a choice rather than outright controlling them? Is that about the sum of this sort of manipulation?'

'Exactly right,' Clara replied. 'But that doesn't make it any less dangerous. In the right—or I should say, wrong—hands, this could lead to devastating consequences.'

'This sounds an awful lot like brainwashing,' Joseph said.

Clara shrugged. 'Yes, but with one crucial difference. Traditional conditioning, like what you'd see in psychological experiments—think Pavlov's dogs salivating when they heard a bell being rung—relies on repetition and reinforcement. Brainwashing, on the other hand, is a prolonged process of breaking down someone's resistance, reshaping their beliefs, often through isolation, manipulation, and fear.

'What we're talking about here is far more surgical. A trigger word is planted after a person has been conditioned. It's hidden in the subconscious, waiting and biding its time. It also bypasses rational thought, skipping the need for reinforcement or coercion. The person might not even realise they've been programmed. When they hear the word, the response is immediate, automatic. It's not mind control in the Hollywood sense. But it can be just as effective in making someone do something they never thought they would.'

'Jesus H. Christ, and this keyword might have had that effect with DCI Hart and the others, and maybe even me?'

'If it was implanted correctly, then yes. It's entirely possible hearing the word could have triggered a pre-conditioned response in DCI Hart and everyone else who watched it. But in your case, maybe the programming wasn't actually complete because you just watched a fragment of a video.'

'Thank feck for that.'

Megan shifted uncomfortably in her seat, casting a sideways look at her colleague. 'But how would that even work? You're saying someone hears a word and what, just obeys?'

'Not quite,' Clara said. 'It depends on what Storme—if it was him—planted in a person's subconscious. If they were hypnotically conditioned to associate the word Chrysalis with a specific action—say, forgetting something, or even harming themselves or others—then, yes, they could act without fully understanding why. The conscious mind rationalises it after the fact, and makes it feel like their own decision.'

Joseph rubbed a hand across his jaw. 'So we could be looking at victims who don't even realise they were being manipulated? Part of them would actually believe they were acting of their own free will?'

Clara gave him a steady look. 'Exactly. And that's what makes it so dangerous.'

'So for Storme to really pull this off, he must have had enough time to brainwash his targets into believing up was down, and vice versa?' Megan said.

'Correct, but this wouldn't be something done in an afternoon. If Storme conditioned them, he'd have needed time—repeated exposure and reinforcement. The key wouldn't be making them believe up is down, but leading them to that conclusion themselves.'

Megan exhaled sharply. 'But that's terrifying. To think they might have acted on a command they didn't even recognise, and that suddenly shifted their whole outlook of the world.'

'Indeed,' Clara said. 'And if Storme did it with a lot of care, they wouldn't question it. Their own mind would defend the programming. I suspect, though, that even then, a deeper part of their subconscious would realise something was very wrong, but would be unable to do anything about it.'

Joseph blew out his cheeks as the implications fully hit him. 'Okay, this all makes a terrible sort of sense, making it very clear how all these people were murdered. But how is it that I saw this keyword in a dream before I even watched this video?'

Clara's brow furrowed. 'That's what has me very puzzled, Joseph. Dreams are the subconscious's way of processing information—fragments of memory, emotions, things we've seen or heard, sometimes without realising. No doubt you became unconsciously aware of the keyword when you watched the original video fragment. But for it to affect you, doesn't make any sense if Storme didn't have the time to programme you, which as I already said, would have taken time.'

Joseph shook his head. 'I haven't been alone with Storme for any real length of time beyond the brief time we both met him at his flat. He certainly didn't try to...' An awful thought struck him. 'Oh shite.'

It seemed he wasn't alone; Megan was already nodding. 'We both fell asleep in Storme's waiting room. And before you judge us, Clara, that's not normal for either of us to do that on the job.'

'That could be significant. How long were you both asleep?'

'Fifteen minutes absolute tops,' Joseph replied.

'In that case, even if Storme had done something to you, that's not exactly a lot of time to do much of anything in terms of moulding your subconscious, although maybe enough time to start to bury the keyword in your minds. Joseph, I know it obviously had an effect on you, but what about you, Megan?'

'Absolutely nothing, and I've seen that keyword since without it doing anything.'

'Okay, that suggests that in your case you weren't hypnotised. Maybe Storm concentrated all his efforts on you, Joseph. Was there any other time you may have been exposed to Storme?'

'If I was, I've absolutely no fecking memory of it. Or are you suggesting I had some sort of clandestine meeting with Storme and forgot all about it?'

'Not forgot, repressed,' Clara corrected. 'Or more likely— erased. If Storme is capable of the level of conditioning, I believe we're talking about here, then it's entirely possible he implanted a suggestion to make you forget the encounter ever happened. You wouldn't even realise there was a gap in your memory.'

Joseph caught Megan giving him a worried look before she refocused her attention on Clara.

'But how's that even possible?' she asked.

'Well, hypnotic amnesia is a well-documented phenomenon. With the right conditioning, a person can be made to forget specific details, even entire events, as if they never happened. Then, when the right cue is introduced, those memories can be restored, or even altered.'

'So you're saying Joseph could have been exposed to this keyword, but it only surfaced in his dream because his subconscious was still trying to process it?'

Clara nodded. 'Precisely. The subconscious picks up on things long before the conscious mind does. So that leads us nicely to the hallucination you experienced, Joseph.'

'It's not exactly every day I'm visited by the equivalent of Dickens's Ghost of Christmas Past accusing me of being responsible for his fecking death.'

Megan gave her colleague a concerned look. 'It makes sense if Storme was trying to target an experience to make you feel guilty, not that there was anything that we could have done to stop Manning from being killed.'

The doctor's expression darkened. 'That's the part that worries me most. Joseph's subconscious dredging up a memory is one thing, but a full sensory hallucination? For me, that points to deliberate psychological tampering. Someone wanted you to see Daryl Manning. More importantly, based on what Megan just said, they wanted you to feel responsible even though you weren't. As I mentioned right at the beginning, if you can make someone doubt their own mind, make them question what's real, you weaken them. You make them vulnerable. And that,

Joseph, is how you manipulate a person without them ever realising it.'

Joseph drew in a long breath. 'So let me get this clear. I met Storme, he got inside my head, and now I've got a blank space where that memory should be? Is that the sum of what you're saying to me?'

'We certainly shouldn't be too quick to write it off as a theory,' Clara said. 'And if so, the real question is, what else did he make you forget?'

An icy feeling ran through the DI's veins—maybe he was no longer entirely in control of his own actions.

'Okay, so let's suppose he did manage to programme me. How can we get rid of it? I don't much like the idea that there's the equivalent of a bomb waiting to go off in my head whenever Storme decides to trigger it.'

Clara tapped her fingers together again. 'Undoing this kind of conditioning isn't as simple as flicking a switch. If Storme really did plant something in your subconscious, we need to approach it the same way it was put there—through suggestion, exposure, and controlled recall. The problem is, if he's built safeguards, trying to break it could trigger consequences.'

Joseph's stomach tightened. 'What sort of consequences?'

'Some forms of deep conditioning come with protective mechanisms—mental barriers that make the subject resistant to remembering. In some cases, forcing a memory too quickly can cause psychological distress. Anxiety, panic attacks, even physical symptoms. In the worst cases, the mind simply shuts down rather than access what's hidden.'

The DI stared, horrified, at the woman. 'What, you're talking about some sort of coma?'

'Nothing like that, but the mind may go into a state of dissociation, where it temporarily disconnects from reality. This could present as confusion, blackouts, even a breakdown. It would certainly be enough to stop you doing your job.'

Megan leaned forward. 'Okay, then what's the alternative?'

'Careful deprogramming,' Clara replied. 'To use Joseph's own analogy, think of this as defusing a bomb. We'd have to find a way to access the buried memories gradually. Hypnotherapy might help, but given the way Storme may operate, it might be risky—as he may have layered in false memories or misdirection to make you question what's real. Having said that, we won't know unless we try. Another option is exposure therapy—introducing controlled reminders to jog your subconscious, Joseph, and see if anything surfaces. Patterns, phrases, even sounds you may have heard at the time of conditioning. But it has to be done carefully, or we risk reinforcing the programming rather than breaking it.'

Joseph clenched his jaw. 'And if we do nothing?'

Clara's expression became grim. 'Then, whatever Storme put in your head stays there—until he decides it's time for you to remember.'

'Feck. Okay, there's no way I'm walking around with that in my head, especially if this is how Storme controlled his other victims. If there is something hidden in my subconscious, we need to tackle it sooner rather than later. Is this something you could help me with, Clara?'

'I can, although as I said, I can give you no guarantees, and it carries a certain element of risk. It will also take time, lots of it. Of course, there's a simpler way. Get Damien Storme to undo anything he might have done to you. That's if he did anything at all.'

'I think there is more than enough evidence stacking up against the man to suggest this is all very real,' Megan said.

Joseph nodded. 'Unfortunately, without concrete evidence and without wanting to tip our hands, we can't risk asking him for his help. Not that there's much likelihood of him doing that anyway. It would be as good as him confessing.'

Megan frowned. 'Okay, but we do now know he slipped these keywords into his deleted videos, which have to count for something. That also begs the question, how did Storme's intended victims get hold of these adapted versions of his books...?' Her eyes widened, and she snapped her fingers. 'Of course, the prize giveaway—that's how that journalist Jackie Hunt was targeted. I bet if we check with the families of the other victims, including Julia, we'll discover they were all sent free copies as well.'

Joseph gave a sharp nod as he warmed to the theory. 'And no doubt all of them were programmed by that first video to go and see him. Maybe not even in person, but over something like a Zoom call. Maybe that's what he did with me?'

'That certainly makes sense. Using that approach, his programming could be spread over weeks, months even. All the while, his victims wouldn't even realise it was happening,' Clara replied.

'In which case, the sooner I start those sessions with you, the happier I'll be,' Joseph said.

'Then why not start now? I have an hour until my next lecture if you want to give it a whirl?'

'That would be grand. I can't tell you how uneasy this all makes me feel.' He turned to Megan. 'Will you head back and report what we've discovered to Chris?'

'Don't you worry, will do.' The DC closed her notebook and stood. Then she gently rested her hand on the DI's shoulder. 'Try not to worry too much.'

'I'll do my best,' Joseph replied, giving her his best attempt at a smile even as his sense of unease deepened.

CHAPTER TWENTY-THREE

CLARA HAD CLOSED the curtains in her college study and turned on the table lamp on her desk.

Joseph watched as she took a seat. 'So how's this going to work exactly?'

'It's going to be less complicated than you might expect,' Clara replied. 'I'm simply going to ask you to relax and focus on my voice, allowing me to gently guide you into a calm and receptive state. But please be assured, you'll remain fully aware and in control throughout this session.'

'In that case, let's get going in case my head goes...' Joseph made the exploding motion on either side of his head, spreading his fingers.

The psychologist raised her eyebrows at him. 'Okay, please close your eyes.'

Joseph did, and settled into the well-worn chair.

'Focus on my voice and allow yourself to relax completely,' Clara continued. 'Let go of any tension and trust that you'll be in the driving seat throughout this process.'

Almost at once, Joseph felt his muscles loosen across his

neck, letting go of tension he didn't even know he'd been carrying until that moment.

'Now, take a deep, steady breath. As you inhale, imagine your mind is like a calm pond, and with each exhale, allow the sense of tranquillity to deepen, any ripples becoming still. Remember to focus solely on my voice and let every word guide you further into a state of deep relaxation.'

Much to his surprise, the DI felt almost an almost floating feeling taking hold.

'I'm right here with you every step of the way, so know no harm will come to you,' Clara continued.

The normal version of Joseph would have baulked at hearing this, especially when there seemed to be some trigger word buried in his subconscious. But not this chilled-out version of the DI, who accepted this as though Clara was an old friend he'd known for a very long time, and would trust with his life.

'Now, we're about to explore whether there is a phrase that has been buried in your mind, which has been designed to trigger a response. Do you understand?'

'I understand,' Joseph echoed.

'In that case, I'm going to say a single word. Focus on it entirely, and let your mind open up to its suggestion. Are you ready?'

'Yes...' Joseph replied, his mind verging on the edge of sleep.

'Good, then the word is Chrysalis.'

The very conscious part of Joseph's mind that was watching this all play out with a slight sense of bemusement, actually felt underwhelmed when nothing happened.

'Are you experiencing anything unusual?' Clara asked.

'No, nothing at all.'

'I see. In that case...'

Joseph heard the tapping of a keyboard. 'I'd like you briefly to open your eyes and watch the video you showed me. I have muted the sound. I want you to concentrate on the geometrical pattern in the background.'

The DI nodded and opened his eyes. With a soft gaze, he looked at the laptop that Clara had rotated towards him on her desk.

Almost at once, the 3D word Chrysalis he hadn't consciously been able to see before, practically leapt out of the screen at him.

The effect was instantaneous.

Joseph's head pounded as though a heavy weight was expanding inside it. Then his vision blurred, and he found himself back in the white void—a sterile, featureless space where every sound seemed swallowed by an overwhelming emptiness. He stood staring at the same geometrical pattern pulsing on the large floating screen before him.

The word Chrysalis was burning into his eyes like a hot poker, and the pain was ratcheting up.

'Just follow wherever the trigger word is taking you, Joseph,' the psychologist said.

In that instant, everything changed again.

Joseph now found himself standing next to the unmarked Volvo V90 in the road. A police transport van with a prisoner in the back had stopped. In front of it, a black BMW 5 Series had skidded off the road. An ambulance had parked in the opposite carriageway, blocking it and the traffic was already starting to build up behind it.

Joseph's heart beat hard in his chest. He knew this place, this dreadful moment in time. It had been a trap.

Two masked gunmen walked toward the prisoner transport from the staged crash with an almost cocky, arrogant stride. One of them levelled his Heckler and Koch MP5 submachine gun at them. Without warning, they opened fire on the police transport van with PC John Thorpe and PC Dave Burford in the cab.

Even as Joseph's heart spasmed and cold sweat ran down his back, part of his mind knew this was just a memory. But it felt like it was happening again.

The other gunman aimed his weapon at Joseph and Megan and fired. Just as he had once before, the DI threw himself and Megan flat to the ground as the rounds whizzed over their heads.

Joseph watched, unable to change the script, as one of the masked men casually reloaded his MP5 and walked up the side of the police van towards the rear, where the prisoner compartment was.

This was it, the moment that haunted Joseph. He'd been the senior officer who'd been there on the ground on that day. Everything about to unfold was on him.

Then the same words sprang to his lips as they had back on that dreadful day. But suddenly he was no longer an observer along for the ride—he was really there.

'Shite, they are going to spring Manning—' The words died in Joseph's mouth as the gunman aimed at the rear doors of the police van and opened fire.

Bullets punctured the bodywork, sending sparks flying. The pungent smell of cordite filled the air as the MP5's entire magazine was emptied into the prisoner compartment.

As their submachine guns rattled to silence, anger roared through Joseph. This might be a memory, but right then, he was reliving it. Without thinking, he pushed himself up onto his hands, intending to charge the fecker, when the other gunman aimed a Glock straight at him and Megan. The gunman raised his other gloved hand and shook his finger slowly from left to right.

'Joseph, it's alright, you're perfectly safe,' Clara's voice said.

The scene started to fade as one of the masked men with an East End London accent shouted, 'Stay down!'

Joseph now knew that man was none other than DCI Greg Charlton from the Cowley station, an officer who'd betrayed everything he should have stood for that day.

'Joseph, follow my voice. You're still here, safe in my study. Whatever you're experiencing was caused by the trigger phrase,' Clara continued. 'Do you understand me?'

Even as the DI's mind reeled from this past trauma, he clung to the doctor's words.

'I do,' he replied with his eyes still clamped shut, but managing to loosen his claw-like grip a fraction on the arms of his chair.

'Then you will become fully conscious in three, two, one...'

Joseph heard a snap of her fingers and he opened his eyes, feeling disoriented by finding himself back in the study. As his conscious mind resurfaced, he sucked in a shuddering breath.

'For feck's sake, that felt so real,' he was finally able to say after a moment.

'I take it by your reaction the visual trigger phrase worked, then?'

'Like a fecking charm.'

The professor typed some notes on her laptop. 'So what did you experience?'

'When you said Chrysalis, it first took me to the empty white space I've already dreamed about. But it was when you showed me the trigger phrase in the video that the fireworks really kicked off.'

'So what happened?' Clara asked.

'I was dragged back to the moment that Manning was assassinated during that prisoner transfer escort I mentioned. But it was so vivid, it was like I was actually back there.'

Clara steepled her fingers. 'Now, that is interesting. That does suggest your mind was programmed to unearth a memory you still carry guilt about.'

'I certainly feel Manning's death was my responsibility as the officer in charge.'

The doctor tilted her head to one side as she considered the DI. 'So you believe you could have done something to alter the outcome of what happened?'

Joseph considered that question for a moment. What would have happened if he'd attempted to body-charge one of the Night Watchmen? But he already knew exactly how that would have worked out—his body would have been riddled with bullets from an MP5, Megan's probably, too.

He slowly shook his head. 'No, because in truth, if I had, more people would have died.'

'I see. So even though you know that, you still feel responsible?'

'Aye, that's about the measure of it. Not exactly logical, I realise, but I suppose that's often the nature of guilt. You carry it inside you like a lead weight. But why that particular memory, Clara? For years, I carried the guilt over the death of my infant son, Eoin. I'd been at the wheel and lost control of the vehicle. So why not drag that memory up instead?'

Clara gave the DI a thoughtful look. 'Have you had some sort of closure with your son's death, or maybe at least some acceptance that it wasn't your fault?'

Joseph's mind went back to the Midwinter Butcher case, and specifically the death of Aaron Fearnley. He'd been the man responsible for the deer that had run out that stormy night and had caused Joseph to swerve and lose control of the SUV. Yes, maybe Clara was right, because after the man had faced justice of a sort, the DI had finally been able to sleep again at night.

'You might be onto something there,' Joseph finally said. 'I don't know what you think, but it seems to me like we've got a confirmation of Storme's MO and his special brand of manipulation here.' He tapped the side of his skull.

Clara nodded. 'Also, if a therapist knows a patient's deepest, darkest secrets, imagine the harm that can be done with that information in the wrong hands.'

'Such as DCI Hart, for example? He and DI Roberts were, by all accounts, the best of friends right up to the moment Simon murdered Alex with a firearm retrieved from the scene of the crime.'

'If Storme really did condition Simon, maybe he was convinced to project all his troubles onto Alex.'

Joseph slowly nodded as he mentally processed all of this and all the implications. 'But why choose a crime scene to murder his colleague? Okay, there was a firearm present, but by all accounts, Simon appeared fine apart from complaining about a headache, something I also experienced before I had the visitation from Manning. According to eyewitnesses, something seemed to change in Simon when he saw the pistol, and he became glazed, for want of a better term. Then he shot his best friend.'

'The presence of the headache is certainly interesting and suggests that part of your subconscious was trying to fight your conditioning. With Simon, maybe the presence of a suitable murder weapon was another embedded instruction for him to act out on.'

'So, you're saying that the pistol itself might have been implanted in his mind, rather than just a keyword?'

'That could be the case, or maybe he was simply programmed to utilise any appropriate weapon if the opportunity presented itself. Maybe that was also the case with Stacey Ellis when she used a kitchen knife. Alternatively, maybe Simon heard or saw the trigger phrase just before entering the crime scene. I assume you've checked his phone in case he was sent a message?'

'Yes, the forensic team has already been through it, but

found nothing unusual. Having said that, I'll ask them to take a second look with this fresh information in mind. There was also a Major Crime Unit at the crime scene where Simon took his own life. Those vehicles are equipped with CCTV cameras. I'm going to make a point of checking that footage to see if they picked anything up.'

'Then my advice is to look for anything out of the ordinary.'

'Will do. Anyway, in the meantime, if I've one of these fecking triggers in my own mind, please do whatever it takes. I need you to get it out, even if it means a lobotomy.'

Clara gave him a wry smile. 'Hopefully, nothing that drastic. But I must warn you once again, I give you no guarantee this will work, Joseph.'

'Please, just do what you can.'

The psychologist nodded. 'Then sit back, relax, and we'll try this one more time.'

Joseph's fingers twitched against the armrest as he forced himself to exhale and shut his eyes. This had to work because, if nothing else, his sanity depended on it.

Clara's voice lowered. 'I want you to focus on my words. Nothing else matters. Just my voice. Let everything else fade away.'

The doctor paused, letting the silence linger. In the distance, Joseph could hear a group of students laughing and chatting to each other.

'Now, I want you to picture the word Chrysalis in your mind just as you saw it in the video,' Clara continued.

Visualising the word, his fingers twitched as he felt a pulse of energy surge through him.

'It's just a word,' Clara continued. 'A harmless collection of syllables. The word and the intent behind it have no power over you.'

Joseph swallowed, forcing himself to breathe, to ride out the storm in his mind.

Clara's voice pressed on, calm and steady. 'When you hear or see that word in the future, you will feel nothing unusual. No reaction, no confusion. It's just a word.'

Joseph's breathing deepened and the tension in his shoulders eased a fraction.

'Say the word,' Clara instructed.

Joseph's lips parted, but for a moment, no sound came out, bracing for the landmine to detonate.

'Say it,' Clara repeated, firmer this time.

'Chrysalis,' Joseph squeezed out through his clenched jaw.

No rush of static in his mind. No blank space where thoughts should be. No raging headache.

'Try it again,' Clara's voice said.

'Chrysalis,' Joseph repeated, with less hesitancy.

Clara nodded. 'Good, now please open your eyes.'

The DI blinked, taking in the psychologist watching him with a steady gaze. In that moment, he realised that it felt like a weight in his chest had lifted. It certainly felt like something had shifted in the depths of his subconscious.

'So how did I do?' Clara asked.

'Very well, I think.'

She leaned back in her chair. 'Good, but it's just a start. We probably need to repeat this a couple more times over the next week. However, I do think we've taken a very big first step towards deactivating the trigger phrase within you. You should be aware enough now not just to jump if someone says it to you, or you come across it another way. But if Storme really was behind this, he'll certainly have to try a hell of a lot harder to bend you to his will after this.'

Joseph felt a surge of relief at hearing that. 'Then thank you. If nothing else, I won't feel like I'm about to jump off the deep end at any moment. But there's another thing I need to ask. Would you be prepared to give evidence as an expert witness? If anyone could sway a jury to believe something as impossible as this, then it's you.'

'Then I'd be delighted to. If Storme really has been doing what it appears he has been, he's a monster and needs to be locked up as soon as possible. This is a betrayal of everything that psychology stands for. I'm also going to put together an initial assessment of the techniques used to program you and will email it over, which will hopefully help.'

'Thank you. I wonder just how many other people Storme has done this to?'

'That's a very good question,' Clara replied. 'Ideally, you might want to get a hold of his client list. That's where I'd start.'

Joseph nodded, although he already realised that the moment they handed over a search warrant for that, the hypnotist would know they were onto him. But as he thought about it, maybe there was another way not to tip Storme off. That would all come down to whether Chris could persuade a judge that they had enough evidence to issue a very different sort of search warrant. Specifically, one that would allow Neil Tanner to remotely hack Storme's computer, and look at footage from a CCTV camera he and Megan had seen over the man's front door.

CHAPTER TWENTY-FOUR

'So, let me get this right,' Chris said, when Joseph had arrived back in the incident room to brief the whole team about the potential breakthrough in the case. 'You're seriously suggesting Storme implanted this trigger word in your head?'

'Even if I've no memory of it, that's exactly what Doctor Winslow seems to think,' Joseph replied. 'Also, based on anecdotal evidence of the whole business of the spectre of Daryl Manning triggering a guilt response in me, I'm inclined to believe it.'

'So, you're saying this is what Storme did to his other victims?' Sue asked.

'Basically, yes.'

'Bloody hell, talk about "I have you in my power" and all that,' Ian replied.

'Aye, tell me about it,' Joseph said. 'But the good news is Clara believes she has reduced the effectiveness of the trigger word for me. After a couple more sessions, she even thinks she'll be able to remove any influence it has over me entirely.'

'But it could still have some effect on you in the meantime?' Chris asked. 'If so, I need to sign you off active duty right now.'

Joseph quickly held up his hands. 'No, I checked about that as well. I should be able to override any of Storme's tinkering in my brain, thanks to Clara's help.'

'That's a relief to hear. But what about anyone else who might still be out there with absolutely no idea they have a ticking time bomb in their heads? If I understand this correctly, they could be activated by Storme at a moment's notice.'

'That's exactly what I'm worried about. God knows how many people he might have had time to work on.'

'Hang on, I think we're missing something obvious here,' Megan said. 'If Storme really is behind this, and there's a direct correlation to the Samuel Dawson investigation, that will be a finite list of people, won't it?'

Joseph gave his colleague a thoughtful look. 'You're not wrong. Maybe we should revisit the list. Then get Clara to examine them as well to check if they have been programmed. Better safe than sorry.'

Chris cast his gaze over the evidence board. 'I agree, but we still don't know why Dawson was so important to Storme that he would want to avenge his death, let alone have waited so long to do so.'

'Well, I do have an idea,' Joseph replied. 'I think it's time to let Neil Tanner trawl through Storme's files and home CCTV to see if he can unearth anything. Specifically, Clara said we should look for any sort of client list he might have. That could help us identify who's been programmed.'

Chris blew out a breath between his teeth. 'That's going to be a tough sell to a judge, granting a search warrant to give our friendly hacker permission to go through Storme's systems.'

'Aye, I know it won't be easy. But we're also so far down that rabbit hole that we really have no choice at this point. Also, I have this.' The DI presented Clara's psychology report, which she'd emailed over, to the SIO.

'What am I looking at here?' Chris asked, skimming his gaze over it.

'Unlike our so-called expert in this area, namely, Doctor Nicky Hunt, who seems to have a very closed opinion about hypnotism, Clara, someone involved in experimental psychology, is a lot more open to the idea. This is her initial assessment of how Storme may have used hypnosis and conditioning to target his victims. I took a quick look at it and I think it will help you to persuade a judge to grant that search warrant.'

The SIO peered at him. 'So basically, you're expecting me to say yes to this?'

Joseph grimaced. 'That's about the measure of it, boss. But I wouldn't push it if I didn't believe it was absolutely necessary.'

Chris rubbed his chin. 'The alternative isn't going to be pretty if we just sit on our hands and another person linked to that bloody Dawson case dies, so I'm not sure we have any choice at this stage. Let's just hope Neil strikes gold. Then we can drag Storme in for questioning so fast that his head will spin.'

'Now that sounds like a plan I can sign up to,' Joseph replied, smiling at his boss.

'I think that goes for all of us,' Sue said, as everyone else nodded.

Later that evening, as Joseph approached Tús Nua, his gaze was immediately caught by Tux. His cat's tail was up as he padded towards him.

'Hello, my whiskered friend,' Joseph said, getting off his mountain bike and reaching down to scratch the side of the cat's head. He expected Tux to guide him to his boat's cabin door and specifically to his empty food bowl inside. Cupboard love, when it came to food, and his feline companion were firm friends.

Instead, Tux went straight up to Dylan's boat, Avalon, with a backward glance over his shoulder as if to say, will you shift your arse already?

Intrigued by his cat's out-of-character behaviour, Joseph followed. But as he neared his neighbour's boat, he heard the raucous laughter of not only Kate but also Ellie drifting from the cabin. Sure enough, Tux went straight up to the door and waited for Joseph to do the honours.

The DI stepped onto his friend's boat and rapped his knuckles against the cabin door. 'What are you up to in there with my two favourite women, Dylan?'

He was answered by the yips of White Fang and Max, who burst through the door the moment it was opened. They did the inevitable sniff-and-greet with Tux, but thankfully, the dogs spared Joseph the same treatment.

Dylan looked out at him, a cocktail shaker in hand. 'Ah, you're here, at last. You better come in and join the party.'

'You've started without me by the sound of things,' Joseph said, heading inside to see Kate and Ellie in armchairs. Both of the women had empty cocktail glasses in their hands, which they were waving at him.

'I'm glad you're here because we need some help persuading Dylan to listen to our advice,' Kate said.

'Sorry, what's exactly going on here?' Joseph asked.

'We're helping him prepare for his hot date with Iris on Friday,' Ellie said.

Dylan shot the DI an imploring look. 'Joseph, please help me out here. These two have got it into their heads I wasn't taking it seriously enough. And now they've insisted they give me...' he leaned in, 'a makeover.' The man practically shuddered as he said the word.

'Oh, dear God in heaven,' Joseph replied. 'What, getting your hair done, and maybe your nails too, with a bit of lippie thrown in?'

Kate and Ellie both howled at that, making Joseph suspect they'd already had more than one of Dylan's cocktails.

The poor professor scowled at him, face reddening. 'No, I mean, in my wardrobe choices. They don't seem to think my current clothes cut a dashing enough figure.'

'Well, I'm sorry, ladies. I don't see Dylan wearing skinny jeans anytime soon,' Joseph said, playing to his female audience.

That was greeted with even more cackles of laughter.

It took Kate a good minute before she could actually draw breath to speak again. 'No, we were trying to persuade Dylan to at least treat himself to a new jacket.'

Joseph gave his friend an appraising look. 'I'd listen to Kate about that sort of thing. Maybe leave the old tweed jacket with the leather elbow patches at home for this one, hey?'

The professor narrowed his eyes at the DI. 'I do not own a jacket like that.'

'Maybe not, but you are not a thousand miles away from it, either, my friend. But if you want the advice of an Irishman, maybe a good-quality waistcoat. It's almost compulsory to wear one if you really want to impress the ladies back in my own country.'

Ellie raised her eyebrows at her dad. 'Maybe if you live in the last century—' She stopped dead as Kate discreetly elbowed her in the ribs.

'Yes, I think you could look very dashing in a good waistcoat, Dylan,' Kate said, quickly steering the conversation into safer waters. 'But please no bow tie to go with it or you'll start to look like a bookie at the racetrack.'

Dylan scratched his chin. 'Actually, I do rather fancy the idea of a good waistcoat.'

'In that case, I've quite a few stored away on Tús Nua you could borrow,' Joseph said.

'Then thank you, my friend, and I may take you up on that.'

The DI gestured to the cocktail shaker in his hand. 'So what's this all about, then? It's not like you to be making cocktails, unless you count a gin and tonic as one.'

'Ah, you can blame your good ladies for that as well. They have both insisted that now is the time for me to dazzle Iris with my culinary skills. The plan is for me to cook her something as part of a pre-theatre meal before the show tomorrow.'

Ellie gave an enthusiastic nod. 'Dylan has even been trying to come up with drink pairings for each course.'

Until that moment, with everything that had been happening, Joseph had completely forgotten about the show he and Megan had free tickets for. Of course, if things went as he hoped and Neil struck gold, he doubted Storme would be able to make that particular appearance. But right now, he didn't want to deflate the party mood.

The professor turned his attention to a collection of bottles on the counter. 'Yes, please tell me what you think of my cocktail creation, gin-based of course. I'm thinking of pairing it with the starter.'

'I'd be more than happy to give you my professional opinion.'

'Good, because we've narrowed it down to this cocktail after sampling some others,' Kate said.

'Well, I suppose that explains why you and Ellie look like you've been having a grand old time in an Irish pub on a Friday night.'

Both women smirked at him.

Dylan set to work muddling fresh-cut ginger with a dash of sugar syrup. 'Then let me introduce you to a lychee and ginger gin fizz,' the professor said, as he measured out the spirit, some juice, and added the ginger syrup into the mix. After popping some ice into it, he began shaking it with vigour, accompanied by some appreciative barks from his dogs. A short while later, he poured the contents into a fresh glass for Joseph, topping it up with Prosecco and a couple of mint leaves as a garnish.

'Okay, taste that and let me know what you think?' the professor said, watching expectantly for Joseph's reaction.

The DI didn't need to be asked twice, and he took a sip. Cool, floral lychee, sharpened by the mint, hit his tongue first. Ginger followed that, warm and lingering, while the Prosecco left a sparkling finish on his palate.

Joseph gave a slow, appreciative nod. 'That, my friend, is excellent. Who knew you had the skills of a cocktail bartender hidden under that bushel of yours?'

'You approve, then?' Dylan asked.

'God yes, but what's the food you're hoping to pair with this nectar of the angels?'

'A starter of Thai-spiced lobster with a mango salad,' Dylan replied.

'Wow, you really are aiming to impress with an opening salvo like that. And for the main?'

'Persian-spiced lamb rack with pomegranate and saffron couscous. The lamb will be rubbed with a mixture of cardamom, cinnamon, cumin, and sumac. I'll also serve it with pistachios, dried apricots, and a drizzle of pomegranate molasses. They'll also be a side of charred aubergine with tahini and za'atar. I think I'll probably pair that with a nice spicy Zinfandel.'

'Fecking hell, you're not messing around, are you?'

Kate smiled at Dylan. 'That's exactly what we said.'

Joseph nodded. 'And for pud?'

'Ah, that will be my pièce de résistance. It will be a Japanese matcha and white chocolate soufflé. Quite a challenge in my little onboard oven, but nothing I can't crack. I'll probably serve that with warm sake.'

'If I were you, I'd go steady with the booze if this is a pre-theatre meal, or you'll both be pickled before you even start.'

'Ah yes, that's a good point, although I am planning to kick things off around three p.m. That way, we can take our time before we head out in the evening for Storme's show.'

'Well, if any man cooked that for me, I doubt we'd even get to the theatre because I would want my wicked way with him there and then,' Ellie said.

Kate stared at her daughter and then burst out laughing, nodding her agreement.

'Dear God, will you look at you two right eejits,' Joseph said, shaking his head at them. 'Dylan, just how many of those cocktails have these ladies been trying out?'

'One too many, it would seem.'

'Indeed. Well, ignoring the notable contribution of my daughter, I do think you're going to sweep Iris off her feet with that menu.'

'Great food is certainly one way to a woman's heart,' Kate said.

'A bit like the cholesterol,' Ellie added, grinning.

'Shush you,' Kate said, slightly slurring her words. 'As I was about to say, before I was so rudely interrupted, the other far better way to win her heart is being your good self, Dylan. Just be yourself because, yes, your wonderful food is beyond comparison, but it's the man making it who's really important. She will be a lucky woman if she lands you.'

'You really believe that?' the professor replied.

Kate gave an emphatic nod. 'Absolutely, and you should, too.'

Joseph patted his friend on the shoulder. 'You better listen to the woman. And a bit more self-belief there, man.'

'I'll try my best,' the professor replied with a small smile.

'Right, with that all sorted out, I'm going to extract these two female reprobates from your boat and leave you in peace. Ellie, I'll call John to swing by and pick you up. He should have finished his shift by now. Kate, I'm going to pour you into my bed and let you sleep it off.'

A grin filled her face. 'Will you be joining me?'

'Ewww, Mum, not in front of the kids,' Ellie said.

Kate responded with a hiccupping laugh.

Joseph rolled his eyes at Dylan. 'Like I said, maybe hold back with the alcohol on your big date.'

Dylan looked at Kate and Ellie, now hanging onto each other and sobbing with laughter.

'There, I think you make a very good point indeed.'

CHAPTER TWENTY-FIVE

The following morning, Joseph had left Kate curled up in his bed with the mother of all hangovers. He'd gone with his grandmother's old cure to help the love of his life rejoin the land of the living. Unusually, against the collective wisdom on this matter, especially at work, there wasn't a fry-up in sight, or even the hair of the dog. Instead, he'd given her a pile of buttered toast, along with a pot of honey. Far gentler on the stomach than a pile of greasy food, based on his own bitter experience.

Now back in St Aldates, fortified with cups of coffee he'd bought from the Roasted Bean for everyone, there was a definite sense of renewed energy in the incident room. Things had finally begun to slot into place in what had felt like a lost cause only a couple of days earlier, based as it was on a pretty wild theory.

'So how long before we can expect to hear back from Neil Tanner now he's got the search warrant?' Megan asked Joseph.

The DI took a thoughtful sip of his coffee and sat back in his seat. 'He was hoping to get something to us by the end of the day.'

'Then let's hope it's a smoking gun. We need something that

definitively links Storme to these murders. I don't know what you think, Joseph, but my feeling is it's going to be an uphill struggle to prove his guilt in court.'

'You're not wrong. But that's where I think whatever Clara can unearth in the minds of the victims he targeted will be the key, including it seems, me especially. Of course, this is where the genius of these murders lies. Storme has managed to keep his hands clean throughout all of this, getting other people to do his dirty work. Even so, this is still an old-fashioned case of using coercion on someone to commit murder. Presented to a jury like that, they might be more inclined to convict him, even if he did use hypnosis to pull it off. But I just wish we knew what Storme's link to the Samuel Dawson case was. With that, we really would have a much stronger case to prosecute him with, because right now we're still lacking a motive. In the meantime, I'm rather hopeful I'll come across something here.' The DI gestured towards his screen.

'What are you looking at?'

'I'm following up on something that Clara suggested. According to our friendly psychologist, a trigger word in one of those videos isn't the only way a person could be activated. That's why I've taken a second look at Simon and Alex's deaths. According to the records, the only incoming call Simon received was from the Banbury Police Station at around six-thirty a.m. And that was to let him know about the drug gangland hit. Nothing else before or after that to the moment of his death. Certainly, no keyword had been slipped to him that way, according to the call transcript, because I checked. So that suggests the DCI was slipped the keyword by another means. That's why I contacted the Banbury team for any footage from their MCU transports present at the crime scene that day. I'm literally about to play the video from it to see if I can see anything suspicious. Care to join me in case you can spot something I miss?'

Megan nodded and wheeled her chair up alongside his.

'Brace yourself, because this is leading up to the moment Simon took his own life.'

The DC's lips thinned. 'Thanks for the warning.'

Joseph hit play at the exact moment one of the MCU van's cameras had captured Simon emerging from the house. They watched the DCI totally ignore the PC stationed outside to guard the front door, who'd tried to speak to him. The Beretta Simon had just used to murder his friend was still clutched in his hand. He half walked, half stumbled towards the gate.

'There's definitely something off with him,' Megan said, leaning for a closer look. 'Based on the tight expression on his face, and the way his hand is clawed around that pistol, it looks like part of him was trying to fight what was about to happen.'

'Which is exactly what Clara said she suspected—that part of his victim's subconscious, even though powerless, would realise what was going on but wouldn't be able to stop themselves.'

'Well, the man on this video certainly doesn't look in control of his own actions.'

'If that's true, imagine the fear he must have felt coursing through his veins in those last seconds, unable to stop what he'd just done, and what he was about to do.'

Megan nodded with a sombre look.

On the video, Simon walked out of shot, and Joseph quickly switched to the feed from the second camera on the MCU vehicle, matching the timestamp to the first. They were rewarded with seeing the exact moment Simon stepped off the pavement in front of the delivery truck. The impact was sickening, and the DI found himself popping a Silvermint into his mouth as Megan watched grim-faced but stoic as usual, taking in every awful detail of the carnage.

One moment Simon was alive, the next his body had been smashed into a bloody pulp and dragged under the van as it came to a shuddering halt.

'Feck, what a way to go,' Joseph muttered.

'That poor man,' Megan agreed.

Despite the gruesomeness of the scene, Joseph forced himself to keep watching, to witness how the aftermath played out in case he spotted something useful.

Shocked onlookers jumped out of their cars and rushed to the man's aid. The PC that Simon had ignored reached the DCI's battered body first and started talking rapidly into his radio. The driver of the truck stared down at the nose of his vehicle, hands locked onto the steering wheel. But none of this was what Joseph was looking for.

Where was Storme?

The DI's had hoped that the man wouldn't be able to resist witnessing firsthand how his handiwork had played out. But even watching the footage for another ten minutes didn't reveal anything further, and Megan eventually left him to it, so she could return to her own work.

If the mentalist had been there, he was either off-camera or so heavily disguised as to be invisible in the crowd. But if Storme hadn't been there at the end, perhaps he'd been there at the beginning to issue the trigger phrase, giving himself plenty of time to get away.

Joseph rewound the footage at high speed until he spotted Simon first approaching the crime scene from his parked car, and hit play. The timestamp showed it was only six minutes before the moment the DCI had stepped out in front of the truck.

The DI scanned for anything out of the ordinary, someone

who didn't quite fit into the scene. But once again, he didn't see anyone who even vaguely looked like Storme among the passersby. Then his gaze was caught by a dark-haired woman walking along the pavement towards Simon. Just for the barest moment, as she passed the DCI, she leant her head a fraction towards him, then without breaking stride, she headed away.

Even though he hadn't seen her face, Joseph realised there was something familiar about her. His heart skipped. Was this what he'd been looking for?

The DI rewound the tape and played the sequence again. This time, when the woman leant in towards Simon, he froze the frame and zoomed in. Even though the image was heavily pixelated, he could see her mouth opening. He stepped through the frames one by one, until it became clear the woman had said something.

Christ on a fecking bike, Joseph thought. 'Okay, I think I've found something,' he called out to the room.

Megan was the first to join him, but within moments, everyone was standing around him.

'What's this, Joseph?' Chris asked.

'Surveillance footage from the Banbury MCU vehicle attending the crime scene where Simon murdered Alex, before killing himself. I think I've just found the exact moment that Simon was slipped the trigger word.'

'Okay, show us what you have.'

The DI nodded and replayed the footage he'd just analysed, first at normal speed, then frame by frame until the SIO finally nodded.

'Okay, you're definitely onto something,' Chris said. 'So, who is that woman?'

'Well, I don't think that's Storme in a wig, if that's what you mean. But let me check out one of the MCU's other cameras to see if it caught her face as she passed the vehicle.'

A few keystrokes later, Joseph had the vehicle's forward-facing CCTV camera view on-screen. He quickly fast-forwarded until he saw the woman appear. Her face was clear, and more significantly, this time the DI immediately recognised her.

'Bloody hell, that's Stacey Ellis,' Megan said.

Joseph scraped his hand through his hair. 'Shite, so not only did Storme get her to kill Gregory before taking her own life, she also did his dirty work for him, by slipping the keyword to Simon before he went crazy.'

'And if she did it with Simon, there's no reason not to believe she didn't do it with all the others,' Chris said.

'So she was quite literally a messenger of death, and probably didn't even realise it?' Sue asked.

'That would be my guess,' Chris said. 'But once again, we have no way of proving Storme had anything to do with this. So let's hope Neil has some luck unearthing that client list, and hopefully Stacey's name will be on it. That correlation could be exactly what the CPS needs for a successful prosecution. The moment we have that list, I want every single person on it pulled in for questioning.'

'We could be talking about a lot of people here, boss,' Ian said.

'I know, but I'm not taking any chances from here on out. More importantly, when we have that evidence, I want Storme locked up in a cell before he can do any more damage.'

'You certainly won't get an argument from me,' Joseph replied. 'And on that note, maybe I should babysit Neil. Then the moment he makes a breakthrough, we can get the wheels spinning.'

'Do it,' Chris said.

Less than a minute later, the DI was in the TR4, heading to Neil's place.

CHAPTER TWENTY-SIX

Joseph sat with Neil, who was flicking his gaze across his numerous screens, which were all filled with data. The search warrant was stuck to one of them, underlining that this man had principles. There was also a techno music track thumping out of the speaker system, threatening to give the DI a non-hypnotised-induced headache. Unfortunately, the programmer had insisted he needed to feel the music through his body to help him get into a flow state, something for which headphones were apparently not an option.

'Are you sure there's nothing else I can get you?' Joseph shouted over the music, gesturing to the Five Guys burger with all the trimmings he'd ordered to help keep Neil going.

'Sorry?'

He gestured to the burger and shouted even louder. 'I said, are you sure there's nothing else I...' His words trailed away as, thankfully, the programmer lowered the volume of the music.

'No, this is hitting the spot,' Neil said. 'Proper brain food.'

'I thought your generation was all green smoothies made from kelp and sandals?' the DI replied.

Neil grinned at him. 'Only on every other day of the week.'

'So sustenance aside, how's it going?'

'Storme's home network is certainly locked down tighter than a paranoid man with a bank vault in his own home. We're talking a high-end firewall, custom encryption, and even biometric logins. But—' He grinned. 'Every system has a weakness. You just have to find the right thread to pull at.'

Joseph arched an eyebrow. 'And what thread are you pulling at right now?'

Neil gestured towards the largest screen displaying some sort of login screen. 'His router. Fortunately for us, most people don't realise their home router is basically the gatekeeper to all of their digital world. If I can breach that, then I can map out his entire network—laptops, phones, smart devices, and the rest using it.'

The programmer tapped a few keys, bringing up a map linked with lines. To Joseph's untrained eye, it looked a lot like a version of the underground Tube map, but more complicated.

'What's this?' the DI asked.

'A Wi-Fi signal map from a portable scanner I already took the precaution of popping into the flower bed outside St Luke's Manor. That's literally the first thing I did when the warrant arrived. It's not exactly hacking, but it's certainly a good initial preparatory step. Thanks to that, I ran a passive scan to see what devices were broadcasting within that building. Storme's router pinged out to a few devices, including a laptop, his phone, and a printer, as well as several security cameras.'

'Several, but we only saw one over his front door?'

'Trust me, he has at least six others spread out across his flat. They all seem to have been purchased about a year ago. That's according to an invoice I found in the buffer of the unsecured printer. Here, let me show you.'

With a few clicks, a building schematic was displayed over the top of the signal map.

'Now we can see where each of these nodes is in the physical space. I've already colour-coded the cameras and their links so you can see them more easily.' Neil zoomed in on the tower section of the Manor's floor plan until Storme's apartment filled the large screen.

Joseph took in the positions of all the cameras spread throughout the flat, including one in the waiting room where he'd sat with Megan. He gestured towards it. 'I definitely don't remember seeing a camera in there.'

'There's a good reason for that,' Neil replied. 'I've already checked the product number of one of the cameras he's using on his network. Have a look at this.'

With a few more taps, an Amazon page popped up on one of the screens of what, at first glance, looked just like a hardback book. But then Joseph took in the name displayed next to it, Decorative Book Hidden Security Camera.

'Feck, so you're saying Storme was filming people in his waiting room without their knowledge?' Joseph asked.

'Absolutely, and it's a similar story throughout the rest of the flat as well. The only exception seems to be the bathrooms.'

Joseph pulled a face. 'Thank God for some small mercies.'

Neil snorted. 'Oh, one other thing of interest is that there seem to be wireless screens everywhere in his flat as well, all linked to his Wi-Fi network.'

'That doesn't sound particularly unusual, especially these days.'

'If we were talking about a few, I would say yes. But there is one in literally every room. This is not a home where you can get away from a screen.'

'Okay, maybe he's just a guy who has something of a Netflix habit.'

'Maybe, but guess when they were all installed?'

'Don't tell me, a year ago.'

'In one. I don't know the significance of that, but I thought you should know.'

'Interesting, but you can probably guess what my next question will be.'

'Can I gain access to what these cameras have recorded?'

'Exactly. That would tell us if any of Storme's victims visited his flat.'

Neil shook his head. 'Not yet. I haven't actually hacked into his router. At this stage, this is all still passive data gathering.'

'Feck, if you can learn all this without even really trying, it certainly puts the police kicking down the front door to shame.'

'Horses for courses, but as you can see, we can learn an awful lot before you even need to head inside. But to learn what Storme is really up to within those walls, we need to do the digital equivalent of breaking in. Talking of which, time for the main course—I'm going to hack his router.'

'So how hard is this going to be?' Joseph asked.

'The good news is that every router has a default admin panel, usually with a lazy password no one ever bothers to change. If Storme's been sloppy, I can easily brute-force my way in.'

Joseph frowned. 'And if he's not sloppy?'

Neil smiled. 'Then I get creative. Packet sniffing—intercepting unencrypted data. ARP spoofing—tricking his network into thinking I'm a trusted device. Or, my personal favourite, a de-authorisation attack—I force his devices to disconnect. When they automatically try to reconnect, I intercept the handshake and steal the credentials.'

Joseph exhaled. 'I've no idea what any of that is, but it all sounds very illegal.'

'Exactly, and that's why I wanted that piece of paper.' Neil gestured to the search warrant. The programmer cracked his knuckles. 'Now, let's see if Damien Storme left a security back door wide open for us to enter through.'

Neil's fingers danced across the keyboard. The screen flickered briefly as a list of numbers appeared. 'Right, there's Storme's router. Looks like it's a NetGear one, and a very common model. So now to test the router's default settings.' He tapped in a series of commands and the progress bar began ticking forward slowly.

'You really think he's left it with the default password?' Joseph asked.

Neil shrugged. 'Most people do, because they don't realise how easy it is to bypass basic security. NetGear's older models default to something like admin and password for logins. You'd be amazed how often that stays the same.' He gave a small shrug. 'Thankfully, most people are just lazy, which is just as well for us right now.'

Joseph frowned, eyeing the lines of code skimming past. 'And if he's set up a stronger password?'

'Then we start playing really dirty,' Neil replied. 'Like I said before, we can sniff the data packets and figure out what's flowing across the network. Maybe find an unencrypted stream from one of his cameras. If that doesn't work, ARP spoofing it is. I'll fake a trusted device, so Storme's system thinks I'm just another laptop in his house. Then the router won't know the difference as we access all his files.'

Joseph shook his head. Neil was one of the good guys, but this sort of knowledge in the wrong hands didn't bear thinking about.

The screen flickered again as Neil's fingers hovered over the keys, waiting. 'Okay, here we go. Time to see if Storme's been lazy.' He hit enter, and the screen filled with a rapid stream of text. Then, just as quickly as it had started, the screen paused.

Neil leaned back with a wide grin. 'Got it. Admin access.

Now we've got full control of the router. We can see everything on Storme's network—his devices, his files, the works.'

Joseph exhaled. 'So what now?'

The programmer was already typing again, and browsing through the router's web settings. 'We still have to go deeper. The real challenge is finding what Storme is hiding. But don't worry, this is just the warm-up.'

The DI couldn't help but be impressed. 'You make this all look way too fecking easy.'

Neil shrugged. 'It's only easy if you know where to look and combine that with years of practice.' He cracked his knuckles again. 'Now, let's see what's behind door number one—the security camera footage from his front door.'

Within moments, the programmer had a control panel up with what appeared to be a scrollable data panel at the bottom.

'Oh, you little beauty,' Joseph said. 'And you have access to everything it's recorded?'

'Yes, and I've already started downloading the footage. The good news is the stored footage is motion-activated, so you won't have to wade through tons of footage to find what you're after.'

'That's great news, but for now, could we look at what was captured on Monday?'

Neil nodded and started tapping again. Six of his other monitors displayed multiple moments caught by the front door camera. Then he spotted Catherine approaching the door. A few moments later, she'd disappeared inside, the timestamp indicating seven a.m.

'Is she of any interest?' Neil asked, hitting pause.

'That's just Storme's assistant. Can we keep playing the video from here? This is the day that Megan and I paid Storme a visit as well. I'm keen to see exactly what happened.'

'Absolutely.' Neil pulled it up on the main screen as a video and pressed play. The footage fast-forwarded to the next event at ten a.m., specifically the moment the DI and DC walked towards Storme's front door.

'What are you looking for in this footage, exactly?' Neil asked.

'I won't know until I see it,' Joseph replied. 'For now, I want to see how many other clients Storme typically sees on a given day.'

Neil nodded, and they continued to watch, including the footage of the detectives leaving the flat together. Then there was a flurry of visitors throughout the rest of that day, at least six in all, one of which was an Amazon delivery driver. Then the day stamp flicked to the next day, and once again there was a flurry of visitors. There was at least one occasion that Catherine left for about an hour before returning. Joseph wondered at the significance of that and whether Storme was busy programming the woman to be his messenger pigeon for his next victim. It wasn't until another day ticked past that something very unexpected happened.

Of all the people he might have thought he'd see approaching the flat, the last person was Megan by herself.

'What the actual feck?' Joseph said, sitting up.

He did a quick check of the timestamp. The video was of the same day she'd left work sick. But an hour after she'd been sent home, the DC seemed to be in perfect health, her eyes clear and expression relaxed.

'She put it all on?' the DI muttered to himself.

'So you weren't expecting to see Megan visiting Storme by herself, then?' Neil asked.

'No, I fecking wasn't,' Joseph replied, a knot of apprehension building inside him. 'She was meant to be ill at home when this was taken. Can you switch to the other cameras to see what happened when she went inside?'

'Of course.' With a few more clicks, Neil had multiple

camera feeds filling up all the screens, including a wide-angle one in the waiting room area showing Megan sitting alone on the sofa. The large screen on the wall was showing one of Storme's geometrical patterns pulsing in slow motion. It was this that Megan was staring at, seemingly unable to tear her eyes away.

A moment later, Storme appeared in the room and walked right up to her. He said something, but there was no audio.

'Can you please turn up the volume?' Joseph asked.

'Sorry, no can do—this is a video-only feed from this camera.'

'Damn, but whatever sweet nothings that bloody man is muttering to her, it can't be good.'

'You think he hypnotised her?'

'Aye, that's exactly what I think. Megan certainly didn't mention any of this, and if my own experience was anything to go by, she won't even remember any of this happened.'

They continued to watch as Storme said something else to Megan. The DC slowly nodded, then stood, before following him out of the room. A moment later, she appeared on another camera in a small white room with a single seat facing another large screen. After Megan sat in it, Storme carefully placed a set of headphones over her ears, before leaving her alone in the room.

'Can we find out how long she was in there?' Joseph asked as his throat went dry.

Neil nodded and scrubbed the timeline forward. Apart from various appearances by Storme, who seemed to talk to Megan at length, she was otherwise left alone. Apart from loo and meal breaks, the hours sped past. Early in the morning of the third day, Storme appeared again, and Megan stood.

The two men watched the DC's progress as she left the flat, the implications becoming more obvious by the second.

A glance at the timestamp confirmed Joseph's worst fears. It was an hour before Megan had appeared back at work that same morning. She must have swung past her flat to pick up her phone and car, before driving into work. But it was as he'd been watching his colleague in that featureless room that another thought had struck him.

'Neil, can you rewind the footage from this camera to just after the moment Megan and I first visited Storme?'

'Of course...'

A few key taps, and Megan had vanished. But now, sitting in that same seat, headphones strapped to his head, was Joseph himself.

'For feck's sake, now I know when Storme started to brainwash me.'

Neil stared at him. 'And you don't remember anything about this?'

'Other than a featureless room in a dream, which must have been that place, absolutely bloody nothing. But the really bad news is that Storme had his hooks in me for a good twenty minutes, unless I crop up elsewhere in one of these videos. Thankfully, in my case, I've had a psychologist deal with the trigger phrase he implanted in my mind. But with Megan, Storme literally had days to programme her. All this time we thought I was the one that Storme was targeting, but it turns out it was really Megan.' As Joseph spoke, the image of Stacey Ellis trying to murder him filled his mind. 'Feck knows what Storme's made Megan capable of by now.'

Neil's expression paled. 'You think she's going to kill herself?'

Joseph gave a rapid shake of his head. 'No. She wasn't involved in the Dawson investigation. But based on what happened with DCI Hart, I find myself wondering if she might be about to target someone else assigned to that old case.'

'Shit, who exactly?'

'No idea. That's why we need to stop her now.' The DI took his mobile out of his pocket and began dialling.

'You're not trying to call her, are you?' Neil asked.

Joseph shook his head. 'No. For all I know, that might trigger her into action to murder whoever she's meant to target. I'm ringing Chris.'

The moment the call connected, Joseph started speaking. 'Is Megan anywhere near you right now, Chris?'

'No. She popped out to do a coffee run—why?' the SIO replied.

'Neil has just successfully accessed Storme's home computer and security cameras. We just discovered that Megan went there when she was meant to be off ill. It seems fecking Storme had plenty of time to programme her. And just for good measure, we've also found footage of when he did the same to me when we visited him the first time. He must have done something similar to Megan, but called her back for seconds. Chris, I'm worried sick of what Megan might be capable of now.'

'Okay, I'll track her phone...' His words trailed away. 'Fuck.'

Joseph's heart clenched at the uncharacteristic swear from his boss. 'What is it?'

'I'm looking at her phone right now, and it's been left on her bloody desk. Either she left it there by accident, or...'

'Shite! We need to bring her in for her own safety, let alone anyone else she might be programmed to target.'

'Oh, I'm going to issue an alert right across the TVP force to bring her in. I'm also going to issue an arrest warrant for Storme. Is he still in his flat?'

'Hang on,' Joseph said, nodding to the programmer.

Neil tapped the keyboard, and all the screens were replaced with live feeds. Storme wasn't anywhere to be seen on any of them. He then switched to the last captured event on the entrance camera, showing Storme leaving the flat two hours previously.

'No, I'm afraid he's long gone,' Joseph said into the phone.

'So where the hell is he?' Chris asked.

Joseph remembered Dylan's date with Iris. 'I know exactly where the feck Storme is. He's holding a final performance at the New Theatre in Oxford...' The DI checked his watch. 'And it started thirty minutes ago.'

'Okay, then I will see you there. We'll stop the performance and arrest him on stage if we have to.'

'Sounds good,' Joseph said, rushing for the door. He gave Neil a backwards glance over his shoulder. 'Download all the footage you can and send it straight over to Amy. Also, if you can search for his client list, do that as a matter of priority. Hopefully, we'll discover everyone else that bastard hypnotised without their consent.'

'Leave it to me, and good luck,' Neil replied.

The DI gave him a sharp nod. He rushed out and headed down the stairs, taking them three at a time. But his stomach was already twisting with fear about where and exactly what Megan was up to right now, and if there was still time to stop her.

CHAPTER TWENTY-SEVEN

JOSEPH SKIDDED the TR4 to a stop just in front of the New Theatre in Oxford. Marked and unmarked police cars were parked outside on George Street. The DI was out of his vehicle in seconds, running towards the entrance where PC John Thorpe was standing guard.

'Is the rest of the team already inside?' Joseph asked.

John frowned as he nodded. 'Yes, they headed in a good five minutes ago. But the strange thing is it's all gone quiet since then. I tried radioing to find out what's going on in there, but nobody is picking up.'

Joseph gave the PC a confused look. 'But Chris should have had Storme in cuffs by now. It's not like the DCI to take his time when making a crucial arrest.'

'You think there's a problem? Because that's exactly what I was starting to wonder,' John said.

A weight was already building inside the DI's chest. Had they managed to underestimate Storme? 'I'm not sure, but you stay here and make sure no one enters, or leaves, for that matter. If I'm not back out here in five, call for more backup.'

'Will do, but just be careful.'

Joseph nodded as he rushed past the young officer and entered the theatre lobby.

The first thing that struck the DI was the lack of anyone around, specifically any members of staff at the ticket desk. It was also eerily quiet, apart from the distant murmur of a performance underway. When the DI followed the signs for the stalls and found no one at the door to check his ticket, his worry notched up another level. This was a very ominous sign indeed.

Joseph opened the door to hear the melodic tones of Damien Storme's voice filling the theatre. 'Just relax and follow my voice,' he was saying to the audience members.

The mentalist was standing on stage, lit by a single spotlight. Behind him on a giant screen was displayed the far too familiar pulsating geometrical image with a single word on it, Chrysalis. This time it wasn't hidden like the others had been, but was in clear text for everyone to see.

Joseph braced himself for the assault on his mind, but apart from a slight itch behind his eyes, there was no sign of a crushing headache. It seemed his mental defence preparation with Clara had paid dividends.

The theatre was packed with people. Whatever Damien Storme was, he was definitely popular.

Then the DI noticed everyone in the audience was sitting far too still, their unblinking gazes locked onto the large pulsating screen. If Dylan and Iris were among them, the DI couldn't spot them. But then he noticed Chris, Ian, and Sue, along with a bunch of uniformed officers, standing motionless in one of the aisles leading up to the stage.

'You are all here to witness a very special performance,' Storme said to his enraptured audience. 'The theme of today's show is one of revenge.'

That really increased the volume of the mental alarm bells ringing in Joseph's skull. Then he noticed the slightly sweet, musky scent filling the room. He'd come across that smell somewhere before, but where?

'As I promised you all at the start, you are all going to be part of an extraordinary mass hypnosis experiment, which you're all now experiencing. But how, you ask?'

He picked up a plant with white trumpet-shaped flowers in a domed glass container, and presented it to the audience.

'I have in my hand Datura Stramonium. This is a remarkable plant from which I extract a substance known as scopolamine, or to use its more poetic name, Devil's Breath. What's that, you ask? Well, it helps to make people who might not normally be open to hypnosis very suggestible indeed, especially when used like now in this very theatre, when it's aerosolized.

'But please don't worry, it's perfectly safe and won't leave any lasting effects. Also, you won't remember anything at the end of this performance. Other than losing twenty minutes of your life, you will all be fine.'

Joseph felt his mind starting to tilt as Storme's words began to echo in his mind. But that smell... Then he knew exactly where he'd come across that scent before—from the vaporiser in the mentalist's waiting room. Was that how the bastard had managed to hypnotise him and Megan, and in such short order? Then his brain caught up with what was happening here. If everyone else was being affected by the aerosolized drug, Clara's help in preparing his mental barriers or not, the DI needed to get back outside into fresh air before the Devil's Breath got to him again.

The detective turned, his legs already starting to feel heavy, but he managed to stagger back out through the doors. The moment John saw Joseph leaving the lobby, he grabbed him by the shoulders. 'Are you okay?'

'Barely. Storme has released some sort of fecking gas in there. Thanks to that, the madman has managed to drop everyone inside into a hypnotic state, including Chris and the rest of the team. Get that backup here now, and call the fire brigade whilst you're at it. Tell them they'll need respirators before they try to enter the theatre.'

'Will do.' John took out his radio and started speaking into it.

Meanwhile, Joseph pulled out his phone and dialled the one person who might have an idea about how to handle this. Thankfully, Doctor Winslow picked up on the third ring.

The moment the call connected, he was already speaking. 'Clara, it's DI Stone here. I need your help. It's urgent. I'm at the New Theatre. Storme has released some sort of gas or something. It's called Devil's Breath.'

'You're joking?'

'I wish I were.'

'No, you don't understand. It's the drug we use on the experimental psychology course, but that's with people's consent.'

'Hopefully you'll know all about it then, because he's used it to drop the entire audience into a trance state. That includes a bunch of my colleagues who went in there ahead of me to arrest him. But here's the thing. I need to get back in there and stop him before he does God knows what else.'

'Okay, but you'll face the same problem as everyone else; it will make you very suggestible to anything he says.'

'Aye, I already discovered that for myself, but managed to get out in time. So without a respirator mask, how do I counteract it?'

'Well, if you're absolutely desperate to go back in, you could use a COVID-type mask with a damp cloth placed inside it. That will mitigate a fair amount of the effect, but not all of it. The other thing you should do is load up on a stimulant like lots of coffee. That will help counteract the effects of the drug to a certain degree.'

'Okay, I'll try that. He also has a massive screen with one of those fecking geometrical patterns of his with the trigger word Chrysalis on it.'

'In that case, try to avoid looking at it as much as possible. I've attempted to deprogram you, but...'

'Understood, but please get yourself down here because the moment we evacuate the audience, I suspect we're going to have a lot of bewildered people on our hands, my colleagues, among them.'

'I was already planning to do exactly that. I know exactly what drug to use to counteract the effect of the Devil's Breath,' Clara said.

'Then please hurry,' Joseph replied, before ringing off.

The DI spared no time in rushing to a nearby Pizza restaurant, one of the best in Oxford, to grab himself five espressos. He downed one after another, almost burning his mouth in the process. It was certainly the first time he'd had to use his warrant card to jump the queue and order free coffee in the line of duty.

Then, one COVID mask from the dashboard of the TR4 later, along with a soaked handkerchief, Joseph was preparing to head back into the theatre, even as the first of the fire engines pulled up outside and its crew spilled out of the vehicle.

'You're not going to wait for them?' John asked, as the DI headed past him to go back inside the theatre.

'No, because every second counts. Just make sure the fire crew are fully briefed before they head inside. Also tell them we need to kill the power to the projector, so we can break the trance people are in. Then they should be able to evacuate them and hopefully fresh air will help them get over the effects of the gas.'

'Will do, and good luck.'

With a nod to his colleague, Joseph slipped the mask into

place and took a deep breath through the wet cloth of the clear air outside.

As Joseph stepped back into the theatre, his heart clenched. Storme now had five people up on stage, all of whom he knew. Among them was the forensic psychologist, Doctor Nicky Hunt. The remainder were old officers he hadn't seen for years, but in one way or another, all of them had been involved in the Dawson case. Before them, on a table covered with green velvet cloth, were five stainless steel knives glimmering under the stage lights.

'Ladies and gentlemen,' Storme said. 'The people you see before you were all involved in an enormous miscarriage of justice that led to the death of this man. A large photograph of Samuel Dawson appeared superimposed on the shifting geometrical pattern. This version of Samuel certainly looked happy and carefree. It was as far removed as the DI could imagine from the haunted man who'd eventually taken his own life in prison.

'This is Doctor Samuel Dawson,' Storme announced. 'He was a wonderful psychologist, but thanks to the ineptitude of those who should have found him innocent, his life was utterly destroyed when he was wrongly accused of murdering his wife, and he ended up taking his own life in prison.'

Joseph's mind was already racing. So this final performance had all been about revenge, but he still didn't understand why Dawson mattered so much to Storme.

'No one involved ever had to face the consequences of their actions, until now,' the mentalist continued. 'But one by one, those people, racked by their own guilt and not able to live with themselves, have taken their own lives. These five people were also directly involved. So let's hear your applause if you feel they should try to atone for what they did?'

The effect was instantaneous, and a round of deafening

applause broke out from the audience. Joseph was horrified to see even Chris, Ian, and Sue clapping among them, blankly staring at the stage. Whatever else was going on here, it was obvious to Joseph in that moment—Storme really did have the entire audience, willing or not, in the palm of his hand. He also knew he had one chance, however slim, to stop this maniac before it was too late.

The DI started to run towards the stage, deliberately avoiding so much as a glance at the pulsating geometrical pattern on the huge projector screen. But he'd only taken three strides before Storme spotted him and turned in his direction.

'Ah, DI Joseph Stone, late to the party, but here at last. Thank you for saving me the trouble of tracking you down.'

'You're welcome, but you can stop this bloody madness before it goes any further,' Joseph called back as he continued towards the stage.

Storme laughed. 'As if I would do that after all these years of training and preparation.' The mentalist turned to the five people on stage and lowered his voice to speak one word: 'Requiem!' The word bounced around the walls, amplified by the theatre's speakers. Then the word was taken up as a chant by the audience, every single one repeating the word over and over again.

The five people on stage all immediately moved towards the table where the knives had been placed. Having witnessed just how far Storme had pushed Stacey Ellis, the DI knew exactly where this was headed.

At that moment, the doors crashed open behind him, and four firefighters fully kitted out in breathing apparatus, burst into the theatre.

'Stop the people on stage!' the DI bellowed towards the approaching fire officers.

To their credit, the men and women didn't hesitate, and all

broke into a lumbering run laden down by their breathing gear, towards the stage.

The DI returned his attention to Doctor Hunt, the first to reach the table of knives.

'Requiem. Requiem. Requiem,' Damien continued to chant with the audience, his arms extended wide like a sorcerer. 'Now is the time to deal with all the guilt that you've been carrying all these years, the guilt that has been eating away at you from the inside. Time to end your pain and atone for your sins.'

'Don't fecking listen to the man,' Joseph bellowed, as he ran up the stairs at the edge of the stage. The fire officers were still a good thirty metres behind him, quite literally a lifetime for the five potential victims up there on the stage.

As Nicky picked up a knife, her hand shaking, Joseph knew he had a decision to make.

'You are about to release yourself from all your torment,' Storme continued, as the music swelled.

The DI recognised it as the soundtrack from the Omen.

Great fecking choice of music, he thought as he sprinted towards the table just before the other four victims reached it. The DI didn't hesitate and grabbed the table, tipping it over, and sending the knives skittering across the stage. All but the one now clasped in Doctor Hunt's hand.

The fire officers had closed the distance and started lumbering up the stairs just behind the DI.

Hunt's whole body vibrated, as she looked up towards the ornate ceiling of the theatre, exposing her neck.

Not fecking this time! Joseph's mind bellowed at him.

Heart roaring in his chest, he launched himself desperately at the woman, pulling her to the ground with a rugby tackle. The DI leapt on top of the psychologist before she'd even had time to move. Using a wrist lock move, he made her let go of the knife. At once, the woman started to buck under him, a wild animal caught in a snare and fighting to break free.

'Resist!' Storme commanded as the fire officers reached the stage and started grappling with the four other hypnotised victims, frantically searching the floor for the other knives.

It was then that the giant video screen at the back went dead. Joseph spotted John emerging from the side of the stage wearing an adapted COVID mask similar to his own. The PC also had a bunch of pulled cables in his hand.

Spotting the DI, John rushed over. 'I killed the projector backstage to see if that can help break the trance people are in.'

'Quick thinking,' Joseph replied.

The PC shot him a smile just as the house lights came up. Immediately, throughout the theatre, people stirred, awakening from the stupor they'd been in only a moment before. The only exception were the five people on stage, including Nicky Hunt who was still struggling like a wild animal beneath Joseph. Whatever programming Storme had subjected her and others to, obviously ran far deeper than the effect of watching a pretty pattern on a screen.

Then the DI's attention shifted back to Storme.

'Fight them and find peace,' the mentalist commanded from the theatre's speakers.

'John, will you shut that little fecker up for me?' the DI said, as Doctor Hunt tried to throw him off again.

'With pleasure,' John said, flicking his baton to its full length, PAVA spray in his other hand.

'You're under arrest, Storme,' the PC called out as he advanced.

The mentalist turned towards him and laughed. 'You really think you can stop me?'

'Don't say I didn't warn you,' John replied, aiming his artificial pepper spray straight at the man's face.

The effect was almost instantaneous, as the PAVA hit him. Storme started coughing and dropped to his knees, rubbing desperately at his eyes.

Seeing the way Storme had reacted to the PAVA spray, had given Joseph an idea.

He fished his own canister from his pocket and sprayed it straight into Doctor Hunt's face. As the artificial pepper spray hit the woman's eyes, it was like a switch had been thrown. One moment she was like a rabid dog, hissing and spitting at him, the next she was whimpering, her eyes focusing on Joseph for the first time through a flood of tears.

'What happened to me?' she asked, between racking coughs.

'It seems you managed to get yourself hypnotised,' Joseph replied, unable to keep the irony out of his voice.

But now he knew exactly what he had to do to break the trances of the people on stage still under Storme's power.

'John, use your PAVA spray on the others. It will pull them out of their hypnotic trances.'

The PC nodded and darted between the fire officers, pinning the other victims to the stage and spraying each of them in turn. Just like that, they began to splutter and cough, and stopped struggling as their programming was shattered. Then another fire officer appeared by Joseph's side.

The woman had a spare oxygen mask in her hand and pressed it to Doctor Hunt's face. 'Breathe deeply,' the woman said.

The forensic psychologist nodded as Joseph finally let her go and the other fire officers did the same with the other victims, who were all starting to relax their grips.

The DI stood and headed over to the mentalist, who was now on all fours, staring at the ground. Joseph grabbed hold of Storme's shoulder and hauled him around so he could look into the man's face. But the string of expletives he was about to launch died in his throat when he saw the mentalist weeping.

'What happened?' Storme asked, echoing Nicky Hunt, wearing a bewildered expression of his own.

'Cut the act,' Joseph said.

But the mentalist shook his head as he looked around, taking in the theatre. 'I don't understand...' He rubbed frantically at his eyes. Then he saw the other people being helped to their feet by the fire officers, including Nicky Hunt. He gestured towards them. 'Who are those people?'

There was something in the way Storme said it that made Joseph realise the man wasn't putting on a performance. 'Inhaled too much of your own Devil's Breath, have you?'

'What's that?'

Joseph was becoming increasingly mystified by the man's behaviour when his phone rang. When he looked at the display and saw Megan's name, he took the call immediately.

'Are you okay?' he asked as soon as he picked up, letting John take over dealing with Storme.

'Yes, but Derrick won't be when I take his life,' the DC said, her tone iron.

The DI's blood iced. 'Bloody hell, I should have fecking known.' He glowered down at the man. 'Storme, you need to break the trance you've put my colleague in, and do it now.'

'What trance?' Storme asked, staring up at the DI.

'You're wasting time, Joseph,' Megan said over the phone. 'I'm in Storme's flat, but come alone and don't tell anyone. If you do, Derrick will be dead before anyone can step over the threshold, and that includes anyone from the tactical unit.'

'But Megan...' The line went dead. He tried ringing back, but the call went straight to her voicemail.

'For feck's sake!' He stared down at Storme. 'If anything happens to them, God help you.' He then noticed Chris approaching, an oxygen mask strapped to his face. 'Are you okay?'

'Better now, thanks to the injection Clara just gave me. She's set up a triage unit outside to deal with the audience members. I've already sent Ian and Sue out to see her.' Then he gestured down at Storme. 'Time to take this one into custody, at last.'

'I agree, but he seems a bit out of it,' Joseph said. 'Maybe get him checked over by Clara first. Of course, he may be playing the mentally deranged card.'

Chris leaned down and pulled the mentalist to his feet. 'You should see Clara, too, Joseph.'

The DI nodded, painfully aware he needed to end this conversation and get moving.

'I don't understand any of this,' Storme whispered as the SIO cuffed him and got ready to lead him away.

Joseph looked at his boss. 'Chris...' he started to say. But stopped himself.

The problem was, with Megan in her programmed state, if she got so much as a whiff of the DI betraying her, she'd carry out her threat. With all her police training, she would be much more aware of the tricks they might use to storm the flat. No, there was only one course of action open to Joseph right now.

'What is it?' the SIO asked, turning back towards him as he led Storme away.

'Just make sure you get yourself fully checked out as well. That Devil's Breath is nasty stuff.'

Chris nodded and led Storme away.

When Joseph headed back outside, he spotted Clara straight away among the ambulance crews, administering injections to the audience members as they shuffled back into the outside world, all looking stunned.

The DI rushed over to her as he ripped off his mask. 'Clara, have you got any of that drug you talked about? The one to counteract the Devil's Breath?'

She nodded. 'Yes, it's Modafinil. It's what I've been administering to the audience and some of your colleagues. It enhances dopamine and orexin activity, increasing wakefulness, focus, and critical thinking—all things to counter hypnosis.'

'Then fill me up, please.'

Clara nodded. 'Of course. Roll up your sleeve.' She opened a bag and took out a disposable syringe, filling it from a vial with clear liquid. One jab later, Joseph was all done and rushing over to the TR4. But deep down, he was also aware he was heading into what had to be a trap. He just prayed he could get through to the real Megan Anderson before she did anything they might both end up regretting.

CHAPTER TWENTY-EIGHT

IT HAD GROWN dark as Joseph had driven over at high speed to Storme's home, but he'd still had time to reflect on what was happening.

The more he'd thought about it, the more he was absolutely certain he was walking into a well-prepared trap. Based on the video footage he'd seen, Storme had certainly had plenty of time to brainwash Megan and bend her to his twisted cause, a ticking time bomb that had now exploded, even though the man himself had been taken into custody.

But where was the why in any of this? If it was to avenge the death of Samuel Dawson, why hadn't Derrick and himself been included in his stage performance? Had it been Storme's plan all along for Megan to murder them both at his home? But if so, why single Derrick and himself out for this special treatment? They'd both been junior officers at the time of the Dawson case, and there were far bigger scalps to claim, some of which were already dead.

Whatever the answer to this riddle, he would soon have the answer. He pulled the TR4 into the car park outside St Luke's Manor, got out, and headed to the entrance. Many of the windows were lit, with one notable exception—those of Damien Storme's flat.

Joseph checked his pocket for the pepper spray and baton, both of which he intended to make full use of with the DC if she left him no other choice. The only question was whether Derrick, or for that matter, Megan, was still alive up there.

Slipping his mask back on, the DI headed into the lobby and walked up the stairs. As he headed along the corridor towards Storme's front door, his attention was focused on the camera. Would Megan be watching him from somewhere inside the flat, ready to jump him the moment he entered?

The DI paused at the entrance, taking his baton out and extending it. He could hear the faint murmur of electronic music from somewhere inside. Ready to deploy the PAVA spray, he nudged the door with his foot and let it swing open.

The hallway was shrouded in darkness, but the door to the empty waiting room was open and illuminated by the flickering light of the hypnotism video on the large TV. Joseph could also smell the distinctive musty scent of Devil's Breath emanating from the room. No wonder the gobshite was so good at hypnotising people if they sat inside there for long enough, just as he and Megan had at that first meeting.

Even though the DI had the Modafinil injection in his system, almost as an act of faith, the DI popped a Silvermint into his mouth. A hit of menthol certainly helped keep him sharp in any other situation, so a belt and braces approach couldn't hurt here.

With a mental breath, ready to duck if Megan came out swinging a knife at him from behind the door, the DI stepped through into the darkened hallway.

Joseph could hear hypnotic music coming from the open door at the end of the corridor—the one he knew led to the tower. The door was open a crack, and more flickering light was spilling out of it.

Neil had mentioned that all the screens had been added a year ago. Was this so there was no getting away from Storme's hypnotic influence, where the man could deepen the conditioning of his victims?

The DI edged towards the door, pepper spray ready to use at a moment's notice.

At the next door, he paused. Was the trap about to be sprung?

Pulse thumping in his ears, he used the end of his baton to push the door fully open into the tower room.

Then his heart clenched as he spotted Derrick standing on a chair, a hangman's noose dangling from the ceiling and looped around his neck, his arms tied behind his back. The superintendent was staring at the screen on the wall with another one of the hypnotic patterns. Joseph glanced briefly to see the word Chrysalis clearly displayed on it. Based on Derrick's trance-like state, it was clear Storme had managed to program him. Presumably, that had happened when the superintendent had been drawn to the flat and had inadvertently been exposed to one of the videos, along with the Devil's Breath.

Joseph was already moving, the urge to protect taking over, but his eyes also scanned the room, ready for Megan if she appeared and leapt for him. But he managed to reach Derrick without incident. He grabbed hold of his shoulders. The DI gave the DSU a good shake, trying to break the trance the man was in. But the superintendent's face remained passive, his gaze staring straight through Joseph towards the screen, as though he wasn't there.

'Please don't do that,' a distorted robotic voice said from the speakers by the TV.

'Who the feck are you?' Joseph asked, aware that Storme was now in custody.

'Wouldn't you like to know?' the voice replied. 'Anyway, the time has come to wrap everything up. Derrick, please listen up. I have some very special words for you. It's time to embrace the void.'

Just like a switch had been thrown, Derrick kicked the chair away from beneath him and dropped his full weight down on the rope. As the noose whipped tight around DSU's neck, his legs started thrashing around in the air and he began to gasp.

Joseph immediately grabbed the superintendent's legs and hauled him back up.

'Help me!' Derrick croaked out, his eyes bulging as his trance was finally broken.

'Trying my fecking best here,' Joseph said, reaching out with his foot to try and hook the chair.

'I certainly admire your dedication to your superintendent, but if I were you, I would be more worried about your own safety,' the robotic voice said from the speakers. 'You and all the others were responsible for Samuel's death due to a miscarriage of justice. And for that, you have to pay.'

'But how do you know it was a miscarriage of justice? That's not what the evidence fecking said.'

'Oh yes, the famous box cutter with Samuel's prints and his wife's blood. That was false evidence.'

Joseph's mind was whirling, trying to rapidly process this new information, even as his back screamed from taking Derrick's weight. 'But how could you possibly know that?'

'Because I was the one who planted the weapon found near the crime scene. But when, thanks to the incompetence of the investigation, none of you could work out it was a false clue, you all helped take the life of the man I loved.'

The parts of the puzzle started to lock together in Joseph's brain. 'Sorry, you're saying you're the one who murdered his wife?'

'Of course I am. She was in the way. But I also wanted to make Samuel pay for rejecting me during my therapy sessions with him.'

Another piece of the puzzle. 'Feck, you were one of his patients?'

'That's right. It was actually from Samuel that I developed my love of hypnotism. You see, he used it on me during my sessions with him. I loved that sense of control he had over me, the power. It was a real turn-on. It was that same skill, that power over others, that I patiently developed over the years, gradually perfecting my abilities as I developed a plan to make you all pay for his murder.'

But something didn't make sense here. 'I still don't understand why you would want to frame him for his wife's murder?'

'I only meant to punish, not kill him, DI Stone. You see, after Samuel spent time in prison, if you had all done your jobs like you were supposed to, I was going to release fresh evidence pinning the blame on one of his patients, thus clearing his name. Then, with his wife no longer in his life, we could finally have been together. But none of you played your part properly, and thanks to that, he took his life. That's why everyone on that original investigation has to pay for your collective incompetence.'

'You do know how deranged you sound?' Joseph said.

A long laugh. 'I've been hearing that my whole life, DI Stone. Anyway, DC Anderson, you are my chosen instrument of retribution—Awaken.'

Joseph just had time to see Megan emerge out of the darkness from the corner of the room. She hurtled straight towards him, a knife clutched in her hand.

'Megan, no!' the DI just had time to shout.

But whatever trance the DC was in was too deep for his

words to reach her. She growled as she swiped the kitchen knife sideways in an arc towards Joseph's stomach. With no other choice, the DI quickly leapt back to avoid the tip of the knife, but had to let go of Derrick in the process. The superintendent dropped down hard on the noose and began to choke. Megan rounded on the DI, ignoring the superintendent's gasps.

The blade flashed towards Joseph's gut again. Adrenaline humming through his system, the DI leapt sideways, just like his instructor in unarmed combat training had once taught him. As the momentum of Megan's blow carried her past him, the DI grabbed hold of her hand and yanked it, pulling the DC off balance and making her stumble forward. Still with his hand on her wrist, he twisted it sharply backwards, making her hand spasm open and drop the knife. Normally, the DI would have then tried to get her arm into a lock, but with Derrick twitching at the end of the rope, there simply wasn't time.

'I'm really sorry about this, Megan,' Joseph said as he aimed the PAVA spray straight into her face and pressed the button. The moment the artificial pepper spray hit her, the DC started coughing. Tears streaming down her face, she collapsed to the floor. That was all the time Joseph needed to rush over to the chair, grab it, and hook it back under Derrick's thrashing feet. The big man immediately stood on it, gasping for air as Joseph grabbed the knife from the floor and hacked at the rope, severing it. Then he cut the bonds around Derrick's wrists, before lowering him into a sitting position.

'Joseph...' the superintendent croaked.

'Aye, you can thank me later,' the DI replied, returning his attention to Megan, who was staring at him with wide, blood-shot eyes.

'I don't know what happened, Joseph,' the DC said. 'The last thing I remember, I was at St Aldates when I received a phone call from an unknown number. And the next thing I knew, I was here, attacking you.' Then she held out her wrists. 'What I do know is you have to cuff me.'

Joseph nodded. 'I think it's better to be safe than sorry.' He took out a pair of plastic zip-tie cuffs he'd bought just in case, and tightened them around the DC's wrist.

A chuckle came from the speakers. 'I would say bravo, but I'm afraid I haven't quite finished with you yet, DI Stone,' the distorted voice said. 'I have one last trigger to make use of, and this time it's one I buried in your mind.'

But rather than fear, Joseph felt a sense of confidence taking hold. Of course, whoever this was, didn't know his trigger had been safely removed. But maybe he could use that to his advantage and extract some more information from this person.

'Okay, as you've got me where you want me and I know there's not a lot I can do about it, please help me out here. I saw Storme hypnotising me and Megan on video, captured inside this very flat, but that doesn't make any sense if you're claiming responsibility.'

'Maybe you did, but you didn't see the person who had hypnotised the famous Damien Storme into carrying out their bidding. It's the sort of misdirection a mentalist uses all the time on stage, so I'd like to think Damien would approve of my little trick. Get the audience to concentrate on your left hand whilst you do something with your right.'

Joseph thought back to the bewildered state Storme had been in. 'You're saying he didn't know what the feck he was doing, and you were actually responsible for all of those murders?'

'That's right. You see, I needed to tidy things up to make sure there was nothing pointing towards me, leaving Damien to be blamed for everything. I've always thought he was such an arrogant man, thinking he could read everyone, could see into their minds. But he never could with me. I was nothing but a closed book to him. Of course, that was all a pretence, so I could learn and steal his techniques to build upon my own expertise. Then I gradually began to brainwash him using the Devil's Breath I'd learnt about during my degree course here in Oxford. Thanks to his constant exposure to it, I was able to gradually take full control of his mind. Once I'd achieved that, I was able to make him do my bidding, including tonight's grand finale. I just wish I'd been there when he killed himself. And now everything has worked out exactly as I intended, and the famous Damien Storme has been set up as my fall guy.'

This person didn't know that things at the theatre hadn't gone according to plan.

It was then Joseph realised who he was speaking to. A person who had been by Storme's side for at least a whole year. A person who had handed him and Megan weaponised versions of the mentalist's hypnosis books. A woman who'd been all touchy-feely with them—something Clara had warned them a mentalist might use to reinforce hidden keywords slipped into sentences.

'Catherine, is that fecking you?' he asked.

He heard a slow handclap over the speakers. When Catherine next spoke, her voice was free of distortion.

'Impressive. It's just such a shame you won't be able to share the breakthrough with your colleagues. I'm afraid all three of you are loose ends I need to deal with, so what better way than to get you to kill them and then yourself? And the beauty of all of this is that once again, everyone will assume it was Damien who programmed you to do it, rather than his humble assistant, who will discover your dead bodies first thing tomorrow morning.'

Joseph knew the moment to reveal his hand had finally come. 'Good luck with that. I had a psychologist deprogram that fecking mind trigger of yours. It's over, Catherine. And thanks to your confession, we know who you are. If you try to run, we'll track you down. The best thing you can do is hand yourself over.'

Of all the responses the DI might have expected, it certainly wasn't laughter.

'So you think you're safe from my influence, do you? And I suppose the trigger you had removed was Chrysalis?'

Joseph suddenly had a very bad feeling about where this conversation was headed.

'Aye, that's the one.'

'Well, that trigger was never actually intended for you. It was simply the one you stumbled across in one of the videos I had Stacey Ellis delete. By watching those, you managed to accidentally programme yourself, but with none of my reinforcement, so it never fully took. Actually, you were surprisingly resistant to any form of hypnosis, just like Alex Richards was. That's why I had Simon murder him. But in your case, I was forced to rely on Megan to be my avenging angel. She was very susceptible to my suggestions. However, I did have just enough time to plant a different trigger word in your subconscious, which did seem to take, at least well enough for my purposes tonight.'

A sense of foreboding filled Joseph's gut. 'You put another one of those fecking things in my mind?'

'I always feel it's good to be prepared for any eventuality. And now I've lured you here with Walker as bait. But since Megan wasn't able to complete the task and murder you, you'll just have to do it for me.' Catherine then uttered one word, 'Metamorphous.'

Joseph felt his mind instantly lock up as his body moved of its own volition, the knife he used to free Derrick, still in his hand. He felt like a prisoner in his own body as he watched his hand raise the weapon and turn it around until it was aimed towards his own chest. The DI fought with everything he had to stop himself, to break the damned trance that even Modafinil hadn't been able to stop. He felt his arm tensing as it got ready to drive the blade into his own heart.

For feck's sake, he just had time to think as he tensed for the burning pain of metal driven into him.

A puff of spray suddenly filled his face, and the effect was instantaneous.

A firestorm roared through Joseph's eyes, searing into his corneas. Instinctively, his eyelids slammed shut, but that didn't help much, either. The burning sensation remained, as if someone had replaced his tears with sulphuric acid. The DI staggered, hands rubbing his eyes frantically, but the more he touched them, the worse it became.

'Sorry about that, but you looked as though you were about to do something fucking stupid,' Derrick said, the DI's PAVA spray in his hand.

'No, no, no, get away from me!' Catherine shouted through the speakers.

Joseph wondered what the hell she was going on about until he heard another voice.

'I'm sorry, we're not about to do that anytime soon,' they heard Chris say over the speakers. 'Hand over that phone.'

'Stay away from me!' Catherine screeched.

'Well, you can't say we didn't warn you,' John's voice said.

There was a high-pitched buzzing sound the DI recognised as a Taser being fired, followed by a woman's scream.

'Are you all okay in there?' Chris said over the speaker.

'Just about,' Joseph replied, still desperately trying to wipe his eyes clean.

'Hang in there; we're on our way over,' Chris said.

'Bloody hell, don't say hang,' Derrick grumbled.

'How did you know we were in trouble?' Megan asked Chris once he'd arrived a short while later.

'You can thank Neil for the timely intervention,' the SIO replied, offering a bottle of water to both Megan and Joseph to help rinse their eyes. 'He was still going through the video footage from Storme's flat when he spotted Joseph on a live video feed he had open. When he checked the other cameras inside the flat, he saw Derrick put a noose around his own neck. Then he spotted Megan hiding behind a bookcase, holding a knife. He quickly put two and two together, and he contacted St Aldates.'

'But how did you know where to find Catherine?' Derrick asked.

'Once again, that's thanks to Neil. When she started talking to Joseph, he overheard the whole conversation. Then he used something called a packet sniffer to run a trace. Thanks to that, he quickly discovered it was a mobile connected to Storme's WiFi network, meaning its owner couldn't be too far away. With the details he gave us, we ran a trace on her mobile number, and located Catherine outside, just around the corner from Storme's flat.'

'Jesus, then I owe that lad a pint,' Joseph said as some semblance of normal breathing started to return to him.

'At the very least,' Chris replied. 'But you and I are going to have words about this. What the hell were you thinking, heading off to tackle this alone?'

'There wasn't exactly a lot of time to think about it. I was told Derrick's life was on the line if I told anyone.'

Derrick nodded. 'You saved my life, Joseph, and you're not going to get a lecture from anyone on my watch.'

'I appreciate the sentiment, but since you saved my life just now, maybe we'll just call it even,' the DI replied.

'Well, throw in a pint, and maybe we will,' Derrick said with a genuine smile that actually reached his eyes for once.

Despite everything that had just happened, Joseph wasn't quite sure how to respond after the animosity the man had previously shown him. Perhaps that was behind them now and they could start to move on. But that was for another day. First, there was an interview with a psychopath called Catherine with his name on it, not to mention a serious debriefing with the team to get through.

CHAPTER TWENTY-NINE

THE FOLLOWING DAY, Derrick hovered at the back of the incident room. John was also in attendance for the debriefing, along with all the uniformed officers who'd assisted at the theatre the previous night.

Clara had also been brought in to help answer any questions after her initial psychiatric assessment of Catherine. There'd been no sign of Doctor Hunt, and Chris brushed off any questions about why she wasn't there. But there'd been a lot of knowing looks exchanged around the room. It was already an open secret that Hunt's failure in the investigation had led to some very direct questions about her competency for the role. Joseph certainly wouldn't be unhappy to see the back of the old warhorse if she decided to take early retirement.

There had certainly been a lot to get through in this meeting —from Catherine Kendrick planting the original box cutter at the scene of the Dawson investigation, to setting up Damien Storme as her fall guy for the murders of those she held responsible for Samuel Dawson's eventual suicide while in prison. After Joseph had assisted Chris in interviewing Kendrick in another all-nighter, they finally had all the missing parts of the puzzle.

'Okay, what I still don't understand is why Kendrick didn't blame herself for Dawson's death?' Ian asked.

Chris nodded to Clara. 'I think your insight might be very useful here.'

The psychiatrist nodded. 'By projecting the responsibility of Samuel's death onto others, it was a way for Kendrick to cope with her own shortcomings, and create a twisted justification for her actions.'

'So it was everyone else's fault, apart from hers?' Megan said.

'In a nutshell, yes,' Clara replied. 'Accepting the truth that she caused the chain of events that led to Samuel Dawson's death would have broken her. It was far easier for her to twist the narrative until she became the victim. In Kendrick's eyes, she wasn't a killer, but an avenger of a wrong the world refused to acknowledge.'

'So, in summary, the twisted logic of a psychopath?' Sue said.

Joseph met her gaze. 'Aye, but at least now, Samuel Dawson's name will finally be cleared in the murder of his wife. Hopefully, that will be some comfort to his relatives.'

'So why the twenty-year delay for Kendrick to decide to take out her vengeance?' John asked.

'Because this was all about taking time to become, and here's the irony, a trained psychologist specialising in hypnotism,' Chris replied. 'It turns out Kendrick had her own practice in Reading until she closed it just over a year ago. Clara, if you'd be so good as to give us some insight here?'

She nodded. 'Becoming a psychologist gave Kendrick legitimacy in her mind. That choice of profession also let her hide in plain sight, while quietly feeding her obsession with control over her own patients. Of course, for her, it wasn't about healing others—it was about studying them. By learning how people break, and what triggers they had, she eventually learnt how people tick, and specifically their weaknesses.

'But it was Samuel Dawson's use of hypnosis that had first struck a chord with her during her own therapy sessions. Thanks to that, she became obsessed with the idea of using it as another way to deepen her control over people. She then spent years researching how to make people even more suggestible. Here's the irony, and full disclosure, she was one of the students I trained fifteen years ago. Of course, I had no way of knowing she was involved at all in this case until yesterday.

'Anyway, it was during the Experimental Psychology course that she came across Devil's Breath. It's a drug Colombian gangs have been using for years—though over there, they call it Burundanga. Victims become compliant, suggestible, and in some cases, even zombie-like. There are stories of people emptying their bank accounts, handing over their house keys, even helping their attackers, all without remembering a thing afterwards.'

The psychologist looked around the room. 'To Kendrick, that wasn't a horrifying notion—it was actually inspiring. She saw it as proof that minds could be taken apart and rebuilt. All she needed was the right blend, the right method, and the right targets to try out skills on. After some further experiments with Devil's Breath, she found aerosolizing it worked well on her patients. That's when she decided she'd finally perfected her techniques enough to be able to finally put her plan into motion —one she'd spent so many years fantasising about and perfecting.'

Chris nodded to Joseph. 'If you'd like to pick up the baton at this point.'

Joseph looked out at his colleagues. 'All Kendrick needed was someone she could frame, namely Damien Storme. She even boasted to us during the interview how quickly she managed to hypnotise Storme, whilst working as his assistant. She followed that with months of exposing him to Devil's Breath and brainwashing until he was completely under her power.

'Meanwhile, Kendrick researched the profiles for each and every person ever involved in the Dawson case, sending out targeted hypnosis books with those specially adapted video course links. She also hypnotised Stacey Ellis, making the woman believe she was infatuated with Gregory Richards and that she'd even had a one-night fling with him. Then, with Stacey under her complete control, Kendrick got her to write a special version of the program that produced the hypnotic patterns used in the background of Damien Storme's videos, using the 3D Magic Eye poster technique to hide specific text she'd chosen.'

'That was why someone's conscious mind might not pick up on it, but their subconscious still would,' Clara added. 'It was quite brilliant in a way.'

Joseph nodded. 'Then all she had to do was send out the free books aimed at addressing something she knew her victims had an issue with. For example, giving up smoking in the case of DCI Simon Hart.'

'In that case, how did she manage to target you, Megan, and Derrick?' Sue asked.

'When she hypnotised Megan and me in Damien Storme's waiting room, she'd first flooded it with the aerosolized Devil's Breath,' Joseph replied. 'Then she really went to town on Megan with some follow-up sessions.'

The DC spread her hands. 'The shocking thing for me is that, apart from the fact she made me try to kill Joseph, I have absolutely no memory of her doing any of that to me.'

'And here's the really clever part—she didn't even hypnotise you and Joseph herself, but got Storme, who was completely under her power by that point, to do it for her,' Clara said.

'But my subconscious did try to warn me something was wrong,' Joseph said. 'I had a vivid dream featuring a white room and the word Chrysalis, which I now know was inspired by something that actually happened when she had Storme hypnotise me.'

'So what about you, Superintendent?' Sue asked. 'How did Kendrick manage to lure you to Storme's flat if she hadn't sent you one of her poisoned pen books?'

Derrick gave Megan a pointed look. 'It might be better if you explained that.'

The DC, looking embarrassed, nodded. 'I remember telling Derrick that Chris had specifically asked him to join Storme at his flat. The story Kendrick had me recount was that Chris had found evidence of a sensitive nature that he wanted Derrick's opinion on.'

The DSU sighed. 'Which was all a lie, of course, just to get me there. And like a bloody lamb to the slaughter, I headed over there, where I came under the influence of that bloody aerosol of hers. I now know from the tapes Chris has shown me that, having been hypnotised by one of Catherine's adapted videos, she then set to work on me over the intercom, convincing me Dawson's death was all my fault, and I should end my life.'

Megan grimaced. 'That's something I'm always going to feel guilty about.'

Derrick shook his head. 'I'm not blaming you for any of it. You weren't in charge of your actions, and neither was I. All I do know is that if it weren't for Joseph's quick thinking, I wouldn't be here now to make all your lives miserable.'

That raised a few chuckles.

'I could say the same for you,' Joseph replied. 'It was only thanks to your swift action that prevented me from stabbing myself.'

Megan gave him a puzzled look. 'About that, I thought Clara had deprogrammed you before you went there?'

'Only for the Chrysalis suggestion. What I didn't know is that she buried another command in my subconscious.'

'Obviously, as soon as you're available, Joseph, we'll remove that one as well,' Clara said. 'I'm going to give anyone else who's been exposed to her techniques as many sessions as we need to try and root out any remaining commands.'

There were several relieved looks around the room.

'Okay, so why did Kendrick lure you and Derrick to Storme's flat to kill you there, rather than with all the others back at the theatre, Joseph?' Sue asked.

'I wondered about that as well, and it turns out it was personal. Derrick and I were the first officers on the scene of Eleanor Dawson's murder.'

'Yeah, I'm not about to forget that in a hurry. Blood everywhere.'

'Do you remember helping me set up the cordon as members of the public started to gather outside, and we waited for reinforcements to turn up?'

'Yes, what about it?' the DSU asked.

'It turns out Kendrick was unable to resist returning to the scene of the crime. Apparently, she spoke to us that night, asking what had happened. That's why, when I first met Kendrick, I thought I recognised her from somewhere. But in her twisted mind, she specifically blamed the two of us for not recognising her immediately as the real murderer and arresting her on the spot.'

'What, she expected us to be bloody psychic or something?' Derrick asked.

Joseph gestured to the psychologist. 'You should probably answer that.'

'Basically, yes,' Clara said. 'You have to understand, in Kendrick's mind, she was testing the police. Subconsciously, perhaps even consciously, she wanted to be caught. Later, after neither of you recognised her for what she was, that confirmed her belief that you weren't just blind, but you were at the top of the pile in a miscarriage of justice against Samuel. Then, after his suicide, that belief hardened into something far more dangerous. She held you both personally responsible for his death. In her head, if you'd stopped her that day, then he would still be alive. That's the narrative she built, and once it took root, it became fuel for everything that followed.'

'Oh, great, so this is all our bloody fault,' Derrick said, shaking his head.

'In no way or form,' Clara replied. 'Don't forget we are talking about somebody who had serious emotional and psychological issues, which was why she was Samuel Dawson's patient in the first place.'

But even as everyone nodded, Joseph couldn't help but feel like his instinct should have kicked in back at that original crime scene, and he should have recognised her for what she was. If it had, then maybe things might have turned out very differently.

'So let me get this right. Basically, Catherine's plan after all of this was to melt away, letting Damien Storme take the fall?' Ian asked.

'Correct, but it's actually even more insidious than that. After being exposed to her techniques for so long, Storme's programming runs so deep he's convinced himself that he's responsible for all of it.'

Ian whistled. 'Well, I have to give it to Kendrick, that's one hell of a cover story.'

'In light of all this new information, shouldn't someone be

trying to clear DCI Hart of the murder of DI Roberts?' Megan asked.

'Don't worry about that. The wheels are already in motion,' Joseph replied. 'I've been in contact with Geoff Flynn, and they're going to posthumously fully exonerate Simon. I know that's going to mean a lot to their widows, not to mention to all his colleagues at the Banbury station.'

'And to us as well,' Derrick said, giving Joseph a pointed look.

'Aye, you're not wrong. We knew Simon's actions were never those of the man we both knew and liked. Now we finally understand why.'

'So how are we going to prevent Kendrick from pulling this stunt whilst she's in custody? Couldn't she simply hypnotise the guards into letting her out of prison?' John asked.

'That's a very good question, John, and one we've discussed with Clara,' Chris replied.

'Yes, and I had two very practical suggestions. One is to flood any cell holding Kendrick with white noise when anyone enters. That will help counter her ability to get her visitor to enter a hypnotic state. Additionally, there should always be two guards assigned to deal with her—one on the outside of the cell monitoring what's happening inside, whilst the other goes in.'

'Those are precautions we've already put in place for her stay in our holding cells,' Chris said.

'I also suggested that anyone exposed to Kendrick for any length of time be subjected to regular random screenings to make sure she hasn't been able to embed any trigger words in their subconscious.'

'So, assuming Kendrick's prosecuted and found guilty, that sounds like a lifetime in solitary?' Megan asked.

'I think that's exactly what they'll have to do, if only for everyone else's safety,' Clara said.

'Make no mistake,' Chris said. 'Kendrick is one of the most dangerous people the legal system has ever had to deal with. The good news is, now she won't be able to hurt anyone else. In the meantime, we have a lot of material to go through before we can finish wrapping up this case. So let's make sure we dot all the I's and cross all the T's. That is apart from you, Joseph, after pulling another all-nighter, you're to get yourself home. Megan, I want you to see Clara immediately after this to have your first deprogramming session.'

'And don't worry, you're not alone in that, Megan. I'll be having a session as well,' Derrick said.

'It will certainly be a relief to know I'm no longer a danger to anyone else in this room,' the DC replied. 'And talking of which.' Megan pulled out a carton of Krispy Kreme doughnuts from beneath her desk. 'My shout, and my way of apologising to you all.'

'Apology accepted,' Ian said, pouncing with the speed of a panther to seize a serious-looking chocolate one.

'Well, on that note, I think we'll draw this meeting to a close,' Chris said. 'But Joseph, can I grab you for a moment before you head home?'

'Of course, boss,' the DI replied, making sure he managed to get hold of a lemon doughnut before the horde ate the lot.

CHAPTER THIRTY

AFTER USHERING Joseph into a meeting room, Chris closed the door behind them.

'I'm guessing by the grim look on your face, this has something to do with the Night Watchmen?' Joseph asked.

'In one. There's been something of an unexpected development. Unfortunately, it has to do with Derrick.'

Joseph shot the DCI a surprised look. 'In what way?'

'I'm afraid we've recently come into possession of evidence conclusively proving he's crossed the line. It's best if I show you.' Chris opened up his phone, pulled up a video, and started playing it, before handing it to the DI.

Joseph was surprised to see footage taken from outside of a coffee shop of Derrick sitting across the table from Chief Superintendent Amanda Kennan.

'Any meeting with that woman can't be good news.'

Chris nodded. 'I'm afraid not. This video was captured yesterday by the surveillance team who's been shadowing Kennan.'

'I see...' Joseph replied, watching the video of Derrick

nodding as Kennan spoke. 'Any actual chance of hearing what's been said?'

'Sadly not. If the NCA agent had got any closer, she would have risked blowing her cover,' Chris replied. 'But you don't need sound to understand exactly what's going on there. If you look under the table, you'll see why.'

Joseph spotted one of the silver briefcases that the Night Watchmen always seemed to favour placed there. 'Shite, is this what it looks like—Kennan attempting to bribe Derrick again?'

'That's what it looks like. We know there's cash in that case because Kennan was first trailed to one of the drug gangs the Night Watchmen are now in bed with. Thanks to our surveillance cameras inside, we saw her pick up that particular briefcase filled with banknotes. Then she brought that same case straight to this meeting with Derrick.'

Joseph was still hoping that he was about to see the DSU throw the money back in the woman's face as he'd once witnessed the big man doing before back at the Old Ink Press pub car park. But this was nothing like that previous encounter. Instead, Derrick was now all smiles. Then Kennan reached across the table, and Derrick shook the proffered hand. Next, she headed out of the cafe, leaving the briefcase behind. Joseph watched with a growing sense of horror as Derrick discreetly picked up the briefcase and headed out of the door a moment later.

'Christ on a fecking bike, is that what it looks like?' Joseph asked as the video ended.

'We believe so. It seems Derrick has finally accepted a direct bribe from the Night Watchmen. He's obviously thrown in the towel and has decided to work for them.'

'But I don't understand. What's changed?'

Chris gave the DI a straight look. 'Why don't you tell me?'

'What, you think this has something to do with me?'

'Not directly, but maybe an indirect consequence of your actions.'

Joseph gawped at Chris as he realised what the man was driving at. 'Are you seriously trying to suggest that Kate and I getting back together has tipped Derrick over the edge?'

'Well, aren't we talking about a man who has lost everything he cares about? The emotional trauma of that aside, I'm sure losing his home has only added to his financial pressures as well. So maybe this was exactly what it looks like. Derrick, broken by everything that's happened to him recently, has finally decided to throw his lot in with the Night Watchmen.'

'With all due respect, I can't see him doing that,' Joseph replied. 'For everything that man is, he does have some principles.'

'I'm afraid this video suggests otherwise. My superiors at the NCA have already seen it and have informed everyone that Derrick is now to be seen as a suspect in the Night Watchmen investigation. Certainly, any plea bargain offer that might have been on offer to the DSU is now off the table.'

Joseph thought back to the previous night when Derrick had saved his life. 'I'm sorry, none of this stacks up. To start with, if he was so destroyed by what happened, why did he step in to save my life last night?'

'Because, like you said, there's still something decent about the man, even if he has decided to bend the knee to a crime syndicate. Even so, he's left us with no choice but to keep him under tight surveillance from now on. Needless to say, you mustn't mention any of this to Derrick, and I would urge you to keep your distance as much as possible.'

'I'm sorry, but the man I know wouldn't betray his colleagues like this.'

'I agree, but perhaps we're talking about the man we both knew. Heartbreak has a way of changing a person, sometimes for the worse. You might not want to hear this, Joseph, but I think you getting back together with Kate was the final straw that tipped Derrick over the edge.'

The DI squeezed his eyes shut for a moment and pinched his nose. 'For feck's sake, just when I thought Derrick had remembered how to be a decent copper.'

Chris shot him a sympathetic look and nodded. 'Okay, that's enough brain ache for now, especially after the night you've had. Get yourself home and catch up on some well-deserved sleep.'

'And what about you? You were right there with me last night, not to mention the night before.'

'There will be plenty of time for me to get sleep later, and anyway, that's why I'm paid those mythical big bucks.'

Joseph gave his boss a small smile as he handed him his phone back. 'Rather you than me.'

But as the DI left the room, a deep sense of sadness settled over him. Derrick was certainly the last person he expected to bow to the Night Watchmen's pressure. But here they were anyway, and part of him couldn't help but feel responsible for what had happened.

CHAPTER THIRTY-ONE

As Joseph parked up his bike next to Tús Nua, he heard laughter coming from Dylan's boat, Avalon, and saw the professor and Iris emerge from its cabin. She turned to Dylan and gave him what Joseph could only describe as a full-blown snog. Passionate would have been a serious understatement as she attempted to melt her face into his.

Realising he was witnessing a very private moment, Joseph tried to be as quiet as possible as he locked his bike up, and tried to slip into Tús Nua unseen. Unfortunately, the professor's dogs had other ideas.

White Fang and Max barrelled out of Avalon's cabin, barking as they came racing towards the DI. Just to add to the general animal cacophony announcing Joseph's presence, Tux also emerged from the cat flap in Tús Nua's cabin door, mewing loudly as he circled Joseph's legs.

'Alright, alright, I get the message,' the DI said as he opened the treat tin and gave one to each of the dogs, who were looking up at him expectantly, licking their lips. He followed that with a cat treat for Tux, who almost bit his fingers off in his haste to get it in his mouth. The DI wasn't surprised when he raised his eyes to see Dylan and Iris had broken apart and were now looking at him.

Joseph wasn't quite sure what got into his head, but before his brain could stop itself, the words were already out of his mouth. 'Nice morning for it.'

Iris exchanged a look with Dylan and burst out laughing. 'Caught like a randy teenager, sneaking out of my boyfriend's flat.'

Joseph raised his eyebrows at them, and once again the words were out of his mouth before he could stop himself. 'Sorry, you spent the night?'

Iris waved an imaginary fan in front of her face. 'A lady doesn't like to speak of such things.'

Dylan's face bloomed bright red. 'You're home late, or I should say early?' he said, in an obvious attempt to change the subject.

'Another classic all-nighter, but this time for a good reason,' Joseph replied, trying to give his friend some breathing room. 'After that stunt at Storme's performance, we finally have the person responsible for all those murders, safely in custody. Talking of which, are you both okay?'

Somehow Dylan's face grew even redder, a colour closer to vermilion. 'I'm afraid we didn't actually make it to the theatre.'

Joseph looked between them and then snorted. 'Well, colour me surprised.'

That was rewarded by another belly laugh from Iris. 'What can I say? This wonderful man cooked me one of the most incredible meals of my life.'

'You like Dylan's cooking, then?' Joseph said, unable to keep the smile off his face.

Iris kissed her fingertips. 'I adored it. I honestly had no idea Dylan was talented in the kitchen, not to mention the bedroom. He did rather sweep me off my feet.'

Joseph was so taken back, that his mouth opened and closed again when he couldn't find a suitable response.

Dylan stared at her. 'Please stop before I melt into Avalon's deck from embarrassment.'

'You should take it as a compliment,' Iris replied in a matter-of-fact tone. 'Anyway, let's just say, Joseph, we had much more important things on our minds than any theatre performance. I take it something happened?'

Joseph managed to find his voice again. 'Storme hypnotised his entire audience last night, but it's even more convoluted than that. You see, it turns out Storme was actually hypnotised himself and brainwashed by his assistant, Catherine Kendrick. She had a year to condition him.'

'Good grief, but surely Storme, being a mentalist, would have realised what was going on and tried to stop her?'

'Maybe in normal circumstances, but not these. You see, Kendrick made an aerosol from something called Devil's Breath that's derived from a plant. She used that in Storme's home to make him highly suggestible. Kendrick did the same to all her victims, including Simon Hart, who was captured on video, visiting the flat. But she didn't stop there. She used Devil's Breath on the entire audience yesterday and hypnotised everyone. And if that doesn't raise your eyebrows, Kendrick also used that same trick on me and Megan when we visited Storme at his home, before then hypnotising us both.'

'Oh my goodness, but you're both okay?' Iris asked.

'We are now, but that's a story for another time. Like I said, I'm rather exhausted.'

'I'm not surprised,' Ellie said from behind him.

The DI turned to see her standing there with Kate.

'John told me everything that happened,' his daughter said.

'Which she then let me know about,' Kate added. 'Is it true you saved Derrick's life, and then he saved yours?'

Joseph raked his hand through his hair. 'Aye, it was quite a night for it.'

'Bloody hell, Dad,' Ellie said, drawing him into a hug.

Kate did the same. 'So what exactly happened? John mentioned something about Catherine Kendrick activating a trigger word buried in your mind.'

By now, Iris and Dylan were both giving the DI an expectant look.

Joseph held up his hands. 'Alright, alright, I can see I'm not going to get away with a quick summary. So, Dylan, maybe get the coffee on as I can see I'm not about to escape to my bed anytime soon.'

'In that case, why don't I make everyone some breakfast Shakshouka with some flatbreads, and make an occasion of it?' Dylan replied.

'Now that sounds like a splendid idea, lover boy,' Iris said.

Kate looked between them. 'Is there something we need to know?'

Ellie nodded, looking between the two professors, her eyes wide.

'Maybe us girls should have a little chat whilst this gorgeous man gets on with the cooking,' Iris said.

'Okay, then whilst you're doing that, I'll at least grab a shower,' Joseph said. 'I'll be back in less time than it takes Tux to change his mind about going outside.'

His cat gave him the look and then presented his pink arse at the DI and stalked off.

'That's good, because Ellie has news she's absolutely desperate to tell you,' Kate said.

'Good, I hope?' Joseph replied, giving his daughter a wary look.

'Oh, I think you're going to love it,' Ellie said, beaming at him.

Despite his fatigue, and having briefed everyone more fully about the night's events, Joseph felt considerably brighter as he tucked into Dylan's rather sensational shakshouka with eggs cooked to perfection in a rich tomato-spiced stew. The smoky paprika, harissa paste, and the sprinkling of melting feta had really elevated the dish to the next level.

'This is absolutely delicious,' Ellie said, mopping up the sauce with her flatbread.

Iris nodded. 'If you keep cooking like this, Dylan, I'm never going to leave.'

The professor pointedly ignored the grins that Ellie and Kate were giving him. The three women had been as thick as thieves out on the towpath, and Joseph had heard frequent bursts of laughter as he'd showered inside his boat. The snippets he'd managed to overhear suggested Iris hadn't held back on all the juicy details of her night with Dylan.

Well-fed, and with a coffee in hand, Joseph turned to Ellie. 'So, darling daughter of mine, what's this news of yours?'

'I had a meeting with Doctor Stuart Hargrave. He showed me around the Centre for Criminology. He's an amazing man. He's already offered me a job there, subject to me graduating from Blavatnik School of Government.'

'So this means you're going to finish your degree?' Joseph asked.

'Yep, and I've already accepted the job offer. It's absolutely incredible the work they do there, and I want to be part of it. Okay, it might mean not working in the police force, but I'll still be helping an organisation that works directly with law enforcement, including the Thames Valley Police.'

'And even better, it means that Ellie will be staying in Oxford,' Kate said, squeezing her daughter's hand.

'That's the best news I've heard in a long time,' Joseph said, feeling a sense of lightness wash over him. He already knew to his bones this was a great decision for his daughter's future.

'Honestly, this job could have been made for me,' Ellie replied enthusiastically. 'And I've so much to thank you for, Dylan. If you hadn't told me about it, I would have had no idea that place even existed.'

'I'm just pleased that I was able to help you with such a big decision,' Dylan said, smiling at her.

'Then, I think, this is a cause for a celebration, at least once I've had a chance to sleep,' Joseph said. 'What do you all say?'

'Now there's a great idea,' Ellie said. 'Maybe we could try out that new Turkish restaurant in Cowley.'

'I've been hearing great things about that, so count us in as well,' Dylan said, smiling at Iris.

'So it's us now, is it?' she said.

'Sorry, I didn't mean to suggest—'

Iris chuckled. 'Goodness, you're so easy to wind up, you dear innocent man. Of course there's an us, especially after last night.' Iris gave everyone a pantomime wink.

Dylan sighed. 'Is there going to be a lot of this teasing from now on?'

'You better believe it,' Iris said, hooking her arm through his and pulling him into her.

'I think she's definitely going to be keeping you on your toes, Dylan, which is probably not a bad thing,' Joseph added.

Dylan sighed. 'You're probably not wrong.'

Nobody disagreed, especially Iris.

'Oh, and one final thing before I forget,' Kate said. 'Joseph, about trying to find a place together.'

A horrified look filled Dylan's face. 'Sorry, you're thinking of moving out of Tús Nua, Joseph?'

He grimaced. 'It's a discussion Kate and I've been having on and off for the last week.'

Kate held up her hands. 'Before you get too worried, Dylan, I'm not about to steal your friend away.'

'How so exactly?' Joseph asked.

'Because I grasp now that your heart is in this boat. I even get the attraction after I stayed overnight by myself. But perhaps more importantly, I understand the community you're part of here, especially with Dylan so close by. So, at least for the foreseeable future, I think you should stay here.'

The DI felt a boulder fill his stomach. 'We're not going to live together, then?'

Kate pulled a face at him. 'I didn't say that. Now that I understand this is where your life is, it's where I want to be as well. So, have you any objection to me moving in here with you?'

Joseph stared at her as he mentally processed her words. 'You want to move into Tús Nua?'

'Well, doesn't her name translate from Gaelic to New Beginnings?' Kate replied.

He smiled. 'Aye, it does.'

'In that case, I think that's rather appropriate, don't you?'

Joseph took her hands in his. 'You really mean that?'

'With all my heart.' Kate wrapped her arms around him.

As she kissed him, Joseph was only dimly aware of Ellie whooping in the background as she led the congratulations from the people who meant everything to him.

Joseph finally pulled away from Kate. 'Feck it. Who fancies a champagne breakfast to kick things off? Suddenly I seem to have a second wind.'

'That sounds perfect,' Kate said, with a smile that lit Joseph's heart up like sunshine on a winter day. Just like it had always done, and always would, forever and a day.

JOIN THE J.R. SINCLAIR VIP CLUB

To get instant access to exclusive photos of locations used from the series, and the latest news from J.R. Sinclair, just click on the image below to start receiving your free content.

ORDER A HEART OF DARKNESS

DI Joseph Stone will return in
A Heart of Darkness

Order now: https://geni.us/AHeartofDarkness